Gunbarrel Highway

by

Sean Bridges

Copyright Notice
This is a work of fiction. Names, characters, places, and incidents are either the product of the author's imagination or are used fictitiously, and any resemblance to actual persons living or dead, business establishments, events, or locales, is entirely coincidental.

Gunbarrel Highway

COPYRIGHT © 2024 by Sean Patrick Bridges

All rights reserved. No part of this book may be used or reproduced in any manner whatsoever without written permission of the author or The Wild Rose Press, Inc. except in the case of brief quotations embodied in critical articles or reviews.
Contact Information: info@thewildrosepress.com

Cover Art by *The Wild Rose Press, Inc.*

The Wild Rose Press, Inc.
PO Box 708
Adams Basin, NY 14410-0708
Visit us at www.thewildrosepress.com

Publishing History
First Edition, 2024
Trade Paperback ISBN: 978-1-5092-5844-4
Digital ISBN 978-1-5092-5875-8

Published in the United States of America

Dedication

For Max, Luna & Riley. I'll see you down the road. SB

Chapter One

The woman arches in her car seat. Her right hand buries between her legs. Her face contorts in erotic passion, and her eyes squint closed as sensual waves spasm through her body.

Her free hand careens the steering wheel to the left.

The woman's Mazda swerves across the road and races for the Bronco like a bullet.

****

The man's eyes widen. The sports car heads straight for him. He braces for impact.

The Mazda torpedoes into his Bronco with a crunch of steel and shower of glass.

The Bronco's airbag inflates and envelops him.

****

"San Marcos City 911. What is your emergency?"

"Yeah, there's a real bad accident here, on San Elijo Road and Beechtree Boulevard. We're part of the Centennial Ridge development. Ahh, close to 271."

"San Elijo and Beechtree. Off rural route 271."

"Yeah, it's the nearest main road. Turn off 271, and we're right there."

"Can you see if anyone was injured?"

"Ahh, I don't know. I'm looking out my living room window right now. I mean, it was loud as hell. I heard this, boom. It was this huge crash. Man, I musta jumped fifty feet. I can see two vehicles. And yeah. It all looks pretty bad."

"What kind of vehicles?"

"It looks like ahhh, an SUV. Like a dark colored SUV, black."

"A black SUV."

"Yep. And a red sports car? I think. I mean, damn. That baby is totaled. I'll be honest, you can't even tell if that was ever a car. Wow. It looks rough. The accident looks bad. I mean, it had to have been a head-on collision. That car is really smashed up."

"What's your name?"

"Uh, my name is Ethan Solis. S O L I S."

"Okay, Ethan, keep your eyes on the scene and let me know if you're able to tell how many people might be inside either vehicle."

"I really can't tell. It's all such a mess. Hey, I think I… No, I am. Yes, I'm seeing smoke. Coming from the red car."

"And you think the car is on fire?"

"Uh huh. It is. The red one, yeah. I can see smoke. Black smoke."

"Okay. We've got help on the way. Do you see anyone inside or outside the vehicles?"

"I still can't see anybody. I can't tell. There's a lot of debris."

"Okay, we're getting help coming your way."

"Okay, yeah, yeah. You might wanna send…send an ambulance. And a fire truck as well."

"Ethan. If you find out there's several injured and we'll need more than one ambulance, you call us right back. Okay?"

"I will. Hey, wait. I can see something. There's movement inside that SUV."

"Police, fire, and ambulance are on the way."

Ethan listens with the phone glued to his ear. He stares out his living room window at the shadows moving inside the smashed Bronco.

Chapter Two

Fifty-six minutes earlier...

His reflection stares back at him as he squints under the harsh fluorescents. It isn't the light that bothers him, but the hangover pulsating at his temples as his razor slides across his chin and cleans up the patch of shaving foam along his neck.

He mumbles to himself, "You look like shit."

He can't remember the last time he drank so much, and it really kicked into high gear for the past week. They were getting to the end, but not quite crossing the finish line yet. Tempers are frayed on both sides. They both try to mask it, keeping a paper-thin cordiality truce between them. A store supply of liquor keeps the dam from bursting. So far.

All that is really left is to go through the motions. They are pretty much finished with the dissection of the house. Their home. Memories and the past and a true love that once was, now just another itemized checklist.

They already went from room to room, claiming this and that. Words were cordial for the most part. He lost track of how many cardboard boxes he assembled. How many rolls of packing tape had he used? All the damn packing. Is it too heavy? Is it too light? Will it all fit?

Then the trips began, back and forth to the storage unit. The contract he signed said the first month was free. And he scribbled his signature wondering how many more months of limbo he would need after that. All the necessary minutia shrouding the big question. They were inching closer to a clean break.

He manages to smile a little at himself in the bathroom mirror. Sure, he might look like death warmed over, but he is proud of how well he and Judy are handling all of this here at the end. No real fights to speak of, although Judy never calls them that. She plays her little word games and talks semantics and calls what they are doing an "argument" or a "discussion," which makes things even worse, and their voices rise, and their anger boils and spills out all over again.

He's seen it with friends and even family over the years. Times like these can be downright dirty until you both manage to make it to the end. And all that's left is to hand over the keys and close the front door for good. Divorce could be a skip down the yellow brick road, or a never-ending slog like the Bataan death march.

It was not quite the world of Oz with Judy, but he has to admit, the liquor helps. And at the end of these blurred together heavy days, a bottle always waits for them. The good scotch is the first to go. He finished off the Glenlivit. She preferred the Maker's Mark some friend gave her for Christmas.

The tequila went fast. There is a lot about Judy that Daniel can't handle anymore, and he is certain she could say the same. But even he would readily admit his wife, well, soon to be ex-wife. Whatever the proper title was now, she sure could whip up some damn good frozen margaritas.

They discovered it by accident on a trip to Cancun some much better days ago.

Daniel had taken bartending classes before law

school took front and center. He was hazy on the breakdown for a lot of drinks, but he knew what went into a frozen strawberry margarita.

Judy wasn't even sure how to work the blender.

Daniel wanted to help, but she was adamant that she could do it all herself. He wasn't buying that as he watched her scurry about their cozy rental kitchen. The end result looked pretty good. But the taste tests didn't lie. Her mix was the clear winner and so much better. Daniel didn't even try to argue the point.

She said it was her secret ingredient. And he believed her. They laughed and danced throughout the hotel room and even made love on the balcony late into the night.

He smiled at the memory in the mirror. The other night, he asked her about the famous secret ingredient as she went through the motions and whipped up a fresh pitcher. But she never responded. Maybe she couldn't hear him over the rattle of the blender? Or... Maybe she was just ignoring the question?

He didn't allow himself to linger at the bathroom mirror long enough to come up with an answer. "Yeah. Another day late to the office." A sharp twinge of pain shoots through his temple as he glances over at the clock on the nightstand. "Daniel Morrison. Husband of the year. Lawyer of the month. Guy most likely to have his shit all together."

He talks to himself as he pulls a suitcoat out of the closet and looks for his belt. "A man in a suitcase. With no idea where the fuck anything is?" He grabs a belt that doesn't match and struggles to put it on as he huffs out of the room.

"Hey. Judy." He thumps down the carpeted stairs.

"Why didn't you tell me I was running so late?"

Judy takes a sip of coffee, wrapped in her terrycloth robe. "That's not my job anymore." She rubs sleep from puffy eyes, her morning hair a mad scientist's mess.

"I don't see it." Daniel frantically paces around the dining room and peeks down the hall towards the garage door. "Where's my bag? I mean, I can't... Goddamn it."

"Where'd you leave it?" She sips at her coffee and grabs a seat in the kitchen nook.

"Come on, Jude." His voice rises with anger. "If I knew the answer to that, why would I even ask you?"

She ignores his snippy attitude and checks her phone. "You keep packing up the Bronco for your storage unit trips." She offers nonchalantly. "Maybe it's in there?"

"It's not in the Bronco. Why would I put it in there? It's my laptop. My case files. It's not small enough to fall through the cracks. I mean... Where the hell is it?

Judy sips at her coffee, her attention glued to her phone as her index finger continues to slide across the screen with the beat of a metronome.

"I gotta say." He stomps into the kitchen. "Thanks for all your help, Jude."

"Uh huh." She doesn't look up. "You're going to be late."

He slumps against the kitchen archway. "I'm already late."

She doesn't respond. Her phone keeps her busy. He watches her repetitive movements like she's a trapped zoo animal behind the glass. "So, what is this? You're not going in today?"

She still doesn't look up. "I called in sick."

"Ha. Right. Sick's a funny way to say hangover."

He goes for a slight smile. She doesn't return it. He talks to the air. "What about your patients?"

She stops messing with her phone long enough to take a sip of lukewarm coffee. "Diaper rash is rarely fatal." Judy reaches for a crumpled pack of cigarettes and lights one with a candlestick lighter.

Daniel plays with a paper towel. "You sure you want to start smoking again?" He stuffs the towel in his pressed pants pocket. "I thought you quit for good?"

"I'll smoke when I want, thank you very much." She exhales with a little cough. "And you're the one who quit. Remember."

"Look…Jude." Daniel grabs a seat across from her. She doesn't pay him any attention. "Do you want to talk about it?"

"What's there to say? You get the car. I get everything else. That's a fair trade." Smoke billows between the two of them.

Daniel looks down at the Formica. "I didn't want us to end up like this."

Her laugh cuts sharp. "Ohhh. And how did you expect us to end?"

He searches for an answer but doesn't come up with much. "Not like this."

"Well, there you go." She exhales a stream of smoke. "Sounds like you've got it all figured out."

He stares at her. "Is that all you've got to say? Some bitchy sarcasm."

"Oh, I'm sorry. Am I allowed to say more?"

"This is for us." His voice rises with a shake. "I'm doing all this for us."

Her voice rises to meet his. "Oh, that's just bullshit, Counselor. You can save that sob story for your clients.

You never do anything that isn't for yourself. And you know it."

He waits for tempers to simmer before speaking. "Jude. If we keep going down the path we're going, we'll just crash and burn."

"Uh-huh. And what's your solution to all our wreckage?" She stubs out her cigarette with a rash of sparks. "You run away. It's what you do. I mean, we went through this same thing with your little pill problem. I'm fine, you said. I can deal with it. Just like a strung-out junkie might say, right? And if I hadn't forced—"

He cuts her off. "You really want to punch below the belt? We both know I took care of my problem. I did. And this isn't me running away. We're just not working anymore. Hell, Judy, we stopped working with each other a long time ago."

"Well, I for one am so glad we had this little talk." She stares back, with a slight quiver at her bottom lip. "It always makes me feel so much better." She knocks over the coffee cup as she gets up from the kitchen nook.

"Judy. Wait—" He moves to comfort her.

"Don't touch me." She tenses up. "I said, don't."

"Hey, I'm sorry. I didn't want to—"

"I don't care. Stop it."

He tries to comfort her again. "Daniel. Just." She steps away from his touch. "Check the closet. You're late." Her emotions start to crack as she turns away and moves out of the kitchen.

He doesn't follow her. His thoughts are cloudy, and his head hangs low. Polished wingtips click across the tile floor as he goes for the hallway closet and opens the door. There, under a few forgotten winter coats hanging overhead, his leather satchel and a stack of manila folders at his feet.

He calls out to her. "Jude. I've got a hearing at ten. I'll give you a call right after. Okay?" He waits for a second but doesn't get an answer.

Daniel snatches up his bag and gathers the loose pile of folders together. He closes the front door behind him.

Chapter Three

Gridlock. Traffic crawls. Endless rows of cars jockey for position in a snail's race down Highway 35. A green sign points out Austin city limits, which is still twenty miles away. San Marcos stretches through the next four exits.

Daniel grips the steering wheel of the Ford Bronco, his thumbs rest at 10 and 2. He hums along with the jingle on the XM radio commercial and mumbles to himself. "Jesus, please us. Five more miles through this shit. I'm so fuckin' late."

A stench of putrid exhaust wafts in the air and the morning heat shimmers off the asphalt. Digital arrows flash as cars and trucks clumsily merge. His eyes stay on the road but the sounds of the traffic fade in his mind.

"White star," he mutters.

The brand of champagne was White Star. Like the White Star Line. It was British or maybe Irish? The shipping company that built the *Titanic*, the ship that couldn't sink. The memory was vivid. It cuts through the traffic haze, and he is there. The eve of the hotel fight. The reminiscence left a bitter taste. It was an ugly one.

He could see himself in the spirits store, staring intently at the colorful label. He knew that she loved champagne but couldn't remember what type. His first thought was that she'd like any kind. But he knew enough to know that was such a dumb husband move.

He needed to get her something nice. A way to mark the occasion. It was a celebration between them.

A toast to the road ahead.

They were heading to New Orleans for a wedding. There was this good friend of Jude's, some rich hospital administrator about to embark on her third marriage. He remembered Jude saying that she desperately wanted a kid but had lousy taste in men. This new husband, number three at bat. He was some retired military sharpshooter with a solid screw or two loose. Daniel met him at some forced luncheon get-together kinda thing. The guy didn't seem much like the fatherly type. He was more of the survivalist—live off the grid, kill his own food, drink his own urine to survive kinda guy.

But Daniel knew enough to keep his opinions of Judy's friends to himself. He focused on the array of champagne selections and settled on the bottle of White Star. At fifty bucks and change, it couldn't be rotgut.

He couldn't for the life of him remember what sparked the fight. Lately there were so many little brushfire arguments that scorched into a full blaze. And this was another one of those. But this time the fires burned hot as neither of them backed down.

When they made it to the Texas/Louisiana state line, they were volleying screams and shouts at each other from the driver and passenger seat. Daniel could have kept driving, but his head was pounding, and Judy was on a tear, and he admitted to himself that he was liable to drive the damn car right off the road just to end their caustic back and forth for good.

Judy hated cheap hotels and Daniel knew that when he snapped and steered across the pocked dirt parking lot, straight for the thirty-five dollar a night, seedy Day's

Inn, right-off the highway.

Judy was out of the car first, but Daniel caught up with her. He wasn't done. He had a sarcastic response locked and loaded for her last screaming shout, but Judy ignored him and headed inside the skeevy lobby.

They tried to play nice in front of the weary Indian guy manning the tiny front desk. Daniel asked for a king, but she talked over him and requested a room with twin beds. She already knew the look on Daniel's face and didn't bother to turn around and verify it. But Daniel was faster and snatched up the plastic key cards before she could react.

They both left the tired clerk behind and headed for their car with the lobby truce holding under an uncomfortable silence. They continued not to talk as they stepped into their dingy hotel room. There was not much to look at, two tiny beds with thin crisp yellowed sheets. In the small, dank bathroom, Daniel found a stack of towels that may have been new sometime last century.

He tried to diffuse their tension with a joke about the lousy room, but Judy ignored him. She immediately grabbed the one chair in front of the worn desk and set it up outside the room.

Daniel didn't talk to her as she snatched up a bottle of screw-top wine and her latest worn paperback. She would have slammed the door behind her if she could, but the best they got was a tired wheeze until the door clicked closed.

She always did this. Set up shop right outside the hotel room door. All she needed was an available chair, her book and a glass of wine. And it was true, most of the time she would go through this ritual before she even unpacked. A glance around and out the door she went. It was one of the things he loved about her. She would talk to anybody. Daniel wasn't like that at all, but he would usually join her, mainly out of concerns for her safety.

He hated talking to anybody he didn't know. It was something he had to work at. But Judy was natural and never had any problems chatting back and forth with random encounters.

Mostly it was bored night watchmen. More than once, they received odd looks from a myriad of hotel guests puzzled at the loud and cheery hello with the tip of her wine glass. She was always trying to get him out of his comfort zone, and he had to admit, he really didn't mind sitting with her outside all those different hotel rooms. Besides, he loved taking her back inside when their flirting and hunger couldn't be suppressed anymore.

But there was nothing loving about the chair outside the faded white and dirty hotel room door in Lake Charles that night. She wanted to get away from him and Daniel couldn't care less where she went.

So, he sat on the side of one ratty twin bed and popped open the White Star champagne and drank alone from the bottle, with a silent toast to the death of their relationship. It wasn't supposed to sink. But it still hit a big fucking iceberg and went down to the murky depths there in some off-the-highway, shitty little dive motel.

Cloudy from the champagne, he still managed to do the math in his head. And the numbers all added up. Their sum total was five years and change. That night was the beginning of the end.

The blast of a car horn snaps him back to reality. He shakes himself out of his funk. Traffic continues to inch forward. Exhaust thick in the air.

Fidgety fingers scan through the radio dial. The speakers blurt through bits of music and talk, as he looks for something to lift his spirits. Classic rock. Deep tracks. New Age. Nothing seemed to do the trick.

His cell phone rings and mutes the music through the car speakers. He clicks a button on the dashboard and takes the call. "Hello."

"Daniel." A stiff voice fills the cabin. "It's Parker."

"Park. Hey, man. Yeah, I know." He shakes his head to no one. "I'm still on my way. It's nasty out here. Traffic this morning is crazy."

"I'll bet." Parker's voice is firm. "But you know. You should already be here."

"Jesus, Park. Give me a break." He grips the wheel. "We're scheduled with, what's his name, Murphy, at 10:00. I mean, it's no problem. A simple DUI. The man is pleading to it. Open and shut. Why are you bothering me with this?"

Silence in the cabin before the voice answers. "Mr. Kramer would like to review the case before we plead him out."

"Are you kidding me?" Daniel laughs. "Do me a favor, wipe your nose, man. I can see brown from here. I swear, Kramer is such a hard ass. Keep the old man on ice until— "

"Daniel." A gruff voice cuts through the cabin. "It's the hard ass. What was I supposed to have here on my desk before you waltzed out on Friday?"

"Mr. Kramer." He sits up in his seat and merges the Bronco into an open space in front of a slow truck. He takes a deep breath before he answers. "Good morning to you, sir. I spoke with Murphy's mother this weekend. Her son admitted to throwing the punch at the arresting officer. The young man was obviously intoxicated. She has assured me that they will drop any further threats of a lawsuit against the county. There was no use of excessive force. We can plead Murphy out. Simple." He grips the wheel and watches the traffic flow as he waits for a response.

"No." It echoes through the car speakers. "None of that answered my question. Let me ask you again. Where is the case file?"

Daniel steadies the wheel and reaches for some loose folders. He looks back up at the road. "It's here with me, sir."

"Okay, Mr. Morrison." Kramer's stern voice rises. "You are staring down the barrel. Now, I want that case file on my desk in fifteen minutes. Fifteen. Minutes. Or I swear, I will shit-can you back to pro bono work for migrant border jumpers. Are we clear?"

"Yes, sir." The leather on the steering wheel pops as Daniel grips it tighter and bites at his bottom lip. "Crystal clear." The call goes dead through the speakers.

He mumbles to himself. "The fuck? Are we clear?" Daniel shakes in his seat and trusts his middle finger at the padded dashboard "Paper-thin tough-guy bullshit. Screw you. You crusty old bastard." He disconnects his phone from the Bronco and shoves it into his pocket.

He hits his turn signal. The sound repetitively clicks in his ear as he maneuvers his vehicle into another lane. The thrill of movement wears off fast as he drives a few feet and brakes hard behind a slow moving 18-wheeler. Horns honk and the stench of exhaust wafts in the air as the dense traffic continues to inch forward.

Chapter Four

The crimson convertible Mazda cushions around the curve and barrels down the blacktop. It dodges and weaves around parked cars parked on either side of the road throughout the dense suburban neighborhood.

At the edge of the curb, a yellowed plastic safety man, standing at frozen attention. Its "Slow Down - Children Are Playing Here" motto stenciled on its chest. The sign falls over as the convertible clips it. The cheap red warning flag flutters into the gutter.

Claudia Grant tense at the wheel. Her foot heavy on the gas and her smooth hands caress the wheel, careful not to stress her freshly manicured nails. She drives down the side streets without a care in the world. The wind blows her long red hair into a fiery mane. Her giant sunglasses shield the morning sun, her face fresh from another Botox treatment at the med spa.

"What the hell else am I doing? That's exactly what I'm doing. I'm following the directions." Her voice carries loud even over the powerful sports car engine. "Hello? Yes, I can hear you. What? What did you say? Are you calling me stupid? Hold on." She adjusts her hands-free headset and banks the sports car hard. It pinballs down another tight neighborhood street.

"How am I supposed to know where the hell I am? It's not me, it's my GPS thingy that took me this way." She catches her reflection in the rearview mirror. Her collagen-treated lips purse into a kiss as she looks for any flaw. "Not enough filler. I told that twenty-year-old with her tits all in my face that it wasn't enough. But no, why should anyone listen to me? I'm only the patient paying for this shoddy work. Bigger. I want them to be bigger. What? What are you…"

Her voice lashes out into the microphone. "No. I told you and I told your people, I'm not ready for a crowd. I'm not ready for any of this. I swear, I hate these events. I hate that I'm required to go to these events. I mean, they're not even about me."

Her Mazda takes another hard turn and slaloms down the tight street. "What? What are you blabbing about? Of course, I want to help the campaign. I'm always there. Right? Uh huh, that's right. It's what I do." She keeps checking her reflection in the rearview mirror. "I am so overdue. I've gotta book an appointment for my eyelashes." Her eyebrows arch and she ignores the rearview and turns her anger to the microphone.

"Hey, if you wanted me there so bad, you would tell me where the hell I am. What? I don't know. I'm on some dinky little side street. What are you even doing out here in the suburban sticks?"

Her car brakes at an intersection. She looks all around and ignores the GPS voice as it continues to cycle through recalculations. She doesn't listen to the digital pleas and picks a direction on her own. The Mazda accelerates. Claudia laughs into the microphone.

"Voters? Are you for real? Well, I can tell you, I wouldn't want these people anywhere near me. All I see are cheap houses, cheap cars. Oh my God, these cheap trash cans are everywhere. This is like driving through some horrid obstacle course."

An angry neighbor on the sidewalk gestures for her to slow down. She isn't fazed as her car flies on by. "Look, there's some cheap people, and there's some more. And you expect me to grovel to this trash for their votes? I don't think so." She guns the powerful engine and makes a sharp turn. Her attitude cuts off suddenly. "Christ Almighty." She slams on the brakes.

The tiny convertible screeches to a halt; the tires leave dual streaks of black marks on the asphalt. The bumper rests inches from a U-Haul moving van, its rear doors open, and a metal ramp extends from the open cargo hold.

"Are you people crazy?" Claudia sits up in her bucket seat and shouts out as a woman who is used to getting her own way. "Who parks their fucking truck in the middle of the road? I could have been killed here." She rakes on the steering wheel, the Mazda lurches and growls around the moving van.

Two college-aged kids struggle with a leather couch towards the van.

"Hello, you. Yes, you." Claudia commands them. "Get this hunk of junk out of my way. You're parked on the street. I could have the police come down on you like a ton of bricks."

The two college kids lower the couch to the walkway. One is happy for the break, the other teenager strides for her car. "Oh, jeeze. I'm so sorry. I thought we pulled the U-Haul far enough over. Parking is tight as hell around here. I promise we won't be here much longer. Are you okay?"

"What are you, dense?" Claudia shouts out. "Do I sound okay? I mean, seriously. Hello. Look at me when I talk to you/ Do you even know who I am?"

"I'm sorry, but..." The young man looks puzzled. "How would I know--"

"You." She steps over his words. "Move this piece of garbage. Right. Now."

"Ma'am. I do hear you." He slowly walks around her car with a slight smirk as he stares down at the manic woman in the tiny sports car shouting up at him in her giant sunglasses. "And I'm very sorry you're upset. But I can't really move the truck right now. We're almost finished. We're moving-—"

"You're in the middle of the fucking street. You listen to me. I don't care what you're doing. Do what I tell you and move this truck." She snaps out the command with a growing screechy pitch to her voice. "This instant. Now."

"Ma'am." The college student doesn't allow her privilege to faze him. He wipes sweat from his brow. "I mean, ahh...can't you go around us here?"

"Why do you keep calling me that?" She gapes at him with an open mouth. "Ma'am? Is there anything you see that looks like a ma'am? You know what you can do, kid? Go fuck yourself." She punches the gas. The young man leaps out of the way as the Mazda burns across the blacktop and fishtails down the narrow roadway.

Claudia grips the steering wheel and grinds her teeth. Her cell phone chimes. She claws at the headset as it snags through her windblown hair. "I don't have time for this." She gets it in position and clicks on the call. "For fucks sake, I swear, I will get there when I get there. Do you know what happened? I nearly got myself killed. And you won't believe what this snotty little punk actually called me. What?"

Her anger melts away and her voice drops to a sultry

tone. "Baby doll. Oh my God. Hellooo. Oh, no, baby. I can't. Not right now. We can talk later." She downshifts around a curve and hits the gas. "I'm in a bit of a hurry. You know how much I hate these meet and greet events. Oh, and of course. I'm leaving one cheap neighborhood development for another. Why not? Fine. That's simply wonderful." She sputters a frustrating sob. "I am so lost. I hate this GPS thingy."

Her spirits brighten. "Baby, now you know it's not like that. At all." She sits up in her car seat. "I swear. Of course, I miss you. I can't wait to show you how much. But right this second, I am in the middle—" The Mazda brakes hard at a stop light.

"Come on." Claudia's foot guns the gas. "Let's go, let's go. No. Sorry, baby. I'm at a stop light. No, I can hear you." She smiles wide. "Yes. He's gone all this weekend. Honestly, I really don't care. It's the campaign trail again. That's his whole life. Morning, noon, and night. It's always some fool thing or another with the goddamn campaign." She shakes away the negativity. "Listen, I don't want to talk about any of that right now. Shake it off, shake it off. What? No. You talk. Tell me something else. I don't know. Use your imagination. Tell me something nice. Where are you gonna take me?"

The light turns. Claudia floors it and stays glued to the minivan right in front of her.

"Oh, really." She smiles at the voice in her ear. "Is that where you want to go? Ahhh-haaaa. Yes, of course I had a wonderful time at the cabin." Her voice drips saccharine sweet. "No, I did. In fact, I'm pretty sure I proved that point to you several times. Remember? Oh, you don't remember? Well, I'll have to see what I can do about that." She enjoys the sensual tease even as she fidgets and strains in her seat as she careens around the slow-moving minivan.

"See. That's right. I knew you would remember. And if you're a good boy, I'll do it all over again." Her balled fist punches at the padded steering wheel. She shouts out. "Will you get the fuck out of my way!"

She returns to the headset microphone. "No, no. Not you, baby. Wait a sec. Hold on."

The Mazda squeals around the slow minivan and burns down the narrow roadway at high speed.

Chapter Five

The Bronco sits deep in the heart of highway gridlock. Daniel drums his fingers on the steering wheel as he stares at the back of a bus. It's an advertisement, and he can barely make out words and images through the exhaust dirt and matted grime. "I see you there, ambulance chaser. Jesus, how many 4's do I have to dial?" He chuckles to himself. "Who am I kidding? If I don't get a move on here, I'll dial any number you want and beg you for a fuckin' job."

He turns around in his seat and takes in the rows of dense traffic packed in on every side. The lane next to him starts to move a bit. He hits his blinker. "Come on. Come on. Let me in." He wishes for a bit of compassion as he tries to force the Bronco into the lane.

A VW bug isn't fast enough to stay with the traffic flow. Daniel takes advantage of the small space and edges forward as he squeezes the SUV into the lane. "Okay, okay." He can't help but smile as the cars move forward. "Here we go. Finally."

The steady flow drips to a crawl until the lane comes to an abrupt halt. The overhead traffic light stays green, but the line of vehicles idles in place.

Someone leans on their car horn. The high-pitched steady noise muffled through the safety glass still manages to pierce Daniel's throbbing temple. He tries to ignore the splitting headache and growing tension at the base of his neck. His fingers drum on the dashboard to some non-existent song.

The Bronco moves a few meters, and stops again as the light flashes yellow and turns red. The traffic knot gets even tighter as vehicles going the other direction close any available gap.

"Jesus, blue fuck. Christ." Daniel violently shakes the wheel and bounces in his seat, his beating heart a speed bag in his chest. He takes deep breaths until he can reel in his anger. He settles for a thin veneer of calm. "What a fuckin' mess." Noxious fumes from the cluster of vehicles seeps through the Bronco's air vents. Daniel smacks his lips. He can taste the oily fuel stench. He claws at the vents and manages to close all of them.

The interior heats up as the morning sun beats down on the Bronco.

Daniel runs a finger under his sweaty shirt collar and sits back with a frustrated sigh. "What else is new?" The traffic light sways overhead. He stares at it and mutters to himself. "A colossal clusterfuck. That's been pretty much your day to day lately, hasn't it?"

He shakes his head to banish the dark thoughts. "Don't do this. Don't." He wipes away beads of sweat forming along his forehead. "Don't beat yourself up over this. Things happen for a reason and you're doing all the right things. Jude knows it. She does."

The traffic light turns green. Daniel hits the gas and the Bronco lurches through the crossroads. He cushions the brake right behind an orange Datsun. They pick up a bit of speed. "All right. Here we go." The Datsun speeds up. Daniel stays glued to the beat-up car. "Come on, asshole. Let's go. *D* is that way, man. Drive."

The Datsun comes to a stop and doesn't have any

working taillights. "…the fuck?" Daniel realizes and reacts. His left foot stomps hard on the brake; tires smoke and squeal as the Bronco lurches to a halt, inches from the Datsun's rusty bumper.

The glove compartment lid pops loose. Daniel slams the lid closed. It doesn't catch and bounces back open. "Jesus Christ Almighty. Please. I'm begging you." He stares at the open hole in the dashboard, defeated. His head collapses to the steering wheel. Eyes closed tight. "Can't anything go right for me today?"

He turns to the open compartment and his eyes widen. A hint of a smile forms as the distant memory surfaces across his expression. He roots around inside the glove compartment, he shoves insurance papers, forgotten receipts and trash aside. Until he finds what he's looking for.

A small metal breath mint tin. The once bright red and white logo faded with age. He shakes the metal tin. Something rattles inside. "No, I don't believe it." He glances up at the stalled traffic, rows of vehicles still lined up and not moving anywhere.

"The last of the Mohicans."

He peers around at all the other cars with a guilty conscience that only he's aware of.

Carefully and slowly. He opens the metal tin. "Hey, boys." Several blue barrel-shaped pills are inside the container. He tilts the tin and lets the pills roll back and forth. "How have you been? Wow. It's been a while." He gently places the open tin down on the passenger seat. The blue pills vibrate against the thin metal. Daniel carefully closes the glove compartment. The lid clicks into place.

Fingers drum on the wheel as Daniel silently wishes

and hopes the traffic would move. But it doesn't. "Okay." He glances back over at the open tin of pills. "Don't do. Think. Think about it. Things happen. I mean, they happen for a reason." He glances at the pills until he forces his eyes back to the road. "Yes, they do."

Traffic moves a few meters before coming to a halt again. Daniel stays with the lane as the line of vehicles move together.

"Yeah, I can hear her. Loud and clear" He grips the wheel and agrees with his reflection in the windshield. "But be honest. Do you really care what she thinks? I mean, face it. Man, your marriage is flatlined. You know exactly what Judy would say. You know it." His fingers slide across and touch the metal tin. "But she ain't here right now. And she never has to know."

Traffic lurches forward. Daniel forgets the tin and steers the Bronco into another lane, behind a car with working brake lights that flash alight until they turn steady red. The line of vehicles comes to a stop.

Daniel grinds his teeth as he stares at the vehicle in front of him. He can make out a fresh bumper sticker showcasing some local politician.

Make Texas for Texans Again—Vote Hayden Grant.

"Think about it." His eyes drift from the windshield and back to the passenger seat. "You know what's waiting for you." The blue pills vibrate inside the tin. "As soon as you walk into that office. Old man Kramer, all in your face. I mean from the first second through the entire fuckin' day. Sorry, pal. I don't want to be the bearer of bad news." His right hand leaves the steering wheel. "But it's a fact." He carefully touches the metal tin like he expects a shock.

"Come on. Admit it. There's no shame in being honest with yourself." Fingertips graze the smooth pills inside. "You need this. Take two. Junkie's orders." His hand hesitates over the tin. "Christ. Go on. Do it." His conscience doesn't let up. "Well, what the hell are you waiting for?"

A honk from a car horn startles him. He gives a little wave as he drives forward and stays with the traffic flow. "Ten minutes." He talks to his reflection in the rearview. "That's it. You've got, ten minutes." He glances at the digital clock on the dashboard. The blue pills vibrate in the tin. "One minute more and a pissed-off boss this morning becomes a full-on, all-day headache. And then. You'll be thankful you have them. Okay?"

He makes up his mind. "Okay."

Traffic starts to move. Daniel steers the Bronco away from the endless rows of stop and start and drives down an empty residential street.

Chapter Six

The red Mazda coupe roars down the road and blasts past the Neighborhood Watch notice and a twenty-five-mile-an-hour speed limit sign. Her foot cushions the gas, and the engine purrs like a jungle cat.

I've got it, baby." Claudia fidgets with her headset. "I can hear you. Can you hear me?" She leans on her car horn and banks fast around a postal truck parked at a mailbox kiosk. "These people park their crappy cars anywhere. What?" Claudia adjusts her large sunglasses. "No, I can't come over then, baby. Because I'll miss Antoine. He's the only one I trust with my hair. I couldn't get another appointment for months. Cancel it? No, I'm sorry. Not a chance."

She turns hard down another residential road. "What?" A sly smile grows across her face. "Oh, you will, huh. Well, I'm gonna have to hold you to that." Her fingers slide around the circumference of the steering wheel. She snaps out of it.

"Baby, no. Not now. Because I said so. Awe, I love it when you pout. You are, I can hear it over the phone. You're such a teenager sometimes. What am I gonna do with you?" She grins and licks her lips. "Ohhh. Is that so. Well…" Her legs close together. "As a matter of fact, yes, I am. Very much. Because you get me like that."

She squirms in her seat. "You are so bad. Yes, you are. What? No, I can't. Honey, don't." She slows down and sinks into her seat, her smile wide underneath her sunglasses. "Ohhh, you are? Right now?" She keeps her eyes on the road, but her mind is lost in the call. "Baby, that's so wrong. Yes, it is. You know how much I love watching you do that." A slight giggle escapes. "You are such a bad boy."

Claudia glances down the empty neighborhood street. The Mazda is the only car on the road. She downshifts the sportscar and slides down in her seat.

"You're serious, aren't you." She bites at her bottom lip. "Yes, I'm listening." She squirms in the bucket seat. "I'm doing it. God, I love it when you tell me what to do." Claudia unbuckles her seatbelt. "Okay, baby. I will. I'll play." She starts to scoot back and forth in her seat. "I swear when you get like this. You are sooo naughty." Her fingers glide along the wheel as she keeps it steady. "I love it." The Mazda swerves a bit, but she corrects it back into her lane.

In the driver's well, a pair of silk panties appear around her ankles. "I can't believe I'm doing this." She takes her foot off the gas and slips out of the thong.

****

Throughout the affluent community, sprinklers pop out of their hiding places and rotate and repeat. They mist manicured green lawns and the sheen of water reflects a rainbow of color in the morning sunlight.

Ornate metal gates and tall hedges hide the houses from the street. Unseen birds chirp in the trees. A few vehicles navigate the wide neighborhood roads.

The Bronco edges past slower traffic. It banks around a turn and heads for a stop sign. Daniel brings the SUV to a hard halt. He bounces in his seat as he waits his turn at the crossroads. "Come on, come on." His eyes go to the dashboard. He reaches out and touches the clock. "And that's the buzzer. There it is. Game over." He glances over at the passenger seat. The blue pills vibrate inside the open metal tin.

A car horn blast jolts him. It's his turn to go. He waves a quick apology and hits the gas. His foot presses into the accelerator. The Bronco races on down the road.

Daniel reaches for the metal tin.

The Bronco bounces through a pothole.

A handful of blue pills leap out from the tin and scatter all over the passenger side. "Oh, fuck me." Blue pills spill off the seat and fall to the floor. Daniel keeps his eyes on the road. Traffic is thin. He reaches over and scoops up some pills from the seat. He leans and gathers up a few more and drops the handful back into the tin. His eyes drift from the road to random pills still loose in the folds of the seat and rolling around the floorboards.

On the neighborhood road, the red Mazda burns down the blacktop. The sports car swerves down the straightaway.

****

Claudia, her high heel pressed down on the gas pedal and her sun dress hiked up in the bucket seat. The back of her neck pressed against the headrest. Her eyes on the road but her mind is lost in the microphone and the voice in her ear. "I can hear you, baby." Her breath caught in her throat. "Don't stop." Manicured fingers grip the wheel while her other hand grinds in her lap. Her eyes lidded, her voice deep and eager. "Oh, God, please don't stop." Her fingers flex. "Ohhh. I'm almost there."

Identical houses line the street, a tightly packed neighborhood with tiny lawns. A few cars scattered in driveways. The morning sun burns hot as it peeks through the clouds.

Claudia's red Mazda roars down the road. It sways down the asphalt and corrects back into the right lane.

****

The Bronco blasts past a Neighborhood Watch sign and doubles the posted twenty mile an hour speed limit. Daniel reaches and grabs the last of the loose pills from the floorboard. "This is all I need." He looks at the three pills in his hand. His attention stays on the road, but the perfect pills keep pulling him back. "Lemme have these for the day. And I'll start clean again tomorrow." He pops the three pills into his mouth and dry swallows. "First thing."

A red sports car turns onto the road and burns towards him. The Mazda swerves and races for the Bronco like a bullet.

Daniel's eyes widen. He braces for impact.

The Mazda plows straight into the Bronco with a crunch of steel and shower of glass. The airbag inflates and envelopes him.

Chapter Seven

His ears ring at a steady decibel, and eyes glaze over like a glass-jaw fighter who took a hard hit. Daniel shifts in his seat with a groggy grunt. His face rubs against a rough canvas material. Startled, he shoves and pushes the deflated airbag out of his face. His breathing was hindered by a thick lump stuck in his throat.

Through spiderweb cracks in the windshield, he sees steam spraying out from a smashed radiator, the engine compartment a mess of mangled metal, the hood of the SUV crumpled in. Daniel blinks aware. In a fog, he glances over at the passenger seat. Blue pills are scattered all throughout the cabin.

Metal grinds against metal as the driver's side door creaks open. Daniel pushes himself out of the wreckage. Unseen bruises throb, the intense pain masked by shock. He stumbles around in a daze, his wingtips skid through wet asphalt. Daniel takes in the scene through a mental haze. He slips and slides through an oily slick and tries to regain his senses.

A burning sensation in his eyes. He blinks in the morning sun. Wipes at his forehead. Fresh blood on his palm and a red stain grows along the starched cuff of his white shirt. He winces as he touches the large gash above his left eye.

Daniel, his ears still ringing with a steady hum, shakes away growing vertigo as he bumbles about the accident scene.

The red vehicle that hit him looked like a mangled grade-school sculpture of twisted iron. A rainbow of viscous fluids flows over shattered chips of windshield safety glass.

Daniel tries to sputter a sound but can't hear anything over the dense drone in his head. He spots something that shouldn't be on the road. Like a colorful artifact on a bleak landscape. He continues to blink until his focus comes in clearer as he wanders over towards it.

A leg. Clad in a sheer stocking and bent upwards into a twisted hook. The dirty foot pointing towards the sun is missing a shoe. His eyes squint at the crooked leg as he stumbles closer. He finds a woman sprawled out on the ground. Her dress dirty and torn, the satin material soaked a crimson red. Her salon-fresh skin a shredded mess of blood and bone. Daniel stares down at the wrecked body, waiting for a hint of life, any sign of movement that never comes.

He can hear a voice. The ringing in his ears subsides a bit, the words sound as if they echo down a deep dark well. "Hey, mister." A heavyset man in a ratty robe calls out from the safety of his front porch. "You shouldn't be moving around like that. You were in a real bad accident. Are you okay?"

Daniel turns towards the sounds and tries to comprehend. The words in his mind translate into a garbled mess of static. He wipes away the flow of wet blood from his forehead.

"Mister." He can hear the faint sound of sirens growing. "You're in shock. Don't worry. I called 911." The man on the porch cranes his neck for a better look. "They're sending everybody. They're all on the way."

The high-pitched whine of the sirens brings him to the surface. Daniel lurches away from the voice and stumbles for his Bronco. Bent metal creaks as he grabs the driver's door and climbs back inside. He tries to focus on all the loose pills scattered in the cabin and manages to snatch up a few.

The sirens grow.

Daniel sits up in a panic and tries to start the engine. All he gets back is an electric whine from the starter motor. "Come on." Words mumble at his lips. "Come on." The starter motor doesn't spark, and the engine won't catch.

He desperately scrapes up a few more pills from the floorboards. He glances in the back seat. Picks up one more. Sirens grow loud as an ambulance turns onto the road and rides up to the accident scene. A kaleidoscope of colorful lights reflects through the Bronco's shattered windshield. He shoves himself out of the wreckage.

"Mister? Hey?" The man on the porch watches him go with an overpowering puzzlement. "No. You can't do that. Where are you going?"

Daniel ignores the loud voice and lurches away from the scene as paramedics grab their gear and race up to Claudia's inert body.

He doesn't look back as he stumbles past the back yard and follows a row of high wooden slats. An anxious and eager German shepherd barks at the stranger and chases him down the length of the fence. Daniel picks up his pace, his breath caught in his throat, his battered body a live wire. He gets some distance from the dog on his heels and trips over a divot of grass. He slips and falls face first into the green ground. The dog bashes against the wooden slats with a vicious and wet snap full of long sharp teeth.

Blood and dirt smeared across his face as he groans and lifts himself off the grass. A rising level of panic propels him forward and he doesn't look back. The dog keeps pace until he runs out of fenced yard. His intense bark never ceases with a steady yawp.

****

"Is she okay?" The man on the porch approaches the two paramedics huddled over the mangled body. He talks to their backs. "I mean, is she gonna be, okay?"

A tired paramedic glances his way. The man takes that as an invitation and steps closer. "I was standing right there in my kitchen when I heard it happen. It was this, I mean, it gave me one hell of a start. I got on the phone, first thing. Called 911. Jesus, she looks rough."

"Sir. We really need you to back away from here." The tired paramedic stands up. "This way. Come on, sir."

"I'm Ethan Solis. S-o-l-i-s." He tightens his robe and obeys the command but points rapidly over his shoulder. "The other guy from the accident. I saw him leave. I did. He walked straight away from here. I mean, you can't do that, right? Isn't that illegal?"

"Please step back, sir." The glassy-eyed paramedic keeps him moving. "We need the room to do our job."

"No." Ethan doesn't let up. "Listen to me. This guy. The guy that drove that SUV. He left the scene. That's a hit and run, plain as day. And he's gone. I saw him take off that way."

The paramedic looks over at the battered vehicle. The engine compartment took the brunt of the hit, but other than the shattered windshield, the cabin looks in decent shape. He notices the driver's door propped open.

"See, I told you." Ethan talks in his ear. "He got out

and walked right the hell out of here. You can't do that? I mean, I would never do that."

The paramedic ignores him and glances down at the length of fence. He can hear a large dog barking up a storm in a nearby neighbor's yard.

****

Daniel emerges from the endless fence line and doesn't look up as he shuffles down a quiet neighborhood street. His polished wingtips are scarred and coated in mud. His dress shirt and slacks are a grimy mess. He uses his red-stained sleeve to wipe at the dirt and blood matted on his forehead. His eyes lock on the sidewalk with every step, his breath catches in his chest and his feet trip up, but he doesn't stop moving.

He finally pauses to try and slow down his internal alarm. His breathing is harsh but steady. He takes in his surroundings and glances up and down the road.

Identical houses and demarcated fences line the dense neighborhood. A quiet street, birds chirp in the trees, a stillness in the air.

In the distance, Daniel spots movement. A young woman pushes an umbrella stroller down the sidewalk. His anxiety rises as he turns around and heads back the other way. He continues to follow the sidewalk. His eyes can't help but dart all around for any movement. A panicked electrical current of thoughts trip through his mind. "What the hell am I gonna do? What did I do? I had to leave. I had no choice. Blue pills. In my system. All that blue. A drug test, first thing. In the ambulance. They'd take my blood. Check it. I wouldn't pass. Hell, they'd see it in my eyes. Pupils dilated. I couldn't hide it. I had to move. Fuck…I'm so fucked."

Battered and bruised hands fish through his soiled

pants pockets, and he finds an old paper towel. He uses it to wipe at the grime on his forehead. His eyebrows matted with dirt and gore. Words caught in his lips. "I must look like a fucking lunatic." The paper towel blotted with crusty blood. He balls it up to throw away but stuffs it back into his pocket.

His wide eyes scan all around. A car engine starts up and he startles at the sound. "Jesus." He turns around in a panic and decides to duck in the shade of a stack of metal mailboxes.

A suburban mom sedan pulls out of a driveway and cruises on down the street.

Daniel keeps his back to the approaching car, knowing he stands out on the barren sidewalk like a sore thumb. He glances over his shoulder as brake lights flash, and the sedan turns onto another road. "They're gonna stop me if I'm out here like this too much longer." He babbles to himself, "Get out. Right the fuck now." Daniel picks up the pace. "I've gotta get off this street." His hackles rise. He freezes in place. "Oh, no. Please. No."

He can hear it. The whiny loop of horns and sirens grows fast and increases with an intense echo. Daniel stays frozen in place on the sidewalk. He shakes in his shoes as the wall of sound grows deafening. He doesn't realize he's biting his lip until he can taste the blood. His wild eyes clench closed tight.

With a blare of horns and sirens, a fire truck turns onto the street and races past him. The blast of windstream blows through his matted hair. His eyes crack open to watch brake lights flash red and the fire truck takes a sharp turn down another road. "Calm down. Down. There you go. It's okay. You got this." He spits out the copper taste from his mouth. "Okay. Think. The fire truck came from that direction. Right? Yeah. Then that's the way to go."

Daniel moves and heads down another suburban street. "I swear, I'm in the goddamn *Twilight Zone*. It's the same street as the last one." He keeps up the pace. He spots a delivery van inching down the road, apparently searching for the right house number. His nerves continue to ride waves of jolts and sparks. He feels unseen eyes all over him. His heavy breathing cuts through the birds chirping in the trees and the stillness of the neighborhood. "Out. Get out." His gaze stays glued to the horizon. The words mutter at his lips. "Move through the maze. Keep going. You're good. Going the right way. Away from here."

His tired eyes brighten. "Wait... There it is. That's it." He heads across another street and zeroes in on the gated entrance to the development. A metal cutout of a cowboy leans against a metal fencepost. Metal longhorn steers flank on either side of the community entrance. A frayed wooden sign speaks to the country road.

Welcome to Centennial Ridge, a homey place to hang your hat.

Daniel keeps moving until the sidewalk runs out.

A faded yellow line separates traffic on either side of the busy roadway. A convoy of cars and trucks keeps a steady pace and rockets down the rural road.

Daniel walks towards the approaching vehicles and stays as far to the edge of the asphalt as he can. His scuffed wingtips kick through grit and gravel. He keeps his eyes glued to the ground as vehicles buffet past him. He squints through a dust cloud and morning haze.

He closes in on a rusted pole and the back of a metal

sign. He turns around for a glance as he walks past it. A dingy white background with faded black ink.

Speed Limit 45 miles an hour.

The sun beats down on his cut forehead, the blood flow crusts and coagulates under the intense heat. Sweat mixed with soot coats his face and runs in a river. Stains grow all through his dirty clothes. He keeps walking, careful to stay far from the side of the road. He passes a collection of plastic debris and glass bottles. Fast-food wrappers are squashed in the muck.

An 18-wheeler tractor trailer thunders towards him. Its roar grows as it races past him. Daniel shields his face from the tunnel of wind that batters him. He watches the truck tear down the road and turns back towards his long walk. His eyes blink under the steady sun.

A slight smile manages to cut through all the matted grime on his face. The tip of a yellow and orange seashell on the horizon. As he closes in, he can see the entire Shell gas station logo, the small station just over the hill. The sign beckons.

His wingtips kick through the dirt as he exerts what energy he has left to propel forward. He plods for the looming sign like a man stumbling towards an oasis in the desert.

The three gas pumps sit empty under a leaning awning. Daniel ignores them as he goes for the shaded glass door.

The blast of air conditioning immediately hits him, it's a shock to his system as it chills the sweat on his body. He freezes in place as the door wheezes closed behind him. Bright florescent lights shine, their crackle competes with the hum from the drink coolers. Rows of colorful snacks, gaudy displays and neon advertisements all vie for his attention.

He's hypnotized by the lilt of the store Muzak. It's peace. He basks in the feeling. Until it's broken by a faint siren in the distance. Daniel turns and watches through the tinted glass as the noise increases to a piercing sharp whine. A police car shrieks down the rural road. He stays at the tinted glass until the siren fades. A river of shakes races through his body and crawls across his pale skin. Daniel's lost in the sensation and fights to get himself under control.

He spots a sign for the restroom. And heads for it.

"Bathrooms are locked. For customers only."

He freezes. And turns towards the voice. A guy with a wiry black beard and corporate T-shirt sits at the counter. His face peeks through the Plexiglas hole surrounded by the back of the register, various scratch-off choices and endless cigarette brands.

Daniel plods towards the counter. The beady eyes above the black beard widen as he takes him all in. Dress clothes a ragged mess, his bleached white skin coated in a dirty grime. Daniel steps up to the register. A single word croaks between his chapped lips. "Coffee."

The bearded cashier stares back at him. "Are you okay, man?"

"Uh huh." Daniel doesn't flinch. "I'm good."

"Okay." The cashier clearly doesn't believe him. "Coffee. It's a few hours old, but it's still fresh. You can find everything you need. Right over there."

Daniel holds out his hand. "Bathroom." Impatient. "The key."

"Sure." The cashier waits." One large coffee. That'll be—" The register rings up the sale. "—$2.99."

Daniel breaks the stalemate and fishes through his

pockets. He pulls out a bloody paper towel and shoves it back inside. Cashier's eyebrows can't help themselves. He watches every move. Daniel brings out his phone and wallet. He thumbs through bills and drops a crisp twenty onto the counter.

The cashier snatches it up and examines both sides. He finally passes over a box wrench with a copper key dangling from a fob.

Daniel takes off. The cashier rings up the sale and calls to his back. "Hey? Don't you want your change?" He doesn't respond and heads for the restroom sign.

The key slides into the lock. Daniel shoulders into the bathroom. He closes and locks the door behind him. A small room with a toilet endlessly running and a small porcelain sink. An overpowering antiseptic smell dominates. Dirty white tiles cover the floor and walls. Every surface seems slick and wet to the touch.

He can't help but have a slack-jawed stare at his reflection in the smudged metal mirror. He wipes away the sheen of condensation and peers closer. He grimaces at the state of his clothes. His shirt and pants blotted with a map of sweat and dirty stains. His scuffed and scarred shoes light-years away from the polished loafers he slipped into this morning. He runs a battered hand across his sunken and shell-shocked face. He winces as fingers graze the deep gash across his forehead.

His hand goes into his pants pocket, and he grabs his cell. He stares at the phone in his hand like a monolith from better days that he unearthed.

Three missed calls from work are highlighted on the home screen. He ignores them and flips through various screens until he can scroll through his contacts list. He finds the right name and pushes the number to dial.

Phone to his ear, he can hear muted ring tones followed by an electronic click. "Come on, Sis." He mumbles to the metal mirror. "Pick up. Please. Please. Be there."

The call connects. A cheery voice echoes in the small room. "Hi. This is Jessie. I'm not in right now but leave me a message and I'll get back to you. If you're calling about the Toyota, please leave your name, number and a good time to call you back."

An electronic beep gets his attention. He talks into his phone. He tries to keep the shakes and tension out of his voice. He doesn't succeed. "Hey, it's me. Dan. I…uh. Listen, I…I need to come over and see you. Something happened here this morning. Something that I can't believe. I mean…I swear, it wasn't my fault. I didn't even see her. You know. I couldn't believe it. I was…I mean, she came out of nowhere. But I'm… I took some…uh…" He stops talking. Silence records over the line. He stares at his haggard face and clears his dry throat. "I'll tell you the whole thing. Okay. When I come over there. I'm on my way. Be home. Please be home. Please." He ends the call and drops the phone back into his pocket.

His hands shake. He doesn't move until they stop. He turns on the faucet full blast. A wild spray of water fills the sink. His fingers test for temperature. He splashes handfuls of water on his face, his eyes closed to the cooling sensation. He repeats it a few times. Water washes out of the bowl and runs onto the tile floor.

He stops as water streams down his cheeks. Daniel stares at himself in the warped metal mirror, the running water forgotten.

Chapter Eight

Two uniformed policemen walk down a manicured garden path, an opulent house over their shoulders. Clusters of fancy dressed patrons part along the pathway and let the officers through. The two uniforms keep a steady pace.

"Excuse me. Officers," a woman's voice calls out. "Please. Could you hold up a minute?"

The two blue uniforms stop as Roya Navarro catches up to them. A gold shield hangs from her jacket breast pocket. She looks at their young faces. The officers could be her sons.

"Detective Roya Navarro. SAPD. I'm with Victim Services."

"Detective." The cop with chiseled cheekbones speaks up. "I'm Officer Charles Perez, this is Officer Walter Kovach. We're with San Marcos PD."

Handshakes are shared. "Sorry to meet under these circumstances." Detective Navarro speaks in hushed tones as people move around them and hustle off in their own directions. "Do either of you have any experience with this?"

Officer Perez responds. "No, ma'am."

"It was a head on collision." Officer Kovach, a rutted red-faced farm boy who looks uncomfortable under the morning sun, speaks up. "She was dead on impact." He wipes at his sweaty forehead. "That's all, folks. Am I missing something here? What else should we say?"

"Yeah." Detective Navarro shakes her head but bites her tongue at his snide attitude. "You better let me tell him." She communicates with the two officers like a woman who's had to deal with some form of the Boys Network her whole professional life." Okay, I can see all the hustle bustle going on around this shindig. So where are we going?"

"On the other side of this hedge maze." Officer Perez points. "They've got a makeshift stage set up."

"Big place. Privileges of the wealthy." Detective Navarro takes in the house and open space. "Pretty sweet. This back yard even has a back yard. Okay, you two. Lead the way."

Kovach and Perez continue to follow the large hedges. Navarro stays on their heels. Perez talks to her. "It's supposed to be some kind of political gathering. Guess the homeowner is a big supporter."

"I'd say." She continues to soak it all in. "Good to have friends in high places."

The three of them break out of the hedge maze, into the midst of a large crowd. A campaign rally for the donor class. The party faithful sit on fold-out chairs in front of the makeshift stage. Homemade signs dot throughout the crowd.

Watch out Washington. Grant is gold. Next stop, the Capitol. Texas needs Hayden Grant in Congress.

The crowd soaks up the rhetoric as an amped-up politico paces back and forth on the stage and rallies the troops. "Four more years! Can we take four more years of this?" The crowd responds with boos and sporadic shouts. "Do you want four more years of your tax dollars going to every welfare program in the state? How about a bleeding-heart congressman, suckin' up to every special interest on the hill?"

Boos rain down as the two police offices and Detective Navarro stride through the horde and head towards the stage.

"I can hear you." Cheers ring out. "And I know someone else who can hear you." Cardboard signs wave and thrust in the air. "That's right. We want new blood. We want a man who gets things done. A family man, full of love and pride. Honor and integrity. A Texas man, born and bred—" Whoops and hollers drown out the politico, but he rides the audience wave and picks it back up. "Yes, that's right. I hear you. And we know what we want. Someone who will stick it to all those Washington insider fat-cats and stand up for all of you."

Shouts and cheers ripple throughout the crowd as the trio of police break around the front and head towards the back of the makeshift stage. A young man speaks into his headset and strides towards them with clipboard in hand. "Hello, excuse me. Yes, I'm with Encore Events. How can we help you officers?" His paper-thin perky smile surfaces amid an ocean of worry.

"Yes." Detective Navarro steps close. "We're looking for Hayden Grant."

"Is there…" Color drains from the event coordinator's face. "I mean, are we—"

She talks at a whisper. "There's no trouble here. We need to speak with him is all."

The event coordinator is smart enough not to ask any further questions and points towards the side of the stage.

As the politico continues to warm up the crowd, a silver-haired man stands off to the side and studies a set of note cards with steely eyes. Words mumble from his lips as Hayden Grant goes over his stump speech. His down-home demeanor topped off with a tailored suit and expensive shoes, he looks like a country-fried politician who is used to eating the competition for breakfast.

"Mr. Hayden Grant. Sir." Detective Navarro slowly approaches him. "If I may. Might we have a moment of your time."

Hayden glances over at the short Hispanic woman and flashes her his used-car salesman smile. "Yes, of course there, little lady." He shakes her hand with the right amount of pressure, by rote. "Right after my speech. There's no autographs until the show's over. See ya then." He drops her hand and turns away.

Navarro plays along until she can get a word in. "Sir, my name is Detective Roya Navarro, with the San Antonio Police—"

He cuts her off with the same broad toothy smile. "Detective. I always welcome the support of our finest. We back the blue here, yes indeedy. First Corinthians, four-two. Moreover, it is required in stewards, that a man, or in your case, a woman, well, that she shall be found faithful. I sure do appreciate your vote." Hayden drifts away, focused on his notecards.

She sputters a response and starts to follow when a meaty hand clamps onto her shoulder.

"Hey, lady." John Smith, a hulking choir boy with a military crewcut in a crisp three-piece suit, steps between them and grabs her arm. "Mr. Grant is busy." Navarro tries to release his iron grip, but he holds on tight. His voice is polite but firm. "Stay away from him."

She stands her ground and speaks in a measured tone. "You mind taking your hand off me,"

He doesn't respond. Or break a sweat in his suit, even under the intense Texas sun. And he doesn't let go.

"Back off." Officer Perez flanks the detective. "Right now."

"And what if I don't?" John leers back and doesn't move. Navarro pinches the skin between his thumb and forefinger and peels his massive hand away. John's calm demeanor cracks. His face goes flush as he grits his pearly white teeth. He fumes with anger.

Officer Kovach watches the situation deteriorate, and his police instinct kicks in. He steps up and joins with his trio.

John is ready to take on all three of them.

"Come now. Brothers. And sisters of the law. There's no need for any of this." Hayden steps between the boiling stand-off and layers on folksy charm. "Please. You must excuse my associate. John Smith here is one of the best body men in the business. But even I admit, he can be a little bit overprotective." Hayden claps his broad shoulders and John never flinches. "I blame his Mormon upbringing. He's never learned how to harness and release any of those aggressions we all have."

John breaks the stand-off with a guttural grunt to his employer and steps away. Hayden never loses his toothy smile. "Now I'm about to walk out on stage here any second. But whatever police charity you're all with. Well, I'm sure we can make amends—"

"Sir." Navarro cuts through his chatter. "I'm sorry to be the one to tell you this. It's regarding your wife."

Grant's political spin and down-home attitude melts away. His steely eyes squint. "What about my wife?"

"She was involved in an accident." Navarro's training kicks in, her words steeped in sympathy "A motor vehicle accident. About half an hour ago. A very serious one."

Hayden goes shell-shocked at the news. Even John's rough and tough gaze cracks a bit at his bosses' reaction. Hayden finally focuses back on the detective. "How serious?"

"Sir." She drops her gaze. "I'm afraid she's…" Navarro swallows before she speaks. "Gone. Sir, I'm so sorry to be the one to tell you this—"

Hayden throws his notecards up in a shower and turns away from Navarro's sympathy. John moves to his side and offers comfort, but he shrugs him away.

Navarro motions to the two uniform officers. "Mr. Grant, if you could come with us. We'll get you out of here and take you right to her."

"That dense fuckin' woman." Grant snaps back an angry bark. "You be straight with me now. It was that plastic piece of shit, death trap car of hers, wasn't it? I swear. She's always been careless. And clueless. But I sure thought she had enough God given sense to—"

Cheers from the crowd drown out his diatribe. The politico on stage frantically waves a ten-gallon Stetson hat. A deafening chant from the crowd. "Grant! Grant! Grant!" The politico tries to shout over the persistent drumbeat. "And now, the man you came here to see. The one you've been waiting for. Your friend and mine. The man who can. The man who will, go all the way. From right here in Stone Oak, straight to Washington. Our very own." Under steady applause, the politico motions him out. "Congressman. Hayden. Grant."

Hayden turns to his body man and gets his emotions under control. John gives him a once-over and guides him to the edge of the stage.

Grant turns back to the detective and two officers. "Well, I appreciate you all telling me the news. But my dumb-shit wife is gonna have to wait." His used car smile returns easily as a Cheshire grin. "The show must go on." Grant walks out on stage to a wall of thunderous cheers and whistles.

John doesn't say a word as he shoves past the trio of police.

Navarro stays and watches from the side of the stage, she can't control the shocked look that's etched on her face.

Officer Perez notices and steps up next to her. "Sorry, Detective. I know I don't have much experience with any of this. But I gotta say, what I'm seeing right there isn't what I'd call the grieving process."

Navarro glances over at the rookie officer. She doesn't respond back.

They all watch the stage as an energetic and pumped Hayden Grant plays to the crowd under steady waves of cheers and goodwill.

Chapter Nine

A rusty screen door screeches open. Bruised knuckles rap at the paint chipped frame. There's no answer. He knocks again. With an exasperated sigh, Daniel rests his forehead against the flaked and faded front door. He soaks up the stillness until he's ready. He takes a deep breath and knocks again.

"Goddamn. All right. For Christ sake." A gravelly voice tempered by too many late nights calls out. "I'm comin'. Who the hell do you think you are? Knockin' on my door this early." Deadbolt locks tumble open. A chain rattles. The door cracks open. Ron Stanton's unshaven and ragged face peeks through the open crack.

"Danny Boy. Hey." His bleary eyes widen as he recognizes Daniel. His sunken scowl turns up into a crooked smile. "Look at you. Here on my front porch. What's up, bro?"

"Hey, Ron." Daniel shuffles and peels some paint off the door frame. "Is Jessica around?"

"Naw." Ron shakes his head. "She's out with the kid. Little guy's been up all damn night, coughing up a storm." He clears his froggy throat. "You know your sister. She won't listen to me. Dragged 'em off to the Urgent Care, first thing."

"Oh. Well." Daniel squirms. "I'm real sorry to hear about that. Hope he's okay." Ron continues to stare at Daniel's numerous cuts and bruises. He tries not to notice, "Yeah, Jessica. I really need to um… talk to her. Do you know when they might be coming back?"

"Nothing fast ever happens in a hospital waiting room." The front door opens wide. "But come on in. Me casa is your casa."

Daniel walks into the house. It smells stale under a cloud of sour milk and no fresh air. The door shuts behind him and seals tight against the frame.

Ron, dressed in a worn tee-shirt and ratty sweats, walks through a living room of thrift-store furniture. A woman's sensibilities try and make it cozy comfortable. Fisher-Price toys scattered across the floor. Daniel hangs by the front door; he stands over a large dirty toolbox and a pair of muddy work boots.

"So, Danny Boy. Dan the Man. It's been a while." Ron circles the worn carpet and kicks out at a stuffed rabbit and a plastic truck. "You're lookin' good. Not counting what that 2x4 did to your face."

"Ahh, it's nothing, Ron." Daniel shrugs it off with a phony smile. "I was stupid. You know, I was messing around with my phone and took my eyes off the road and ran into a ditch. I really should call for a tow."

"A ditch did all that, huh?" Ron keeps a straight poker face. "You sure you don't want to go to the doctor? I mean… Damn."

"No, thanks." He shakes him off. "I appreciate it though. I'm okay. Really. It looks worse than it feels."

"Oh yeah? Well, I'm standing way over here and it feels bad as hell. You need some liquid painkiller?" Ron glides over to a pressboard cabinet and slides open the thin glass door. "Grab a seat and take a load off, Danny. I got ya covered." He rummages around the cabinet. "Let's see. What have we got? Hmm. You want some whiskey?" He looks at another bottle. "Or whiskey?"

"Thanks a lot." Daniel stares back, clearly an uncomfortable guest. "That'll work."

Ron tips the bottle his way. "Good choice. Think I'll join you." He grabs two cheap dollar-store glasses and heads for the fridge. "Drove into a ditch. How's that Bronco of yours? Is it pretty banged up?" He opens the freezer door, cold air escapes into the humid room. The motor hums in the quiet as Ron slides an old ice tray out and twists it with a crack. Shards of ice fall to the sink and floor. He salvages what he can.

"Yeah, my car." Daniel breaks the quiet. "She's seen better days. Hey, uh, Jess said you were gonna be gone this week?"

"Nah. Job site is shut down." Ron fills the glasses with chunks of ice cubes. "Foreman's haggling with the corporate dicks over at Lawson. Same old shit. They don't want to cough up any more overtime." Ron heads back to Daniel with frosty glasses and a bottle. "Can you believe that? I'll bet you ten bucks those rich stuffed suits are all Shylocks." Ron pours the drinks. "Jess don't like me talking like that out loud. But what else can you say? Call a spade a spade. And these pointy heads are doing what they do. You know how they are. They're doing it sure as God on high, stealing it right out of my hard-earned paycheck."

Daniel doesn't really listen to his ramble but chimes in when he's done. "Tough break." He takes a drink of whiskey and grits through the acrid taste.

Ron picks up his glass and tips it towards Daniel. "Tough as hell is right, Danny Boy." He knocks the drink back like it's water. And lets it go down smooth. They sit in the quiet. An uncomfortable tension builds.

"Dan the man. We're family. Right? Blood thicker than water and all that shit." Ron slides a little closer on the couch. "Now, I've driven into my fair share of ditches. And I gotta say, I wasn't nearly as busted up as you are. I mean. You see what I'm gettin' at here?"

Ron waits for an answer. Daniel polishes off his drink and puts the glass on the table before he speaks. "It's nothing. Really. I forgot to wear my seatbelt and paid for it. I got bounced around and banged up a bit. I'll be sore for a while, but I'll heal. That's all there is to it."

"Well, thank God for that. You gotta watch out. These dirty cops are all over out there. Lookin' to fill their quota. You know? Their numbers for the month." Ron agrees with himself as he refills Daniel's glass. "Even if you slip into the seatbelt after they pull you over. You're still screwed. They got you on tape. Surveillance drones. Japanese electronic things flying all over the damned place. The deep state. They've got eyes everywhere. And they'll get you. Don't ever doubt that. You wear your seatbelt. I'm forever on Jessica about it. You go on and ask her."

He stands up and claps Daniel on the shoulder. Daniel winces. Ron doesn't notice or care. "Lemme get cleaned up, and we'll see if we can get your Bronco out and back on the road. Save you the cost of the tow. That sound about, right?"

Daniel agrees back. "Yeah. Thanks, Ron."

"Family. Do what you can for 'em because you never know when you're gonna need 'em." He smiles a toothy grin and takes off down the cramped hall. "Drink it all up, bro. Liquid gold. It'll take away your pain and make you feel like a king." He slips out of his tee shirt.

Daniel lets out a sigh and sinks down into the old

sofa. His gaze drifts to the TV. On the screen, a game show host hucksters an overweight contestant to pick a price. The red-faced contestant bounces under the weight of his imminent decision. Daniel finds the remote and flicks through the channels. He glances down the hall and turns down the volume as he searches.

He stops on a local news channel. A young newscaster gathers up her notes and flashes her serious look to the camera lens. A breaking news crawl scrolls across her chest.

Daniel turns up the volume a tad. "…the accident occurred over an hour ago, in the residential section of Centennial Ridge. If you're joining us, Claudia Grant, the wife of Congressional candidate Hayden Grant, dead this morning from the result of a fatal car crash. KTXU's own Gary Grey is on the scene."

The TV screen switches from the newsroom to an outside view of a pristine glass and steel structure. Gary Grey stands off the side of the camera shot with a microphone in hand. His slick charm masks a cocky bravado. His camera voice is tempered with the lilt of a fake Australian accent. Everything he knows, he learned in the tabloid school of journalism.

"Thank you, Sarah. I'm here outside Methodist Hospital, where the body of Claudia Grant, may she rest in peace, awaits the arrival of her husband, candidate Hayden Grant." Grey walks and talks, he moves with the microphone like a professional at work on his stage.

Alan Stubbs, his stocky camera man in pocket-filled jorts and a T-shirt, keeps in step with him and follows his cues. Grey steps around a parked ambulance, his camera shot framed with the emergency entrance loop of the hospital.

"We've learned that Mrs. Grant was here at this very hospital no less than three days ago. For what friends and family call, stress and fatigue." He cozies up to the camera. "However, inside sources tell us that Mrs. Grant was here to have her stomach pumped. Due to an overdose of some suspicious nature."

Grey's index finger goes to his left ear as Sarah Spivy in the studio speaks up. "Gary. Are the local police investigating Grant's possible drug use as a cause for this horrible accident?"

Grey takes in the question and picks it right up. "Sarah, as far as we can tell. San Marcos PD and Metro Units from SAPD are all keeping their lips sealed." He steps off the sidewalk and dances with the camera as they move closer towards the emergency entranceway. "However, it's a possibility that cannot be ruled out. With this political horse race ever so close, if these revelations do play out, they would clearly be a devastating blow to the congressional chances for candidate Grant."

Emergency sirens whine and grow in the distance. Bubble lights flash as two police cruisers and a town car with tinted windows pull into the hospital parking lot and head for the emergency entrance.

A surge of media swarms as the vehicles come to a halt. Reporters and microphones joust for position. Uniform officers try and hold the media horde back.

The front doors to the town car open. Detective Roya Navarro steps out of the vehicle and bellows over the noise. "Come on, people. Please. Give the man a break. No pushing. Back it up. Back up. Now."

John Smith climbs out from the driver's side and muscles his way to the rear of the town car. He opens the door and helps Hayden Grant out.

Reporters surge forward and shout out a jumble of questions. John helps shelter Grant through the media phalanx. Navarro elbows her way forward and keeps up with the men.

The hospital emergency doors loom. Reporters keep pace and shout out questions.

"Sir. Sir. When did you first learn of the accident?"

"When was the last time you spoke with your wife?"

"Your poll numbers are on the downslope. Care to comment?"

"How are you feeling right now? Hey."

Gary Grey glides through the jackal pack and picks his moment. He slides up with his microphone at the ready. "Gary Grey, KTXU News. Congressman. Any comment about the drug allegations? Is it true your wife was here two weeks ago to have her stomach pumped? Congressman."

"No comment." Navarro shoves him aside. "Jesus, Grey. Get lost, huh."

Grey swats her concern away. "It's a free country, Detective. I have the right to ask pertinent questions and my viewers have the right to know."

Hayden Grant stops as the emergency doors slide open. Gary Grey jostles with a group of reporters. Hayden flashes his political smile and leans in close to Grey. "I ain't the congressman yet, son." Grant gestures to the crowd of reporters and tries to get them all to settle. "All of you. Simmer it on down. Thank you. Now, I will make a formal statement to the press very soon."

Shouts from the rabble, Grant waves his hands and gets them back under control. "Wait. A short while. It's all I ask. And until that time, please allow me to visit with my wife in peace. Thank you."

Reporters surge forward and shout a barrage of words. Detective Navarro shows the way and escorts Hayden inside the hospital. John takes a position at the edge of the sliding doors, acting as a stoic bouncer to the undulating mass of media, all trapped on the wrong side of the velvet rope.

Daniel hits the mute button on the TV.

He grabs the glass of whiskey from the coffee table and drains it. He shakes off the strong liquor taste.

His breathing is harsh, his eyes heavy. He inches down the hall towards the closed bedroom door. He can hear the shower running. He walks back into the small living room; his hands run down his face and tug at his hair. He's trapped in a claustrophobic prison, and the walls close in tight. Shaky hands thrust into his pockets, and he pulls out his phone. His finger flips through screens fast, and he presses a number to dial. His left-hand still shakes as he holds the phone to his ear. Muted clicks until the call connects.

"Hello." Judy's voice filters through the phone. "Hello? Is anyone there?"

"Jude." Daniel swallows the throbbing frog in his throat. "It's me." He takes a deep ragged breath. "Listen, I don't know… There's a lot to tell you." He can't keep the raw feelings in his voice at bay. "I… I can't. It's… Something's happened."

"I don't understand?" The tone in her voice is soft. Judy treads slowly. "What's wrong? What is it?"

"Fuck. I…I don't know." He tries to reel in his emotions. "I don't know what to do here. I'm trapped. I'm lost."

"Are you okay?" She talks over him. "Honey,

you're not making any sense. Calm down. Why do you sound so upset?"

He can hear her concern and worry. He spits it out in a shaky voice. "There was an accident. A bad one. And all of a sudden, there she was. Right in the middle of the road. I saw her. I thought she might... I don't know."

"Are you hurt? Dan, talk to me. Please. Tell me what's—"

"It all happened in an instant." He talks fast and shakes his head at the voice on the phone. "Just like, that." His voice trails off, haunted by the memory.

"Come home." Judy gets his attention, her tone full of compassion but tempered with command. "Right this instant. Listen to me. You come right home."

"I..." He stammers back. "I can't."

"Okay." She picks it right up. "Then I can come to you. Wherever you are. I can do that. Tell me where you are. Please."

"I..." He's about to say but his mind shuts it down. "I don't know how. But I gotta be the one to fix this. It's up to me. To make this right."

"Wait. We can do it together." Judy tries to get his attention. "Daniel. Honey, please, don't do this—"

He ends the call, stares at the phone in his hand and sobs.

****

Judy sits at her kitchen table and hangs up the phone.

Six police officers hover around her. A police technician removes his headset and offers her canned praise. "You did good."

Judy lights another cigarette.

"It looks like the call wasn't long enough to complete the trace." A junior officer works on her laptop;

her fingers fly across the keyboard. "We've got it narrowed down to anywhere in Hays County. Maybe Caldwell? But I can't pinpoint a physical address."

A plainclothes detective speaks up. "How are we doing on that tracking app thing?"

"His phone is equipped with it, but he doesn't have it turned on." Junior officer clicks through her laptop. "We've reached out to the telecom company. They can work around it, but no word back yet."

Plainclothes detective calls out. "Get someone on the horn who can get that done, ASAP. My kid works faster than this."

The junior officer closes her laptop and leaves the kitchen. A squad of blue uniforms move throughout the house.

Judy sits in the center of the storm, with her burning cigarette in hand.

"Your husband." The plainclothes detective sits across from her. "Where do you think he is?"

"I don't know." Judy shakes her head fast. "But he's scared." The detective reaches out and touches her hand. Judy flinches away.

He's unfazed as he sits back in his chair. "I'm sure he's afraid." He studies her every reaction. "Now, where would he go?"

She doesn't respond. "Come on." He leans forward. "Talk to me. You know his routines." He doesn't blink as he watches the jittery woman try to ash her cigarette.

"What else do you want to hear? He left for the office. That's where he goes, every Monday morning. He goes to work. That's his routine."

"Uh huh. Well, he's not there." The detective looks for any crack he can use. "So, how about outside his routines? Family? Friends?"

"His family. They live in Maryland." Judy exhales a plume of smoke. "You can start there. Friends? I don't know of any. There are a few couples we occasionally have dinner with. But anybody else? Not a clue."

The detective listens intently but doesn't respond. He continues to stare at her.

Judy takes another long drag as a pack of police roam all throughout her house. She shuts out the waves of noise and stares out the kitchen window, knowing where her husband might be.

Chapter Ten

A bleary-eyed orderly leads the way. His shoulders hunch over a haggard expression as he plods forward. Detective Navarro keeps an eye out everywhere as she heads down the white hallway, faded linoleum under their feet. Hayden Grant strides on with a light skip in his step. His cheery demeanor seems more at home on the cocktail circuit than a tiled causeway.

They all head into the bowels of the hospital.

Grant glances over at Navarro's suit jacket and the badge hanging from her breast pocket. "Detective, I wish to see my wife alone."

Navarro studies every face they pass as a potential problem. "Of course, sir."

Grant never loses his smile. "That's mighty good to hear." He studies her as they move, looking at her clearly for the first time. She notices the attention. Grant speaks as they walk, his voice soft but firm. "I'm a plain-speaking man, Detective. So, allow me to speak plainly. Because if I'm ambushed by some scumbag paparazzi, or frankly any living soul with a cell phone camera, I'll make it my business to see that today is the last day a shiny gold shield hangs from your suit jacket. Do you understand me?"

The detective hears the threat but doesn't show it. She keeps her thoughts to herself and returns a firm, "Yes, sir."

Grant waits for more but it doesn't come. Over the sound of their shoes on the linoleum, he continues to put on the pressure. "I am putting you on notice. Anybody means anybody. You may not think this is your problem, but I'm telling you, with one hundred percent certainty. It is your problem."

Navarro hits it right back. "You won't be disturbed."

They all walk through multiple sets of swinging doors. Faded black signs point towards the morgue. A chill grows in the air. The temperature seems to drop as they continue down the stark white hallway.

The tired orderly stops in front of a metal door and jacks a key into the lock. He talks to the door, his voice as bleary as his expression. "I'm the only office with a light on down here. I'll be there at my desk. You all let me know when you're finished." He opens the door and walks off down the cold hallway.

Grant watches him go and waits until he's completely out of sight. "Talk to me." His calm politician demeanor fades into a vicious snarl as he turns on Navarro. "Why is this taking so goddamned long?"

"I'm sorry to say, sir." She looks puzzled. "I don't follow you?"

"This son of a whore, pill-poppin' lawyer who killed my wife." Grant snatches her forward with a grip on her jacket lapel. "Do you plan on filling me in? Where the fuck is he?"

"Sir." She slowly takes ahold of his hands and peels them off her. "You're forgetting yourself. Once again."

Hayden doesn't let up. "I want this murdering druggie prick. Whip and strip the hide clean off him and plant his worthless guts in the ground." Hayden gets closer, "Shit-fire, I want a wooden stake shoved straight through his demon corpse to make sure he never even thinks about gettin' up again."

Navarro lets him rant. "Every precinct is on alert. Every squad car in a thirty-mile radius is out on the prowl. We've got a crew sitting and waiting at his house. He will not get far."

He steps back, but his fiery eyes don't let up. "You better not be jerking me." Hayden pushes open the morgue door. "Because if I haven't made myself Crystal Pepsi clear. It's your ass on the line, Detective."

He waits for her to break. She doesn't. But she finally speaks. "When he comes up for air, he's ours."

Hayden's smile returns and he pats her on the shoulders. "You know what? I believe you. Now, get the fuck out of here. I wish to be alone with my wife." He doesn't wait for her reply as the heavy metal door closes on Navarro's stone face.

Harsh florescent lights hum over a sterile and cold room. Cubicle drawers line the walls. A gurney stands in the center of the floor next to a metal examining table.

Grant takes in the sanitized space, and his wingtips echo throughout the bunker as he steps up to the gurney. He stares down at a body covered in a white sheet. His firm hand starts to shake as he peeks under the sheet. "Jesus, Claudia." He lets the sheet fall back down. Grant slides her stiff arm out from under the sheet. The dead skin bleached and battered. He cradles her cold hand in his. "I swear. How do you always have a knack at making my life miserable?"

Hayden slides a large diamond ring off her rigid finger. He looks at the ring in the palm of his hand, as Claudia's bruised arm hangs in limbo. Grant slides it back under the sheet.

He takes a deep breath and checks his pockets. Checks his suit jacket until he finds his phone. He paces the tile floor in the cold room as he scrolls across the screen and pushes to dial. He holds the phone to his ear as the call connects. "Monica. Yes, that's right. Can you hear me?" He paces around the gurney. "Hold on. Wait, I can barely… Reception is for shit down here." He moves throughout the morgue.

"There you are. I can hear you now. I said I can hear you. What? Messages. Yeah, I'm sure. Let's hear them. I said, go ahead. What do you have for me?"

He listens to the voice on the phone. "That's enough. You can stop, I'm not calling her back. Let's hear the next one. Okay. Yes, fine. Set that up. I don't know. Sometime next week. You keep the schedule. You check the schedule." His eyes perk up. "Hmm, no I remember. How much did she give to the cause?" He leans against the gurney. "Wow. That much, huh. Okay, set up a lunch at, ahh, Signatures. Let's see how much more we can squeeze out of her."

He paces the room. "Monica, stop whining. This is not my problem. Well, if they're booked up, then book us someplace else. Make it nice. She's worth the effort. What that woman doesn't spend on her face, she'll drop on every sob story out there." He smiles at the thought. "It's the rubber-chicken circuit all over again. I don't even have to change my talking points. Promise to hurt the people they want me to hurt. Cut taxes. Bash the queers and build the wall. It's boiler plate. After my song and dance, all that's left to do is cash the checks."

His free hand goes to his forehead. "Christ, I could use some coffee." He massages his temple with a deep sigh. "No, Monica, I'm in the fucking hospital. What?"

He stands over the gurney. "Still dead as far as I can tell." He smiles down at the white sheet. "At least she's no longer useless now."

Hayden steps away from the body and fiddles with the sink on the metal examining table. "With Claudia's help, there's no way this vote in November isn't a straight up shatter the glass slam dunk. You can start calling me Congressman Elect. Next stop, Washington." He runs his hand under the cold tap and rubs his tired face. "What's that? No, I'd call it a lucky break." He grabs a paper towel and pats down his wet face. "I've been thinking about it since I got the news. You'll see. I'm going in front of the press. Fuckin' jackals. What?"

He drops his arm with deep sigh. He shakes it off before he brings the phone back up to his ear. "Monica. Stop it. Of course, I love you. How many ways can I prove it? You are so much more than a secretary to me. Baby, please. We don't even have to worry about a divorce. Problem solved."

He waits for her to take a breath and pause before jumping back in. "I hear you. I do. Now listen to me. I have every intention of taking you to Washington. Yes, and making you the next Mrs. Hayden Grant."

His hand fishes through his pockets and he pulls out the diamond ring. "I already have the ring picked out and everything." He rolls it around in his palm. "Baby. Watch the news. And record it. This one's gonna be a keeper." He clicks off the call.

His smile melts in the quiet. Hayden turns away from the body of his dead wife and paces the room, lost in his thoughts.

Chapter Eleven

Daniel sits sunken into the old couch with toys and clutter all around him. He swirls the last of his whiskey around in the cheap jelly glass. Shades of light from the muted TV set flicker and dance across his haggard face.

"Good to go, all squeaky clean." Ron thumps on down the hall. He snatches up his muddy work boots and plops down on a splintered wooden chair. "Okay, bro. Let's go see what we can do about you." He laces up his boots. "The winch on my truck should pull you right out of that ditch, toot sweet."

Daniel downs the dregs of his drink. He gets up from the couch on shaky legs. "Hey, Ron. Did you ever wish you—" He takes a deep breath and tries to shake out of the liquor haze that clouds his mind. "—you could take back…" He clears his dry throat, but it doesn't hide the undercurrent of nervousness. "A split second. To take it back. Or give anything, to do it all over again."

Ron stops messing with his boot laces. He doesn't respond and leans back in the chair. Sharp creaks from the warped wood cut through the quiet.

Daniel takes another deep breath before he speaks. "I didn't run my Bronco off the road."

Ron doesn't respond.

Daniel can't help but utter a little laugh. "You know, she ran into me. I swear, like…" His voice falters. "I mean, it all happened so fast. So goddamned fast." The emotions are overwhelming. "It was fine. It was perfectly fine. And then—it wasn't." He tries to shake away the memory. But he can't. "She...it was like a torpedo." He mimics the sound. "Straight into me." Daniel waits for any kind of response.

Ron stares at him. Until he finally speaks. "You mother-fuck." He slaps his knee with a callused hand and belches a booming laugh. "Ha, I knew somethin' was up." Ron leaps to his feet with a broad smile. "Sorry, bro, but this is from the heart. You're a lousy fuckin' liar. I could see it all over you, clear as day. Bam!" Daniel startles at the loud exclamation and he doesn't share in the excitement. "I mean, there at the door." Ron strides over and claps him on the shoulder. "When I opened it. You were on the porch, all clammy and white, like a dead fish. Christ, you still look like that."

Ron laughs, but Daniel doesn't. He closes his eyes tight and shakes his head. "I left her there, Ron. It's what I..." His body shivers. "I did. I left the scene. Of a crime." He starts to hitch and crack.

"Hey. Hey? What are you doing?" Ron drops his broad smile, uncomfortable with the rising display of emotion. "Bro? No, don't. You don't need —to— "

"She's...I mean, I left her there." The dam breaks and Daniel gushes a raspy sob. All the built-up tension pours out in a halting tear. "To die. Right there. I saw her on the road, I saw her body. She didn't move. Her leg all twisted around, like she was folded in half." He covers his face with bruised hands and utters a high-pitched whine as he whimpers and cowers under the torrent of ugly images that trip through his mind. "I couldn't believe any of it. I was on a tear, and... I panicked. I did. I ran. I ran away."

"Hey, bro. Uhh, you know." Ron isn't sure how to react to this flood of sentiment. As Daniel struggles to pull himself together, he can't hide a snarl of disgust. He settles for a few friendly pats on the back with the palm of his hand. It's the best he can do for comfort. "Pull yourself together, huh. Stop it. It's not this bad. I mean. Lemme ask you. Hey. Listen to me."

Daniel's ragged, tear-streaked face stares up.

"I hear you saying she was dead when you left. But was she really? I mean, think about it. How do you know?" Daniel doesn't respond; Ron keeps his attention. "Maybe she was fooling? Hey, it happens. It's a fake set-up to fuck you over. Take away your rights."

"Oh yeah?" Daniel barks back a nervous laugh. "I don't think so, man." Daniel wipes tears away and tries to calm himself down.

Ron's glad to see it. "It's true. Guy on the radio talks about it all the damn time. They hire these actors to do their dirty work. It's happening everywhere, man. Hell, the government knows all about 'em. Think about it."

Daniel gets himself under control and offers Ron a slight smile. He can't help but find a bit of levity in his brother-in-law's bullshit talk radio seriousness. That fleeting feeling fades under the weight of his reality. "Back in the Bronco." Daniel plops down and sinks into the old couch. "I have these…uh…pills. These blue pills. I found them in the glove compartment."

Ron takes a seat. "What kind of blue pills?"

Daniel stumbles a response. "Something to get me through the day." Ron continues to stare as he stammers, "Not all the time. I don't take them every day, I mean, I'm not addicted."

"Yeah, sure." Ron nods along. "I get it."

Daniel doesn't. "I don't use them all the time, is what I'm saying. Every now and then. They help keep me even."

"Yeah, I hear you. Makes sense." Ron shrugs his shoulders. "So, what?"

"The pills that I take." Daniel picks up the empty jelly glass and fiddles with it. "That were in my vehicle. They're not a…legal substance. Do you understand?"

"Sure, you've got a little habit. Who doesn't?" Ron goes for a smile. "I've got an Ambien prescription myself. When I can get the damn thing filled. I've even had Jessica down at the clinic. With a bad back, hurt foot, whatever. But you know these quacks, they don't—"

"Jesus, Ron." Daniel snaps back. "Will you listen to me. Both vehicles speeding. There's a collision. The police show up. And find a mind-altering, an illegal mind-altering substance, scattered all inside my…" He suddenly springs up from the couch. "It's over. That poor woman, spread all over the asphalt. I turned that road into a crime scene. That's what I left behind."

Ron stands up. "Hey, bro. Calm down—"

Daniel doesn't listen. "I'm so fucking dead. Like that woman I left there on the road. I'm done. My life is all over."

"Bro. You're okay." Ron grabs him. "It's okay. You're safe. You did the right thing." Daniel, his eyes glazed over in panic, starts to flail about. Ron reacts and stays with him. "Easy. Go easy. Do me a favor. Put the glass down; you're gonna hurt yourself."

Daniel stares at his hand, the empty jelly glass gripped tight in his fist. He places it on the table. Ron snatches it up. "That's good, bro. Let's keep it nice and easy. Sit back. There you go."

Daniel listens. Lost in a daze. The words fall from his lips. "I killed that woman. There's no way around it. And I'm going to prison. For what's left of my life."

"Hey, don't do that to yourself." Ron takes the empty glasses over to the Formica kitchen counter. "You shit-can any prison talk. Right now." He opens the freezer door. "You had an accident. That's all it was. An accident." Ron pulls out an old ice tray. "And you walked. You did. Now that may seem like a big fuckin' deal, but it's not." He twists the tray with a frozen crack and drops slivers into the two cheap glasses. "Don't go making it anything more than it is. Tell the cops the truth. You hit your head. You were dazed like a motherfucker. And with you being all messed up and shit, you wandered away. That's it. Case closed. Cops would buy that." Ron unscrews the whiskey bottle and pours two large glasses.

Daniel sits in a funk, and he doesn't say anything.

"Bro. I'm not trying to blow smoke. I hear you. I get it. You're fucked, yeah." Ron carries a glass over to Daniel. He takes it. Ron clinks his glass against the side. "Well. Best we figure out a way to un-fuck you."

A breaking news scroll flashes across the muted TV.

Daniel stares at the kaleidoscope of colors and graphics as he takes a large belt from the jelly glass. "I think…" He lets the harsh liquor wash over him and weighs his words. "If I really want to un-fuck this. I think…I've got friends I can call." He takes another long pull and this one goes down smoother. "Well, I wouldn't quite call them friends. Maybe, colleagues at best. But I can call them. And turn myself in."

"Hey, bro." Ron tries to break through. "What are you talking about? You've got plenty of options here."

"No, I don't." Daniel shakes him off. "I've gotta live in the now. Right now. And right now, my reality is—" He swallows his words. "—the longer I stay away, the worse it's gonna get."

"You can run." Ron lets the thought sit out in the open as he takes a drink. Daniel stares at him. Ron continues his thought. "I'm serious as a heart attack. Run. You can."

"Right." Daniel utters a wheezing laugh. "Run. I'll do that. Sure thing. Where the hell am I supposed to go?"

"Go anywhere." Ron waves his arms and manages to keep the whiskey in his glass as he gestures all around. "Any-where. Throw a dart at the map and go. But first off, you get the fuck away from here. Come on, bro. You said it yourself. Your life is for shit. So why not start over? Clean your slate. Erase the whole clusterfuck chalkboard." He calms down convincing himself. "Hell. Maybe this is the wake-up call you needed? Think about it. A new life. New opportunities. Get to begin again." Ron settles himself back on the couch. "I mean, who wouldn't want that?"

Daniel lets it soak in but washes the thought away with whiskey. "No. It sounds too good to be true. Because it is. Run? Can't run forever. Your past always catches up to you."

Ron's flat expression molds into a puzzled glare. Daniel watches it happen. "You okay there, Ron?"

"I don't fuckin' believe it?" Ron stares. "Will you look at that." He points to the screen. "You're on TV."

On the muted screen, Hayden Grant stands in front of the hospital emergency room doors. He holds up a picture of Daniel. Ron grabs the remote control and turns off the mute button.

At the hospital, various cameras click away. A bevy of reporters hover all around.

Hayden Grant commands their attention in front of an array of microphones attached to a podium. He holds a blown-up photo. It's a motor vehicles driver's license portrait. An unflattering image of Daniel, who looks like a deer caught in the headlights.

Grant waits for the scene to calm a bit before he speaks. "As you all know, I've been inside visiting with my wife. For the final time." He projects a hint of sadness on cue and gets himself together. His fake feelings are overpowered by anger. "My lovely wife, Claudia Grant. A brilliant, vivacious woman. The love of my life. The woman who owns my heart and soul. My person. My partner." His voice rises. "But no more. Her life ended suddenly. Ripped from this world. Cut down in her prime, by this drug-addled degenerate."

Grant shakes the photo and turns to make sure it's caught by every camera. "A Mr. Daniel Evers Morrison. This man. Right here. This human waste. This garbage. This inhumane monster. Today, he killed my wife."

The bubbling audience of eager reporters give Grant their rapt attention.

"I pride myself on my southern roots. A better man than me. He said it best. 'Justice is God's idea and Man's ideal.' Justice. Done right and fair. Now as a candidate for political office, one who stands for law and order, what kind of a man would I be to allow such a despicable person to get away with this crime?"

He holds up the photo again for the cameras. "So, today, I ask the good citizens of central Texas, far and wide. To know this face. And know it well." He shakes the image in a manufactured rage. "This man. He is out there, somewhere. Get a good look."

Grant places the picture down on the podium. And let his camera emotions wash away, down to his best politician face. "I offer a reward. Not drawn from your kind donations to my campaign. Or special interest dollars trying to steer my official decisions. No. These funds are from me. From my heart."

He soaks in the moment and holds the anticipation long enough. "I offer a reward of one million dollars. Cash. For his capture. Alive or otherwise."

Reporters rumble under a raft of camera clicks and shutters. Journalists surge towards the podium. Grant tries to keep them under control. They calm down as he starts to speak again.

"Read your Bible. It's right there. An eye for an eye. My dearly departed wife meant more to me than life itself. And I understand that no amount of money will bring her back. With your help, I only ask for justice."

Reporters shout. "How much?"

"Sir, is that even legal?"

"Can you repeat that? Did you say, in cash?"

"Is this a bounty? How will it be paid?"

"One million dollars?"

The questions are a jumble of frantic words.

"God bless." Grant smiles at the chaos. He ignores the questions and offers a broad smile and his politician wave. "Let justice be done, though the heavens fall."

His hulking body man steps up to the podium and helps Grant move away from the melee. Cameras click and flash and follow their movements until Hayden and John are enveloped by a phalanx of uniform police.

"There you have it." Gary Grey steps in front of his remote news camera with his microphone at the ready.

His voice breathless. "In a surprise announcement, a whopping one million dollars in cash reward offered by congressional candidate Hayden Grant. There is no telling how local law enforcement will handle this turn of events. I can tell you I'll be out looking. Back to you in the studio, Sarah."

Ron clicks off the TV. They both sit stunned. Daniel stares at their reflection in the blank screen. Ron breaks the silence. "Well, so much for turning yourself in. No, we've gotta hide ya. But not here. We can't stay here. Not long, anyhow."

"But…they can't do that." Daniel comes out of his stupor. "Legally, you can't… A bounty? I mean this is anarchy." He stands up and pulls out his phone. "I gotta clear this whole thing up. This mess is out of control—"

Ron grabs him. "Bro. Legal or not, who gives a shit? You. You're guilty as fuck. You know how I know that? I saw it on the TV. That there is right now kinda real." He points to his cell phone. "And turn off your damn phone. Sure as shit, Bill Gates can track those things. He gave all that technology over to the government."

Daniel ignores the crazy but turns his phone off anyway. He plops back down to the couch, his face pale as a ghost. He looks like a rat caught in a trap.

Ron crouches down and gets his attention. "This whole damn city is gonna be in an uproar." He shakes Daniel's leg. "Hey. You listen to me and listen good. A million bucks? All these crazy Vato immigrants, they'll string you up and slit your throat clean for two bits. Hell, they find you in this neighborhood, they'll screw and tattoo you for no extra charge."

Daniel doesn't blink or move.

"Now." Ron stands up in front of him. "You stay

put. I've got an idea. A lead on a place that might work. There's this old cabin out by Geronimo Lake, down near Seguin. Me and the boys go out there a few times a year to hunt and fish."

Daniel doesn't respond.

Ron talks it out. "Have some time away from the wives. It's a get-away. Yeah. A real good one. Let me get us a key and we're out of here. Okay?"

A pasty Daniel manages a slight utterance.

"I'll take that as an okay." Ron smiles back. "Right. You sit tight. I'll call my buddy and set it all up. His cabin, it's so clear in the middle of nowhere. Nobody's gonna find us out there."

Daniel doesn't speak. Ron is fine with that. "Okay. I'm on it."

Ron strides down the hall. A thin smile stretches across his face. "A million bucks." He mumbles to himself. "Jesus howdy." He glances over his shoulder.

Daniel continues to sit and stare at his reflection in the dead TV screen.

Ron closes his bedroom door behind him.

Chapter Twelve

Detective Navarro leans against a San Marcos police patrol car shrouded in caked dirt. She slides a finger through the grime and wipes it on the arm of her suit jacket as she watches a black town car speed away from the scene.

All around the hospital emergency entrance, a horde of media gathers under flood lights. Various reporters preen and postulate in front of remote camera rigs.

Navarro stays with the squad car. "I just...I can't believe this. I mean. We did hear him correctly, right?" She continues to stare at the scene. "I apologize about my language upfront. My momma taught me better. But seriously. Are you fucking kidding me?"

Officer Kovach sits half in and half out of the open squad car. He has the radio mike in hand. He waits for a second before he repeats his call to dispatch. Radio squelch is all he receives back.

"No need to apologize, ma'am." Officer Perez stands close to Navarro and watches the media circus unfold. "I agree with you. But offering that kind of money? Look, this whole damn thing might be some kind of sick joke is all." Navarro turns and looks at him. "It could be." Perez continues his thought. "I mean, Hayden Grant is a sleazy politician. No doubt. But first and foremost, he's a politician. Since when are they ever on the level?"

"You're right. Politicians and lying go hand in hand. But honest or not—" Navarro points over to the unfolding media circus. "—that crazy mother declared open season on our missing Mr. Morrison. And frankly, on any other poor bastard that might even look like him. Mobs out for blood tend not to be too picky."

"You think this whole thing is a smokescreen?" Perez raises an eyebrow. "The money offer's not even for real."

"I'm saying at this point, what does it even matter? Grant lit the damn fuse. There's no taking that back until it blows." She leans inside the squad car. "Kovach, any luck? Are you getting anybody?"

"Sorry, Detective. Nada. It's dead air." He puts down the radio mike. "I can keep trying, but all I hear back is static. Our switchboard's gotta be lit up like a Christmas tree."

"Okay. Perez, you stay with me." She slaps the passenger door. "Kovach let's get you on over to the Morrison household. They're gonna need all the help they can get keeping the press and public at bay."

"Affirmative, Chief." Kovach closes the driver's side door. "I'm on it." The engine fires up, and bubble lights flash. The patrol car burns out of the hospital parking lot.

"Let's go. On the fly. Come on." Gary Grey jogs over with his cameraman in tow. "Roll tape. Do your thing. Keep the camera rolling." Grey gestures at Navarro with his microphone and puts on his 'Made For TV' reporter face. "Two-shot. Get us both in a two-shot."

Navarro turns away from the approaching spectacle.

"Alan, are we good?" Grey moves fast to get close to her. He points at the lens. "Two-shot. Hospital in the background." The cameraman gives him a thumbs up. Grey keeps up the banter. "Sound, speed. All set?" Alan never leaves the viewfinder. "You're good to go."

"Detective Roya Navarro. Gary Grey, KTXU News." Grey talks to Navarro's back. "So pleased to see you again. What an interesting turn of events happening out here. Wouldn't you say?"

She ignores him and dodges the camera. She heads for her unmarked vehicle.

Officer Perez tries to block Grey, but he's nimble and keeps on the detective's heels.

"No comment? Not even a sound bite? Our viewers deserve answers. We both heard a congressman elect lay down a million-dollar marker and fire the starting gun. I'd say the hunt begins. I'm sure you have some thoughts about that. Yes?"

Navarro stops in her tracks and faces Grey. He closes the gap and brings his microphone to her mouth. "Go fuck yourself, Grey. And you can quote me on that."

"Short. Sweet." Grey keeps his smile. "I love it."

Navarro snaps away from the microphone. Grey keeps badgering and talks to her back. "Come on, Detective. Some straight talk, between you and me. Our viewers have the right to know." She continues to ignore him. He doesn't let up. "Nothing. Zip. For real? Are you still sore about that interview? I can let bygones be bygones here. How about you don't shoot the messenger. Save that for the ex."

"Okay. You're all done here." Officer Perez gets between them. "That's enough now. Turn your camera off. Turn it off."

Grey talks over the order. "Alan, you can ignore his fascist demands. We are not in Mexico, Officer. I don't know if they taught the Constitution in the Academy. But here in this country, we still have a freedom of the press."

Perez returns a slight chuckle and bats the subtle racism aside like someone who's heard it all before. "I was born in Marble Falls. Jack-hole." Alan re-positions the camera rig but Perez keeps himself in front of the lens. "And you two can have all the freedom you want, back there under the patriotic glow of the flood lights. You know the drill. Let's go. Back to your pen. I won't say it again."

Alan gives up the fight and drops the camera lens. He follows the commands. Perez watches him close.

Grey takes advantage of the moment and sprints after the detective. He closes the gap fast. Navarro gets to her unmarked vehicle. She opens the driver's door. Grey comes up on her.

"I'm sure being back at this hospital is hard. Old memories surfacing kinda thing. Don't be that way, Detective. You should see the stuff I didn't bring up. How about you throw me a bone. For old times' sake."

"You're a scumbag, Grey." Navarro turns on him and snatches his cheap coat with a snarl. "You were then, and you sure are now." Grey keeps his cool as she shakes and tightens her hold.

Officer Perez races over to the unfolding scene.

"Temper, temper, Detective Navarro." Grey smiles in her grip. "This is very unbecoming of a SAPD dick. Oh, I apologize. As a woman, you don't take offense to that term. Do you?"

"Walk away, Grey." She lets go of him with a lip curl of disgust. "Go."

"Manhandled, or woman-handled, by the police." Grey straightens out his rumpled suit jacket. "Oh, I sure hope someone got this all on tape. Maybe this time you'll be suspended for even longer."

Perez grabs Grey with both hands and jerks him back off his feet. "What the—?" Grey frowns. "Hey, watch the suit."

Perez ignores his bickering and looks over to Navarro. "Are you okay, ma'am?"

She bottles up her thoughts and feelings tight. "Get him the hell out of here."

Perez doesn't need to be told twice. "Let's go." The officer hauls him away.

The squad car radio squawks. Navarro takes a deep breath and a beat to herself before she leans inside and grabs the mike. "Dispatch, this is Navarro. That's a 10-9 on your last transmission. Come again." A squelch of static on the radio.

"Not so rough, huh." Perez guides him through the parking lot and Grey continues to protest. "This is news. Don't you understand? I'm only doin' my job." Perez doesn't listen or let up. Grey cajoles. "Come on, Officer. How about one soundbite? Gimme one for the record. You're sure to impress the *mamacita* and all those kids down at the station."

Perez doesn't take the bait. "We're all finished playing." The officer shouts out to Alan. "Hey, you. Camera guy. Wait up a sec." Alan stops walking. Perez approaches fast. "What I should do is fine you for littering." He throws Grey to the ground. "You forget to take your trash with you."

"You think I'm playing out here?" Grey gets to his feet with a huff and brushes off his pants. "This is my job. A job I do very well, I might add. And the story of the day, hell, our time. It's unfolding right here in front of us. A powerhouse politician declares war on a local citizen. Tell me that doesn't get your dark Latin blood pumping, Officer."

Perez ignores him and talks to Alan. "Do your boss a favor and escort him back to the reporter's pen. Before he gets into some trouble he can't brush off."

"Texas justice. Here and now." Grey gets in his face. "It's like that John Gotti case. The New York mafia boss guy. Remember what he did to that neighbor who ran over his son?"

"One more step. I swear." Perez pulls out a set of handcuffs. "You take one more step and I'll drag you in for obstruction."

"Uh huh. You can spare me the tough-cop bullshit." Grey puffs out his chest and stands his ground. "You'll never make it stick."

"Stick hard enough to hurt." Perez smiles. "You really wanna try me?" A stand-off ensues. Until Grey breaks it and backs down.

A car horn cuts through the tension. "Perez." Detective Navarro shouts over. "10-33 on Morrison." The officer replaces his handcuffs and hurries over towards the unmarked squad car.

Grey and Alan watch him go. Alan holds the heavy camera rig down to his side. "So, what happened to the guy?" Grey stares at the officers with a sneer. "He's a dumb-ass kiddie cop on a short leash of an even dumber lady detective. One who's too stupid to realize I did the SAPD a favor. That interview. My interview. It made them famous."

"No, I meant the neighbor." Alan watches Perez climb into the unmarked vehicle. He turns to Grey. "The John Gotti neighbor. What happened to him?"

"What happened? Well..." Grey keeps his eyes on the vehicle. "It was a normal day in Queens, New York. The guy driving was a nobody. Until he ran over John Gotti's twelve-year-old son. The poor kid was playing around and darted out into the middle of the road. The car hit him. And killed him." As he talks, Grey watches Detective Navarro crank the unmarked vehicle to life and place a bubble light on the roof. "It wasn't deliberate. Not at all. An honest to goodness accident. Call it an Act of God. But the driver was devastated. He was a good guy, and the sad son-of-a-bitch was really busted up about the whole thing. He was also a dad, you know. So, he arranged a meeting with John Gotti. Man to man. Father to father. To try and heal the wounds he accidently caused."

The unmarked squad car peels out of the hospital parking lot. The red bubble light flashes in its wake.

"Let's go." Grey smiles at the scene. "We're on the move." Alan looks over to the press pool under the floodlights. "Back to the reporter pen?" Grey stares at him. "No, you idiot. To the van. Weren't you paying any attention? Navarro. She called for a 10-33."

"So." Alan shrugs his shoulders. "What's that?"

"That is the police code for an emergency call. All officers immediately respond. If I had to guess. Someone's found our 'Where's Waldo.'"

Alan works up a sweat as he lifts and lugs the camera rig. "You mean Mr. Morrison?"

"You're not for real, right?" Grey keeps Alan in tow. "This big dumb oaf thing is an act. Or are you really that dense?" Alan's about to speak but Grey shuts him down. "Please don't answer that. I guess it's time to take you back to school. Student. Meet Teacher. Lesson one. You always watch and listen. That's the only way you learn." They both hustle towards the parking lot and head for the KTXU News van. Grey keeps up his banter. "You wanna grow in this field? Hell, you wanna keep your job? Then on this job, your eyes and ears stay open."

They weave through parked vehicles until they stop at the van. Alan pops open the rear doors and loads in the camera rig. Grey doesn't offer to help. He slaps the side of the van. Bits of primer flakes to the asphalt. "Move it. Let's get this heap on the road. And crank up the police band. We need a physical address on that 10-33."

Alan climbs inside and starts up the engine.

"Can't you feel it?" Grey can't stop smiling as he climbs into the passenger seat all excited like a kid ready to open their birthday presents. "Something's afoot."

A belch of exhaust as the van bolts and burns out of the hospital parking lot.

Chapter Thirteen

The bubble lights strobe on top of the unmarked vehicle. All along the road, cars and trucks part in their wake as Navarro weaves through the dense traffic.

Officer Perez rides shotgun. "Unit 121. Detour from the main residence." He has the radio mike to his mouth and speaks with urgency. "We've got him. Hays County address. Eight, eight, six South Guadalupe Street. Repeat. 886 south Guadalupe." He keys the mike again. "Kovach. Come back."

"Unit 121 responding." A tinny voice cracks through the static. "10-4 on that address. 886 Guadalupe. I'm on my way. Meet you there."

Perez clicks off the mike and places it back on the radio. Navarro keeps her foot on the gas and both hands on the wheel with her eyes locked on the road.

"Ma'am." Perez bounces along with the ride. "Can I be honest with you?" Navarro threads her way through a traffic snarl. She has enough attention left over to answer. "I sure hope so. Shoot."

"This whole, served up on a silver platter." Perez speaks his mind. "I don't buy it."

She glances over. "What do you mean?"

"I mean, put on your detective hat." They pick up speed and race through an intersection. Perez holds on to his seatbelt strap. "Morrison's panicked, he's on the run. Why would he go to his sister's house? That's like hiding behind a bush or something. It's too easy."

Tires squeal as the vehicle makes a hairpin turn. Navarro doesn't let up on the gas. "I'll take it. There's nothing wrong with easy." The vehicle burns down a straight-away. "Besides, it's human nature to stay close to home."

Perez grunts in agreement. The sound of the engine roars over them as they sit quiet. The car barrels through dense traffic.

"You back there at the hospital." Perez clears his throat. "Was that all. um…" Her foot stomps on the gas as they pass a slower FedEx truck. Navarro glances over. "All um, what?"

"There on the hospital lawn." He sits quiet for a bit. "You and that little *pinche* reporter. I mean, the whole thing looked pretty tense. And it felt personal."

She keeps her eyes on the road. When she finally responds, her voice sounds off in the distance. "Did it now? Hmm."

"Hey." Perez picks up her mood. "If I'm out of line, please—"

"No." She shakes him off. "You're good." She keeps her hands on the wheel and heads down a frontage road, parallel to Interstate 35. Perez doesn't say anything more. He waits until Navarro decides to talk.

"That reporter was with KTXU. Gary Grey. He's a real piece of work. I'd say, maybe about a year ago, he sets up a series of interviews with SAPD personnel. Fluff pieces on the nightly news. Get to know your local beat cop. Stuff like that."

The unmarked vehicle banks hard and takes the ramp onto a highway overpass.

"Now, I'm not one for the spotlight. But they came

calling. And I listened to the sales pitch. I was polite, but not interested. They persisted. And I had to make it clear. This wasn't my thing. To me, TV interviews were a waste of my time. So, thank you, but no." Navarro merges onto the highway and weaves around slower traffic. "Then my division chief called me up to his office and I understood. He thought different." She finds a pocket in the fast lane and cruises. "I think the chief had stars in his eyes. He was all gung-ho about the idea. What's the harm? We need good community outreach. The least you can do is try. Make a nice impression. Blah blah blah."

"You want Exit 205." Perez studies the GPS map. "It's coming up in about three miles."

Navarro speeds up. "Exit 205. Got it." She passes another slow car and gets back into the fast lane. They race at a steady pace down the highway. She eases back into her story. "Frankly, with Division over me. I really didn't have a choice. So, I sat down for the interview." Perez looks over at her. She's concentrating on the road but lost in her story. "Grey. He was what you saw out there. One smarmy bastard. A kiss-ass with a smile until he got me in the hot seat. As soon as they turned on that camera, he immediately started to grill me about a medical report I thought was dead and buried."

They sit in silence. Tires hum on the highway. "I apologize, Detective." Perez speaks up. "You don't have to tell me about any of this. It's none of my business."

Navarro agrees. "Yeah, I know." An overhead highway sign shows Exit 205 approaching. She checks over her shoulder and it's clear. She shifts lanes and heads for the off-ramp. "My ex-husband. He was an executive with Valero Oil. Gunning for a senior VP slot.

And one Saturday night after some schmoozy corporate event, he had a bit too much to drink, and his jealousy got the better of him." She bites her bottom lip before deciding to proceed. "He was upset, shouting. Apparently, I had spent too much time talking to some young man at the party. I really had no idea what he was on about. Didn't make a lick of sense. He was on a tear, and I tried to calm him down. But he got rough." Navarro drives off the highway and races through an intersection, her voice calm and her eyes locked straight ahead. "In fact, he got rough enough to land me in the hospital. With a broken collar bone." Vehicles part in her wake as she drives down the road. Her eyes stay on the road as she talks to Perez. "Hey, don't leave me hanging. What's our next turn?"

"Um, yeah." Perez snaps out of his thoughts and checks the GPS. "Okay. You wanna take a right on Rattler Road. It's up here in about a mile."

"Rattler." She understands. "On the right."

He continues to gawk at her. "*Puta madre*. It's... I'm sorry you had to endure that, ma'am. I didn't mean for you to dig all this up—"

Navarro cuts him off and answers matter of fact. "I'm not digging up anything. I can see the whole mess like it was yesterday." She slows down and searches for her turn. "Grey knew exactly what he was doing. Pushing my buttons. So, with the floodlights and camera on me, and that asshole peppering me with question after question about my ex, I made a firm decision. I got up out of my chair and slapped him across the face. Hard."

"Damn." Perez shakes his head. "What a prick. I knew I didn't like that guy."

"I gotta tell you." Navarro smiles a little at the

thought. "It felt damn good. But as you can imagine, that ended the interview. Grey went full-bore at my chief. Said I attacked him. He had it all on tape. He was gonna sue. He wanted my job. I was a danger to the precinct. To the community. One big mouthful of Greek salad."

Perez perks up. "What's that mean? Greek salad."

She drives past another intersection. "It's like, ahh, a bunch of fancy talk that doesn't mean a thing." A slight chuckle to herself. "Which pretty much describes Gary Grey too."

Perez checks the route. "We're coming up to it. Okay, take a right at that next light."

Navarro perks up. "There it is. I see it."

Perez still stares at her. "So what happened?"

She makes the turn onto Rattler Road. "He wanted to resolve the whole thing on air. But I wasn't playing that game. Legal went back and forth. And they settled on me submitting a formal apology to both Grey and KTXU. I got written up. It's in my permanent record. Along with a two-week suspension with pay."

Dense traffic and city sprawl on both sides of the road. The vehicle moves past traffic pulled to the side.

Navarro gives a crooked smile to the memory. "Grey had a restraining order issued against me. Which was fine. We were all done talking anyway." She grips the wheel. "And discussing my loser of an ex-husband on the evening news wasn't my idea of a good time." They glide through another intersection. She beeps her horn at a lagging car. It gets out of the way. "And that was the last time I saw that smug little jerk's face. Until…today."

They sit in the quiet and listen to the tires hum on the road. Perez clears his throat and checks the route.

"We're less than a mile away."

Gated communities crowd on either side of the two-lane road as they close in on the address.

****

Two filtered voices banter over the police band radio. "Unit 121. Detour from the main residence. We've got him. Hays County address. Eight, eight, six. South Guadalupe Street. Repeat. 886 south Guadalupe. Kovach. Come back." The radio goes silent. A blast of static through the speaker and a tinny voice responds. "10-4 on that address. 886 Guadalupe Street. 121 on the way. Meet you there."

"Did you hear that?" Gary Grey bounces in the passenger seat. He strikes Alan on the shoulder. "Exactly like I said it would happen. If you're smart enough to listen and learn."

Alan drives the KTXU news van and brakes at a stoplight.

"Guadalupe street." Grey fiddles with his phone and plugs in the information. "And bingo. I got it right here. Ha. Look at that. We're only eleven miles away. Let's go. Turn us around."

"Now?" Alan glances over his shoulder. "But I can't right here."

"Do it anyway." Grey huffs back. "Come on. I'm good for the traffic tickets. Go." Alan flinches at the barking order but he responds.

Two cars in the opposite lane come to a screeching halt as the van makes an illegal U-turn. Car lights flash and horns blast. A ranting driver silently shouts inside his vehicle. The boiling angry mime thrusts out his middle finger. Grey returns a broad toothy smile and waves back.

A belch of exhaust and the van trundles back down the road. Grey can't contain his glee as he watches his phone. "We'll be the only ones on the scene when they take this Morrison guy down. I can see my Pulitzer Prize from here." He laughs at the thought. Alan glances over. Grey points to the windshield. "Watch the road. Get us on the highway." The van slows. Grey shouts out. "What are you doing? Run that light. Run the damn light."

Alan punches the gas and the van barrels forward through the intersection as the light flips to red.

"Good man." Grey smiles. "Drive like you've got a purpose." The van climbs the on-ramp and merges with heavy highway traffic. "Pick it up." Grey leans over to look at the dashboard. "Will you get in the fast lane? Let's go."

Alan snaps back. "I'm going as fast as I can." His shoulders hunched and tense, Alan's glued to the steering wheel.

"Okay. Jeeze." Grey backs off a bit. "Don't have a heart attack." He sits back in his seat and watches his phone. "Get us there as fast as you can." Grey watches the distance to their destination tick down like sand in an hourglass.

Alan settles the van into the middle lane and keeps the pedal to the floor. "So. Tell me what happened?"

"Like I said." Grey perks up. "Lesson one. You listen and learn. Be aware of what's happening all around you. They sure left that hospital in a hurry. Didn't they?" Alan agrees. "Exactly." Grey dramatically agrees with him. "Something was going down fast. And I knew it." He throws a snide aside. "Here's some more solid gold, and I won't even charge a finder's fee. If you want a future in this business, you better be ready to hustle."

"I am hustling." Alan drives past a slower truck and settles back into the middle lane. "But I meant that story you were telling. About John Gotti. His kid gets hit by a car. It was some neighbor guy driving. And…"

Grey looks up from his phone. "What do you care?"

Alan shrugs. "I want to. I'm a trainee reporter. I was being curious."

"Ha. Good. You don't want to lose that." Grey settles back in his seat. "A journalist's curiosity should always be in his back pocket. Sometimes the whole story isn't there on the surface. You've got to dig down a little to get to the good stuff."

"Dig deeper." Alan agrees. "So, what happened?" He passes another truck and merges back into his lane.

Grey checks his phone. "Well, Gotti got the message. The driver was devastated about the accident and wanted to express his feelings. Gotti's people arranged for a meeting between the two men. They set it up in some house in Queens." Grey checks a passing highway sign and looks back at his phone. "You want Exit 205. It's coming up here in a bit."

Alan repeats it. "205. Okay."

Grey turns in his seat. "When the driver arrived for their meeting. Gotti's thugs roughed him up and dragged him down to the basement. Handcuffed the poor bastard to a boiler pipe. And John Gotti was down there ready for him." Alan glances over. Grey returns a grin. "They beat the man senseless. And while the sap was still alive. Gotti cut him in half with a chainsaw."

"Good God." Alan goes pale as he grips the steering wheel. He swallows back his sense of revulsion.

"I don't think God had much to do with it." Grey snickers at his reaction. "Lesson two. You don't want to fuck with the rich and powerful. They never have to play by the rules."

Alan goes pale as he can't shake the vile image from his mind.

"There it is." Grey flicks Alan's flabby cheek and points to an overhead highway sign. "Snap out of it. Don't miss our exit."

The van takes the ramp and drives off the highway.

Chapter Fourteen

Daniel stays tucked in the shadows down a long hallway, calmly checking out a myriad of framed pictures. He studies various images like an interested patron at the art museum.

Recent family photos of his sister and two nephews. A picture of Jessica and Ron happily beaming at the camera and showing off their new baby. A staged studio photograph where the family dressed in their Sunday finest all stare off to the left.

Daniel stops at a faded image from his past. A happy family backyard barbeque. Mom and Dad smiling from the great beyond. His baby sister Jessica, a tomboy in worn overalls. He squints to see himself, a kid he forgot he once was. He peers at the faded pixels, a young boy's frozen smile, light years away from the sunken and haggard expression reflected in the picture glass. Daniel runs a finger across the dusty frame. He licks his dried lips and calls out in the empty hallway. "Hey, Ron." His voice echoes in the tight space. "Listen. I think…" He cracks a smile, like the one on the little boy in the old photograph. "Yeah. I'm gonna take off."

The closed bedroom door jerks open. "What? Danny Boy." Ron stands in the frame with a shocked look across his slack jawed face. "How about we wait a minute. What the hell are you talking about?"

"I've made up my mind." Daniel takes in the

statement. He's sincere. "I'm leaving."

"Hey. No." Ron frantically shakes his head. "That's not smart. Not at all. I mean…" He mentally grasps for another angle at a response. "Think about it. We've got a solid plan. It'll work. And you up and walk away from that? Huh uh. No way."

"I can't do it." Daniel steps down the hall, glancing at the wall of family photos. He touches a recent picture of his nephews playing on a rickety rusted swing set. "I can't drag my family through this mess. Through my mess." He looks at Ron. "No reason to get you all dirty." Daniel turns away and walks on down the hall.

"This is way too sudden." Ron frantically sticks with him. "You're not thinking straight. Listen, bro. Leaving? You gotta shitcan that talk, right now." Ron reaches out and stops him in the cluttered living room. "You and me. We're a team here. We've got a plan in place. It's gold. It's foolproof." Ron snatches him up by the shoulders to get his complete attention. "It's too late. Parts are in motion. The two of us, we stay put right here." Ron spits out his words like an excited child. "Now, my friend is on his way over. I get the key to his cabin. And we're gone. You and me. We're good to go. Home free."

Daniel waits for his babble to stop before he speaks. "No." Ron starts up, but Daniel cuts him off. "I don't want any part of some half-assed plan. I'm not going to sit forever in some cabin out in the middle of nowhere. That's it. I've made up my mind."

Ron doesn't respond. Daniel steps close. "I can't run away from this any longer." He turns and starts for the front door. "I'm going home."

Ron utters an angry grunt and kicks out at a plastic toy car; it bounces off the wall.

Daniel jolts a bit and stops.

"You can't go." Ron closes the gap and shakes his head in a panic. "Think about what you're doing here. Think clearly. Before you make a big mistake, bro."

Daniel chuckles at the thought. "I am making a big mistake. And I'm done with it. Hell, Ron. I don't even have to make the effort to call ahead. I've probably got the police all lined up and waiting for me at home." Daniel stares at the closed front door. "All swarming my house." He takes a deep breath as his hand reaches out and grasps the doorknob.

Ron reaches to the small of his back and brings out a Smith & Wesson revolver. "I said. Stop." The gun shakes in his hand as he aims dead center between Daniel's shoulders.

"Cop cars up and down the street." Daniel holds the doorknob, lost in his own world. "In the driveway. Packs of 'em on the front lawn. Waiting for me." He pulls on the doorknob, it's locked. "I'm sure they made a mess of Jude's flower beds. Man, she's gotta be pissed." He tumbles open the dead bolt, it clicks in place.

Ron pulls back the hammer and cocks the wheel gun. "I can't let ya leave Danny Boy." A gun shot thunders through the front door. Wood splinters; sunlight streams in from the fresh hole and pools on the carpet. In started shock, Daniel stumbles and crumples to the floor in front of the door.

"Shit, that was loud as hell." Ron towers over him with the revolver aimed at Daniel. His ears ringing, lost in a deep mental haze, Daniel swims through consciousness and glances up in a daze.

"Hey. You all right?" Ron stares down at him. "Can you hear me?"

Daniel tries to get up on his elbows. Ron pushes him back down with his boot and pins him to the floor. "I told you to listen to me." Daniel starts to squirm. "Don't start. You stay put." Ron doesn't let up. "I like you right where you are, bro."

Outside the front door, right before the crazy chaos erupted, it's an early afternoon quiet on Guadalupe Street. Hidden birds chirp in the oak trees. Row houses aligned next to each other, separated by wooden fences and shades of green where the cut grass from a lawnmower sets the demarcation lines.

Two figures hustle down the quiet residential road. They freeze in place as a single gunshot echoes out. "Did you hear that?" Officer Perez has his service revolver up.

"Shots fired." Detective Navarro takes shelter against a hedge row. "It's our house."

Perez motions to a hidden figure across the street.

Officer Kovach acknowledges the signal and moves. He crouches his way across the worn asphalt and follows the walkway pavers on up to the little row house at 886 South Guadalupe Street.

A solitary splintered hole shows through the worn front door. Kovach has his service revolver at the ready.

Navarro and Perez inch their way across the front lawn of the house. Navarro takes out her 9mm automatic.

Kovach motions for them to stay back. He taps his throat and holds up two fingers.

Perez closes the gap with Navarro. He whispers. "We've got two voices, right inside." She understands and moves a little closer to the porch.

Inside the house, Daniel stays pinned to the floor in front of the closed front door. His voice croaks as he speaks from the ground. "Ron. Put the gun down."

Ron stands with his boot on Daniel's back. The wheel gun trained down on him. "Not for a million bucks." He gets his tension under control. And takes his boot away. "Well, maybe I'd do it for that." He steps back but keeps the gun trained on Daniel. "That man on the TV said he would pay a million dollars for you." He grins at the thought. "Now, you're a real good egg. Always helping me out here. You keep the wife and kids off my back. And I sure do appreciate it. But I gotta tell ya. That ain't nearly enough to tip the scales. I'm getting that money."

Tendons pop and Daniel utters a deep moan as he stretches and extends from his flattened fetal position.

"Nope." Ron pulls the hammer back on the pistol. "You wanna stay right where you are, Danny boy." No response. Daniel starts to lift himself off the ground. Ron bellows a nervous frantic shriek. "I said, don't move." He pulls the trigger. The gunshot thunders. Another gaping hole punches through the front door.

****

On the front porch, Officer Kovach flinches from the shock of the deafening sound and blast of wood splinters. He stares at the singed hole through the door, right at his eye level. His hand goes to his temple and brings back wet blood coating his fingers. Over the light and shadows from the holes through the door, a figure moves around inside. Instinct kicks in as Kovach automatically raises his service revolver and fires multiple rounds until his weapon runs dry.

A rain of gunshots punch through the wooden door and repeatedly hit Ron. A red mist sprays on the couch and wall as he jerks and dances in place from the rapid consecutive hits. He collapses to the floor in a wet heap.

Blood pools out on the carpet and vinyl. Ron's pistol falls and slides under the couch.

On the porch, Kovach stands shell-shocked in front of the Swiss-cheese door. His empty revolver locked tight in both hands. Blood trickles down his cheek. Officer Perez snatches him back by his uniform collar and pulls Kovach to safety. He checks his bleeding wound and gives him a look-over. Kovach mutters under a thousand-yard stare. Perez quietly mouths to Navarro. "He's in shock, but okay. Looks like shrapnel damage."

Navarro motions to the door. Perez keeps his weapon trained.

"Mr. Morrison." The detective calls out from the porch. "Can you hear me in there?" She gets no response. "This is the San Antonio Police. You've got nowhere else to go. Drop your weapon. Now."

She glances at Kovach who holds a makeshift compress to his temple. "You turned this into a goddamn clusterfuck." She spits out a harsh whisper. "This ain't the wild west, Cowboy." Kovach nurses his wound and doesn't respond.

Perez leaves his side and slides up onto the porch. He edges up against the door and steadies his breath and tension. His revolver gripped tight in his hands.

****

Inside the house, shadows play on the floor. Daniel can hear a voice speaking, the words sound like a distant echo. He hears his name, stretched out like a record at slow speed. The growing pool of blood on the vinyl spreads. It oozes towards his cheek. A second before it touches his skin, he lifts off the floor like lightning.

Ron is dead on the ground, his eyes lifeless. A surprised expression frozen in rigor across his face.

Daniel doesn't give him a second look as he crab-crawls towards his objective. His shoulder connects with the edge of the couch and shoves it aside. The discarded pistol gleams up from the sea of dust bunnies and bits of forgotten food. He snatches up the gun and stumbles off down the hall.

The front door is kicked open. Perez and Navarro sweep inside the living room in a commando motion. "Man down." Navarro goes for Ron on the floor. She's careful not to step in the growing pool of blood.

Perez glances down the hall but moves into the kitchen. "Kitchen clear. Is it our guy?" She doesn't answer. Perez snaps out. "Detective, is it him?"

Navarro turns the pale face towards the sunlight. Ron's dead eyes stare back at her. "Negative. It's not Morrison." She stands up, her weapon out and down. "Let's go. Room to room. Sweep and clear."

They carefully start down the hall.

Perez checks a closet and moves to the next closed door. "Bathroom. Clear."

Navarro glances at the display of smiling family photos as she inches forward.

In a small room at the end of the hall, a young boy's choice of poster art and prized magazine pictures are taped haphazardly to the walls. Yesterday's after-school snacks left on a dresser, the spoon congealed to the plate and piles of clothes scattered on the floor.

Daniel bounces through the minefield and lunges against the dusty window frame. Through the smudged glass he can see a torn metal screen hanging by a thread. Next to the window against the house, a cluster of tubes run from the electrical meter.

The pistol forgotten in his hand knocks over a

leaning tower of PlayStation games. They cascade to the floor as he tugs and struggles to open the window. The window doesn't budge. It's locked. His panic bubbles as he thumbs the latches open and lifts the window with a squeal as the warped wood rubs against the frame.

Navarro stands at the open door of the master bedroom. Her eyes check out every corner and focus on every shadow as Perez carefully opens another door and peers from floor to ceiling inside a small bathroom suite. "All clear."

Navarro nods back and looks towards the last closed door.

Daniel struggles to lift himself up on the windowsill and drags his left leg out. The threadbare metal screen falls to the grass as he uses an electrical meter pipe to steady before he drops to the ground.

He bolts around the house and into the backyard. Frantic glances over his shoulder as he moves, he runs smack into a rusty metal swing set. The metal chain clangs like a church bell against the chipped steel bar. Daniel stumbles and scrambles for the perimeter chain-link fence, and with a wheeze he lifts himself up and over.

Navarro pushes opens the closed room door and peeks inside. A child's choice of colorful images covers the walls. Video games scattered on the worn carpet. She crouches down so she can see under the bed. A pile of board games and the shadows of discarded clothes.

Navarro stands up and slips into the room. She freezes on the open window. "He's on the move." She peers out the open window and sees the metal swing set bobbing back and forth.

Perez steps into the room.

Navarro snaps over her shoulder, "He's in the backyard. Go."

Perez doesn't have to be told twice. He runs down the hall to the living room.

"We got 'em." Officer Kovach sits frozen on the couch, blood congealed and drying down his cheek. He continues to stare at the dead body on the vinyl floor. "Didn't we?" He thinks for a second and agrees with himself. "Yes, we did. We got 'em."

A jumble of frantic words spills from Perez as he races into the room, leaps by Kovach and clambers for the front door.

Kovach stays on the couch and watches him throw open the gunshot-splintered door and bolt outside. The door squeaks back on its hinges and eases closed.

"We got 'em good." He tells the dead body again. Ron's glassy eyes stare up at nothing.

Chapter Fifteen

Detective Navarro drops down from the windowsill and heads for the backyard. She takes careful and steady steps as her 9mm automatic sweeps out in front of her. Her eyes dart all around as she moves past the rusty swing set and heads for the chain-link fence. She peers up and down the alleyway. Either way looks all clear.

"Morrison." She calls out to nobody. "I know it's you." She waits to hear any kind of response or movement in the quiet neighborhood. "Stop this. Now."

Daniel can hear the shouts over his shoulder. He's not nearly far enough away for comfort. Sweat pours off his forehead. His shirt sticks to his skin. His haggard breaths catch in his dry throat. He follows the dirt and dandelion covered pathway between two privacy fences. The rutted trail snakes and dips through a drainage culvert. His scuffed dress shoes slipped in the mud. Rocks tumble down a gravel embankment. Daniel skips and stumbles forward until his feet land on firm pavement. He casts frantic looks over his shoulder as he propels forward, towards a residential crossroads and a four-way traffic stop.

A minivan slows to a stop at the edge of the sign, its turn signal flashes, and it drives forward. Daniel leans against a coarse metal stop sign and catches his breath. His bulging eyes can't turn away from the opening of the alleyway and the slope down the gravel embankment.

Detective Navarro holds onto links of the metal chain-link fence as she starts to climb. Her weight on the flimsy fence causes it to shake in her hands. She moves cautiously, until she can manage to swing one leg over, even as the chain-link continues to jiggle.

"Hey. Detective," Perez shouts out from the rusty swing set.

Startled, Navarro swings her other leg around and lands hard on the other side. She winces at the sharp pain and drops to her knees.

Perez races over to the fence line. "Are you okay?"

"I'm super." She probes at the torn knee of her pants, then looks up from the grass. "Get over here."

Perez easily leaps over the chain-link fence as Navarro struggles to get to her feet. She winces at the tenderness of her ankle. She crouches back down and carefully massages the swollen joint.

Perez catches his breath. "Which way did he go?"

Navarro shakes her head. "No idea. We split up. You head uptown. I've got downtown."

He doesn't move. "Did you hurt your foot?"

"Yes." She snaps back. "Any more stupid questions?" Perez doesn't say anything. "Go." Navarro points the way. "Go get him." He takes off and hurries down the alley way.

Navarro hobbles a bit and tries to walk off the pain. She grits her teeth as she navigates past the privacy fences and can see the drainage dip up ahead.

Daniel leans against a stop sign. His eyes dart from the crossroads to the gravel-lined culvert right over his shoulder. Vehicles continue to navigate through the four-way stop. Daniel can't help standing out like a sore thumb as he glances inside the passing cars and trucks.

A tan Oldsmobile with two men inside waits their turn and moves into the intersection.

An old Honda wagon drives behind the Oldsmobile. A clan of kids bounce all around. The suburban father leans on the steering wheel and ignores the chaos over his shoulder.

Daniel can hear the faint sounds of sirens in the distance. The piercing wail grows closer.

A Mercedes sedan with a purple vanity license plate pulls up to the stop sign. The bold letters on the plate spell out Ability. A female driver sits alone in the vehicle. She waits her turn. Daniel stares right at her.

"Morrison." The word shouted loud enough over the traffic at the residential crossroads. Daniel looks back.

Detective Navarro starts to navigate down the slope of the gravel embankment. He can hear her from across the street. "Stop."

He turns away in a palpable panic.

Tricia Kelley sits in the air-conditioned comfort of her Mercedes. She can feel Daniel's eyes on her through the tinted windshield. She glances for a quick second at the unkept man standing at the side of the road and mutters to herself. "God, these panhandlers are everywhere. Stop looking at me, you freak." Her manicured fingers wrapped around a large Yeti thermos of coffee with faded lipstick embedded along the lip. She takes a sip. Her foot hovers over the pedal as she waits for a pickup truck to pass all the way through the intersection before it's her turn. She cushions the gas. The Mercedes accelerates forward.

The passenger door is ripped open. Daniel holds onto the frame and his foot drags in the road. Panic sticks in his throat. He blurts out one word. "Drive."

"What the Christ?" Tricia can't believe what's happening. She shouts out in bewilderment and anger. "Get the hell out of my car—" Her eyes drop to the pistol in Daniel's other hand. She slams on the brakes.

Daniel's thrown forward inside the car. His shoulder bashes against the padded dashboard. The passenger door bounces and clicks closed. The Mercedes stopped in the middle of the intersection. Tricia screams at the top of her lungs.

Navarro makes it down the gravel embankment and her feet land on the pavement. She starts moving towards the cars and commotion at the four-way intersection. Police sirens wail in the distance. Navarro knows they're heading for the house that's now a crime scene. She hurries as fast as she can with a hitch in her step, the pain from her swollen ankle kept at bay behind gritted teeth. Her automatic pistol is down at her side. She's alone on the street as she closes in on her elusive prey.

A red Mustang grumbles into the intersection. A muscle-bound, tattooed Good Samaritan pops out from behind the wheel and runs over to the Mercedes.

Inside the vehicle, Tricia pinwheels blind punches at Daniel. "Out. Out. Get out. Get. Out." Her panic masked under the frantic blows. "Get the fuck out of my car."

Daniel takes a barrage of punches and smacks. He struggles to shove them aside. He's pinned to the closed passenger door.

A closed fist thuds against the safety glass. Through the window, beady eyes and a bald head peer inside. He tries the handle and it's locked. His gruff voice muffled. "Open the door." He jostles and tugs at the handle. "Open the fuckin' door."

Navarro hobbles up to the intersection. She's smart

enough to keep her gun down and out of sight. "San Antonio police." She tries to control the chaos with her voice. "Stop. Right now."

The Samaritan tough guy continues to hammer on the passenger window. Tiny cracks splinter through the safety glass.

Tricia flails in her seat and keeps up the constant bombardment of blows. "Lady." Daniel manages to deflect a few. "Stop it. Stop hitting me." She doesn't listen. He closes the short gap and pushes his body weight against her. "Move, lady. Will you get this car moving?" Through the back window, Daniel sees the policewoman coming up fast. "Drive." He shouts out and jams the pistol into her side. Tricia jumps in her seat. Her hands grip the steering wheel.

Cracks grow through the passenger window. The Samaritan tugs at the door and thuds against the glass. The Mercedes lurches forward. Samaritan leaps back.

Navarro hammers on the trunk with the butt of her pistol as the car moves forward. The Mercedes bucks and accelerates through the four-way stop.

Navarro reaches out and tries to steady the Samaritan. He spins on her with juiced adrenaline and throws a wild punch. It glances off her cheek. Surprised, she punches back and connects with the man's glass jaw. He drops like a sack to the asphalt.

The tired detective towers over the unconscious man and reels in her tension. She catches her breath as she stands in the intersection and watches the Mercedes speed away.

Chapter Sixteen

Hayden Grant liked to tell people on the political trail that politics didn't find him. He found politics.

Loretta, his second ex-wife, was from Texarkana. A border town right on the Texas and Arkansas line that grew into a monster industrial truck stop for endless interstate commerce. The city played up its Texas bonafides as the gateway to the Lone Star state with images of cowboys working on the range and big blue sky shining down on wide Stetson hats and longhorn steer grazing all on the prairie. Even when the reality was acres of concrete and steel covering whatever green valleys used to be there and 20-lane highways with streaming traffic flowing across the state border.

But bustling Texas cities might as well have been on the dark side of the moon to a young man right on the edge of failing out of high school and barely existing day to day, living on the wrong side of the tracks in East Alton, Illinois.

Friends his age volunteered for the military meat grinder. Hayden considered it. He was a proud American. But not proud enough to die for his country in some overseas shithole.

Still, he couldn't wait to leave his hometown behind.

All his father seemed to amass was a line of creditors and collection agencies on his trail. The man was always overwhelmed by a mountain of paperwork made up of overdue traffic tickets, bounced checks, property liens, lawsuits and frivolous counter suits.

It was his mother who taught Hayden how to survive using his smooth tongue and wits that she knew he got from her side of the family. Her boy could convince you there was an ice storm coming on a hundred-degree sunny day. Some folks called it outright lying. But she preferred little, tiny fibs or at best, maybe stretching the truth a bit. She believed her only son's charisma and sense of self-worth could take him far in this world. She kept the little nagging voice in the back of her mind quiet, the one that said, down to brass tacks. Hayden Grant didn't have much else to fall back on.

Hayden made it through high school by the skin of his teeth, and his D+ grade average wasn't good enough to get into any kind of serious university. Trade schools weren't an option. A blue-collar life was beneath him. He never liked getting dirty. Physically anyway.

And he was smart enough to understand that the road ahead isn't smooth or easy with a high school diploma. So, he enrolled in Lewis & Clark Community College over in Godfrey and searched for some new direction in life. His compass landed on the most beautiful woman he'd ever seen. And it was there on campus that he met his first ex-wife, Sara James.

Hayden saw her as a conquest. He wanted her. And it was only a matter of time before he convinced her that he was right. It wasn't so much courting or dating. More like circling a potential client. It wasn't long after that he closed the deal over one three-day weekend, and they were married. Sign the papers on a Friday. A backyard barbeque with friends and family Saturday. And a Honeymoon suite at the Redwood Ramada Inn with a

Sunday morning late check-out. They didn't have much else but each other. And that was enough.

Honestly, he saw their relationship more like a mental challenge. An experiment. Could he mold this lifeless clay into the perfect partner? He hoped he could change her into something she wasn't. Take this quiet girl who went with the flow her entire life and open her eyes to all the potential beyond their dead-end little town? It was only a matter of time. She never once complained. At her core, she was a solemn church mouse who was more than happy to let him call their shots and set out a solid life for the two of them.

Hayden moaned about their mundane day-to-day existence and all his untapped potential going to waste in a handful of community college classes that didn't add up to a damn thing. But he was sweet and kind when he would talk about their soon-to-be life. He could see it for the two of them. It was currently out of reach, but he was positive it was outside of Illinois. And Sara was always more than happy to simply listen, and all was right in their world.

They spoke about children and growing their family tree. Sara had her heart set on two kids, a boy and a girl. And Hayden began to get comfortable with the idea of being the head of a household. He liked the status as a father and provider, and he figured there was no way he could be worse than his own dead-beat dad. But talk of kids and family was put aside when a work opportunity came knocking. And Hayden was more than ready to answer the door.

Sara wasn't sure, but after a strong interview in St. Louis, Hayden made the decision for the both of them, and they dropped out of community college with a solid job under his belt.

His smooth tongue was put to good use as a salesman for John Deere out of Wood River. His specialty was agriculture and construction equipment. Big ticket items. His bosses took notice as he climbed the sales-floor ranks with ease. His supervisor testified that Hayden could sell a tractor to a blind paraplegic and even overcharge the bastard before they rolled the cripple on out the door. The man was a natural salesman.

That fall, John Deere executives sent their best and brightest Midwest sales division to an annual farming convention in Dallas, Texas. And it was there that he met Loretta Banks. She was the top salesperson for heavy construction equipment who worked out of the St. Louis branch. It was love at first sight.

What began as a series of tradeshow one-night stands didn't fulfill their intense hunger. Office days went into after hours. Multiple receipts piled up for several seedy motels outside St. Louis and Wood River. Every other weekend was a work trip that never even existed. It all took priority over his dreary settled home life with Sara.

Hayden wanted a divorce. But Sara wouldn't give him one. So he called in a favor from a drinking buddy with a law degree and got the county court to grant a default judgement. His-no fault divorce was official.

Sara cried for days. She peppered him with screams and shouts and suicidal threats if he went through with it. But he never believed her fits and didn't care what she did. He told her to stop talking about it and just do it. Slice away. She'd be doing him a favor.

Hayden Grant left small-town Sara behind shortly thereafter. Loretta's big tits and even bigger bank account made life much more interesting than a nature/nurture experiment on a quiet church mouse ever could. With the divorce final and suicidal Sara out of sight and mind, they both decided it was time to put all their torrid affair pillow talk into motion. With the flip of a coin, a final decision was made. Loretta and Hayden put in for work transfers.

Texas was bigger and better, and John Deere sure sold a lot of tractors in that state. It was worth the risk. They would leave the Midwest in the rear-view mirror. Take a chance and move down to her hometown of Texarkana. And there they would build a future together.

Hayden never had Texas on his bingo card. In fact, all he could see in his mind's eye were oil derricks and tumbling tumbleweeds. Roy Rogers alongside his stuffed horse. And faded TV episodes of *Dallas*. Still, he fell hard for the big attitudes, sun-kissed weather and wide-open spaces of the Lone Star state. Life was good.

Loretta came from old family money and seemed to know her way around all the elite country clubs, local golf courses and tennis resorts. She was on a first-name basis with every med spa and Botox clinic in the area. A thin champagne glass was never far from her grasp, and she enjoyed being rich and being comfortable.

Hayden went from a lifestyle of scraping pennies and scrounging cigarette butts back in Godfrey to Texas-sized fancy dinners and a fleet of European cars and high-end retail shopping assistants at his beck and call.

He rose through the ranks and managed to sell an assembly line of harvesters and combines, and his quarterly numbers made the folks at John Deere very happy. Raises and promotions were handed out like candy, and he bought his secretary slash mistress a pair of Louboutin heels that cost more than his monthly rent back in Illinois.

Hayden sat back and enjoyed every bit of the ride. But he didn't see what was coming. And it didn't take long before real boredom began to seep in.

He got to a point where he happily went through all the motions, but the truth was it wasn't the same. All those days of selling over-priced farm equipment over corporate expensed steak dinners. Along with a closet full of designer clothes and a revolving door of call girls and sugar babies. That life didn't have the same spark anymore. There was no denying all his needs and desires were more than satisfied.

But his fire, the one deep in his belly, that badly needed tending.

It was a casual conversation after a pleasant Sunday church service that finally gave him a real sense of direction. While Loretta was already off in space riding her Xanax wave. Hayden found himself lost in a deep back and forth with Vance Jackson about seriously running for local political office.

At first, he thought it was a joke. Hayden never really considered the idea. He believed all politicians to be cut from the same corrupt cloth. And they ended up either crooks or suckers. It seemed about as far-fetched as anything he could imagine. But Vance sure could talk a good game. He almost rivaled Hayden in that department. Almost.

The way Vance told it, there was a clear pathway set out. He called it Candyland.

See, you start at the beginning and make your way through the Gumdrop Forest. Become a school board member. Whatever the topic and whatever you do, you always say you're doing it for the children. It might sound corny but that's what worked for this crowd.

After that, your next stop. Climb the Peppermint Mountain. The city council. It's a little harder, a steep climb that requires a man to shake all the right hands and grease all the palms. But if you play it smooth. Have the right people on your side saying the right things.

Well then, it was a clear glide path down to the Hard Candy Castle. And after that, the road ahead was all tasty and sweet. You move upwards and onwards, straight into the state legislature.

Simple twists and turns of a board game. The whole thing really was that easy.

Hayden considered himself a Democrat, in as much as he ever cared about his vote or general politics. Basically, he had a live and let live mentality. And he learned young that there were unspoken rules you had to follow if you wanted to survive in the big city.

Rule one. You always know when and where you're going. For the local papers it became an annual summer event. Publishing stories about random tourists who were robbed and occasionally killed for the crime of wandering down the wrong street.

Rule two. You always stay away from certain neighborhoods. That goes for all hours of the day. Be careful what you say out loud, because commenting on those neighborhoods is full of political and social landmines. Make sure you show kindness and say sympathetic buzzwords in the public square. But in private, hell, let the crazies continue to arm and kill each other. What else were the miserable wretches gonna do? It was survival of the fittest in East Alton and St. Louis.

Rule three. Nevers. You learned to never give a shit.

Never look anyone in the eye. And never talk to anyone you didn't know. Rules of thumb that never changed. It was the facts of life for a long-term life span in Midwestern small towns and big cities.

But down in Texas, from the Panhandle to the Gulf Coast. Rules were up to interpretation. Basically, if you were smart enough to keep what you were doing on your own property. You're in the clear. Good fences make good neighbors. Make sure that whatever happens, it always happens behind closed doors and gates. That was more than enough to keep the peace.

But calling yourself a Democrat in Texas? Out loud and in public? Hell, you might as well call yourself a damn Communist. It wasn't the kinda thing said or done in good company.

So, Hayden became a Republican. And even though technically he was a carpetbagger from Illinois. Well, a good pair of Lucchese tailor-made boots and a jet-black Stetson with a wide brim was enough to keep any of the "outsider" talk down to a minimum.

First up, an open seat for the Texarkana School District Board of Trustees. A three-year position to help guide the superintendent with creative and effective leadership. Hayden was nervous at first but took to the political arena like a duck to water.

The formula was simple. Whatever the question was, it was all in the name of the children. Those impressionable minds needed to be protected and guided. But under the expressions of care was a litany of scare tactics and borderline hate speech that the audiences ate up like red meat served on a silver platter.

Some days, it was the fear of city sprawl. All those urban hellholes that were an utter infestation. A poisonous breeding grounds for heinous crime. Full of rapists and murderers.

And the multitude of gays that were out there, masquerading among us as decent citizens even as they practice their decadent and depraved lifestyles behind closed doors. All of them, working and scheming to indoctrinate all those fresh young minds.

There was never a foreign caravan far from the border. Made up of Central and South American migrants that were storming the gates on a constant basis. Sure, the border was eight hundred twenty miles away. But as far as Hayden and the rally audiences were concerned, the unwashed masses were right outside their church house doors. And all those ragtag immigrants, who didn't have the common decency to even speak English. Well, they, of course, were a vital threat to all the children. Plus the women. Plus the jobs.

His easy targets varied. It really depended on his overall mood and the real-time audience reaction to his basic stump speech.

His dismissed his opponent for the school trustee position as some skirt named Wanda Bowers. He felt she had several strikes against her. First off, the reality was, she was a woman. And as far as Hayden felt, a female opponent meant a flawless victory. It was game over for the little lady.

But she persisted in the race, much longer than he thought. She had this nasty habit of talking about the actual issues pertaining to Bowie County and the Texarkana School District. She pressed the flesh. She listened intently and answered direct questions. And she made her campaign all about their local needs and desires. It was an effective strategy.

Instead, Hayden focused on the big picture. An endless conveyer belt of rainbow gays, the mass of illegal immigrants and a swarm of conniving urban outsiders who were all coming for your children and the good people of Texarkana. They needed a valiant protector in these times of great turmoil. Someone who would put their own needs aside to watch out for them.

The waves of crowds seemed to grow as the May election date approached and Hayden Grant stayed on the stump day after day. Vance Jackson told Loretta he had never seen someone with the gift of gab like Hayden. They watched as he handled the voters with the charm of a megachurch preacher who was born for the stage.

When the ballots were finally counted. He won the election by over 20 points.

Team Grant cheered into the night and celebrated the win at the Gem of the Hills Civic Center. When he got on stage to give his acceptance speech, Hayden was gracious. He thanked all his supporters and highlighted his voters. He promised to be a guiding light for all the impressionable school children of Bowie County.

Later at Vance Jackson's palatial estate home, they had a real wrap party. Top-shelf liquor flowed like water. Key bumps of cocaine were there for the taking. Along with a gaggle of young campaign volunteers who were more than eager to show the donor class a good time.

Loretta was deep into her champagne and Xanax cocktail. And Hayden Grant was introduced to a group of clean-cut fresh-faced fraternity brothers who excelled at what they called a take-no-prisoners politicking. Sometimes it involved ballot stuffing. Churning up the rumor mill. Spreading conspiracy theories of all types. They played it off as boyish pranks or dirty tricks. But

Hayden preferred the simple term for it. Ratfucking.

As the victory party raged on into the night, he soaked in all the adoration. His first taste of political power. Sure, it was on an admittedly small scale. What could a school district board of trustee member really do? He was certain that would be answered soon enough. And he was proud of his accomplishment. Like his mother always said, if it's a worthwhile endeavor, the first steps were always the hardest.

But there at Vance Jackson's victory celebration, he was the center of the universe. And with his wife passed out in the living room and two thirsty female volunteers draped on each arm, Hayden Grant was no more. Official School Board Member Hayden Grant took his place and he clearly understood what was at stake. With the right person out in front, and with some trickster weapons whispering in his ear and powering the throne. There was no limit to what could be achieved.

That night, Grant's future seemed bright. Endless. Candyland was there for the taking. And he was already on his way up the Peppermint Mountain.

Chapter Seventeen

As the Mercedes pulls away, Daniel sits frozen and can't shift his piercing stare from the rear window. He watches the policewoman dwindle in the distance, the crazy commotion at the four-way intersection left far behind. The wheel gun gripped in his right hand; he squeezes the pistol tight. His razor focus simmers a bit as he takes in the driver.

The frightened woman keeps both hands glued to the steering wheel. She's polished and scrubbed in her pristine designer clothes and expensive jewelry. The barrel of the pistol is wedged into her side.

Dark thoughts flash through her mind. A short trip to the HEB market catapulted her instead into this nightmare. The smooth skin on her face, with a hint of make-up, barely masks the erupted volcano of stress and blind panic. Her eyes bug wide as she stares straight ahead. "What…what are you going to do—" Shivers ripple down her forearms. Her voice croaks between chapped lips. "—with me?" Her breath skips, and she pants with fear.

Daniel pulls his gaze off the back window with a sense of short-lived relief. Utter exhaustion replaces taut tension. "Hey." He eases up on his tight grip and removes the wheel gun imbedded against her waist. "Lemme ask you. What's in that thermos?"

"Coffee." She takes her eyes off the road for a brief

second, surprise in her expression. "With cream and sugar. And collagen."

"I'm dying of thirst." Daniel points his chin towards the Yeti sealed cup. "Do you mind?" He takes a big pull from the thermos and wipes his mouth with a grimy forearm. "Yeah, that's good." He places it back into the cup holder. "Thank you." He licks the residue of cream from his lips and sits back in the chair. Spiderweb cracks run all through the passenger window.

She hesitates. "I…I want to…know—" Fingers clench and grip the wheel tight. "— where are we going?"

Daniel sinks slumped into the comfortable leather seat. "Drive." A pallor of quiet falls in the cabin until he turns to look over at her. "What's your name?"

"Tricia." She doesn't say anything more.

"Tricia." He prods her for more information. "Tricia. What?"

"Kelley." The thin dam of her calm façade breaks apart. "I… Look, you can have my money. I've got some cash on me, maybe a few hundred dollars." Her voice rises and falls in a sea of panic. "But please…don't shoot me." She can't help it as her body quivers in the seat. "Don't kill me. Please, don't do it. Please." She glances over at him. "I'm sorry. I didn't mean it. I'm so sorry I hit you. You can let me go. Okay? Please--"

"Shhhh. Stop it." An exhausted Daniel talks over her rant. His tired voice at a whisper as he tries to soothe her down. "Stop. And listen to me. Okay. I'm not gonna hurt you. I swear, I'm not. Do you understand what I am saying to you?"

She shakes her head, yes. A happy relief in her response. "Yes. Yes. I do. You need a car. That's it.

That's all this is. And my car. It's yours. You can have it. It's fully insured. I won't tell. Anyone. I can say it was stolen. I was going to the supermarket, and I'll say, someone stole it. Right out of the parking lot. That's what I'll say."

"Yeah. We can talk about that." He watches out the windshield at some passing road signs. "For now. Go ahead and get us on the highway."

Tricia glances over at him with a lilt of surprise to her voice. "Where do you want to go?"

He mutters back. "Away from here."

The Mercedes glides through traffic and heads for the highway frontage road.

****

Detective Roya Navarro hobbles down the narrow fence line. Her right hand still throbs from the unexpected punch she delivered back at the four-way intersection.

Her police credentials kept the Good Samaritan she hit from continuing to shout about pressing charges. He skulked back to his muscle car with nothing more to show for his noble intentions than hurt pride.

A group of cars and trucks pulled off to the side of the road. A few civilians had their cell phones out recording her every move as she flashed her badge and commanded people to get back into their vehicles and move on. She ignored random questions and snarky comments until the intersection was back to normal.

Finally, she was able to make her way back up the gravel embankment and headed back towards the suburban crime scene.

Her suit jacket is tattered and torn, and her blouse stained with sweat. Her dirty red face is covered in a sheen of grime. Like a Mobius strip, her split-second thoughts and reactions loop around in her mind.

He was right there. God damn it. I had him. I almost had Daniel Morrison. Mercedes. Purple vanity plates. "Ability." The single word slips out. He didn't have any. It was blind luck that he got away. No. Not luck. *It was my fault. What a stupid rookie plan to chase after him on my own.*

Under a heavy cloud of embarrassment and anger, she continues to stride forward. Until she perks up to a wave of sound. Words mumble at her parched lips. "What the hell is that?" Sporadic shouts seem to echo off in the distance. But she can't make out any specific words. Navarro picks up her pace until she stops at the chain-link perimeter fence. She can see divots in the dirt where she earlier twisted her ankle.

Audible voices drift from around the front of the house. Roya wipes sweat and grime from her neck and face. She catches her breath and follows the fence towards the front lawn.

A beat-up KTXU news van sits parked in front of a squad car. Gary Grey waves his microphone around and peppers numerous questions at Officer Perez. Alan shoulders the camera and records every second.

"So who's the corpse sprawled out in the doorway? Hello. Officer, is that our man?" Grey doesn't let up. "Come on. Ignoring what's right in front of our eyes doesn't make it all go away. It's an easy yes or no question, Officer. Which is it?"

"No comment." Perez weaves and dodges away from the thrusted microphone and he tries to avoid the camera lens. "We have no comment at this time."

Grey doesn't stop and lays it on thick. "Is that a *no*?

That sounds like a *no* to me. Did you kill Daniel Morrison? Is that what you don't want to say? Officer? Answer the questions."

A Blanco County EMS ambulance turns down the residential street. The vehicle tries to pull up close to the house. Perez ignores the harassing reporter and steps onto the road for traffic control. He waves and motions for the vehicle to move in closer.

"Grey, you blood-sucking parasite." Navarro shouts out. "Get the hell out of the way." Roya hobbles towards the scene. "That's obstruction. Clear-cut."

Grey sparks up a smile when he sees Navarro. "I want the dead body in the shot." He grabs Alan by his sleeve and points at the camera. "Me, the detective, and the body all in the frame. You got it?" Alan peers through the viewfinder as he focuses the camera. "Let's go." Grey eggs him on. "We good. Are we good?" Alan adjusts the lens until he gives Grey a thumbs-up.

"Detective Navarro. It is always a pleasure." Grey watches Navarro continue to hobble closer to him with a smug smile. "Are you okay? Aw, did you hurt your foot? Yeah, I wouldn't advise running out here in high heels."

"Get out of our way." Navarro spits out her words through clenched teeth. "I won't say it again. Stay the hell out of this."

Grey lets the harsh warning wash right off him. "Yeah. I guess we were too late to see the gunfight at the O.K. Corral." He thrusts his microphone forward. "So, who's the dearly departed in the doorway?"

She ignores the question and hobbles over to Perez. "Cordon off the scene. I want this house locked down." Perez holds up his hands and the ambulance brakes to a halt. Doors bounce open as the EMT crew hustle for their gear. Navarro looks up and down the residential street. A few nosy neighbors peer out from behind curtains or stand watch on their porches and driveways. Roya speaks in hushed tones. "These lookie-loos won't stay put for long. Why are we still the only ones here? Where the hell is anybody? I heard sirens—"

"Sorry, ma'am. I thought we had him but came up empty." Perez steps out of the way as a pair of EMTs pull out more gear from the ambulance. "That man is a ghost. Long gone from here. But I gotta say, this whole town has gone completely mental. Every radio band on the box is squawking about a Morrison sighting. Hell, dispatch had to call all the way to Blanco for the meat wagon." The EMTs brings out a stretcher and set it up. "Police. Fire. I mean, there's nothing available county wide." Perez stays with Navarro. "I guess they're all out searching. What a trainwreck. It's like Elvis meets Bigfoot. People are seeing him everywhere."

"Yeah." Navarro sighs. "Well, our Mr. Morrison's not mythical or dead." She leans in close. "We need to talk to Air Support. But I want it off the radio."

He arches his eyebrows. "You onto something, Detective?"

Grey hovers over their backs. He tries to hear what they're saying. "Come on, Navarro. You got your man, or you didn't. Either way it's a story."

"*Dios mio.*" She swings on Grey. "I want you far away from here and even farther away from me. Right now. This is police business."

Two EMTs roll the empty stretcher down the walkway. "Get on it." Grey shoves Alan in front of them. "Keep filming. Keep filming." Alan hurries onto the porch and stands inside the open doorway. His camera zooms in on the dead body. Ron lies in a pool of his own coagulated blood, his lifeless body in a state of rigor. The lens zooms and focuses but can't get a good shot of Ron's expression of shock and surprise. With the EMTs right at his back, Alan is careful not to step in the gelled pools of blood. He nudges Ron's face with one sneaker. His stiff dead head rolls to the side. Alan smiles behind the camera as he gets his shot.

"You." A gruff voice bellows from the shadows. "Don't you touch him." Officer Kovach, with dried blood all down his cheek and stained into the collar of his uniform, lunges at Alan. "I saw what you did, you goddamn ghoul." Alan utters a surprised squeal as Kovach manhandles and shoves him back through the open front door. Alan trips and stumbles over the door jamb. Kovach doesn't give him a second to get his bearings. He wrestles and rips the camera from his hands with a crazed wild look carved into his face.

"Kovach." Perez shouts from the front lawn. "What are you doing? No."

He doesn't acknowledge or listen to the plea as he repeatedly smashes the camera against the wooden doorframe. Alan cowers as chunks of plastic, glass and bits and pieces fly.

The two EMTs stand and watch the disturbance from the safety of the crime scene like additional nosy neighbors.

"Crime in progress." Gary Grey races down the front lawn. "That's a constitutional crime." He shouts out. "Mark it. All of you are my witnesses." He gets in Officer Kovach's stone face with his finger pointed. "What you did here is criminal. Freedom of the Press."

"What was that?" Kovach drops the remains of the

shattered camera to the porch. "Freedom of what?" He steps off the warped wood as Alan scurries on his hands and knees and gathers up all the smashed parts.

Grey yammers at his back. "That was private property you destroyed. I'll have your job. I'll have your ass." He cuts Kovach off on the front walkway. "What's your badge number?" His index finger thumps against Kovach's broad chest. "I'll sue you for assault and battery. A civil suit for the San Marcos precinct. And everyone up and down the ladder that let an ape like you off the chain. You're a menace—"

Kovach doesn't flinch under the onslaught.

"That's enough." Perez intervenes. He snaps at Grey. "Stand down. And stay back." Perez guides Kovach down the front lawn.

"Hey? Fuck. No way." Grey watches dumbfounded. "You're not walking away from this. Get back—"

"Grey." Navarro gets between Grey and the two officers. "I think we're all done here. Let's try and bring it down a notch."

"The hell with that." Grey shakes off her calm attitude. "We can start with the total destruction of KTXU property. I want restitution. For me, for the studio. In fact, I demand it. I demand redress—"

His warm breath and spittle splatter her face. She doesn't blink or flinch. "*Lo que sea*. You be sure to send me a bill for the busted camera. Okay?" She turns away and leaves him flustered on the front lawn.

"Roya Navarro." Grey shouts to her back. "You better listen to me. This isn't over, Detective. Not by a long shot. You hear me?"

She doesn't turn around to acknowledge him.

He walks away in a huff and heads for the front

porch as Alan cradles the remnants of the camera. "You ever hear of Stand Your Ground, doofus." Grey chastises him. "What the hell did you let him beat you up for?"

"He's a goddamn cop." Alan drops a few broken parts as he tries to explain. "What was I supposed to do?" Grey ignores him and snatches the camera remains from his hands. Plastic bits fall to the warped wood.

Perez guides a stoic Kovach towards a squad car. Navarro catches up with them. "You didn't see it go down." Kovach breaks his stone face to plead his case. "I was right there. And I saw it all. That ghoul kicked out at the body. It was sacrilegious. I had to react."

"Uh huh." She shakes her head. "I'd call that a bit overreacting." Perez holds back a slight smile. He drops it fast as Navarro doesn't smile back. "Right." A sharp command to her voice. "The two of you head back to your precinct. And Kovach." His rigid expression returns as he keeps his mouth shut and pays attention. "Clean yourself up. And then plant yourself at a desk and explain, in detail, exactly what happened out here. And for your sake, it better be a damn good read. Do you understand?"

He keeps any thoughts to himself and returns a single word. "Yes."

"And you." She turns to Perez. "Take it up with your lieutenant if you have to. But you talk to Air Support. In person. We want them to focus all along the I-10 corridor. If I'd had to guess, I'd put eyes in the sky out by Comfort. Maybe Kerrville."

"Not a problem." Perez follows. "I'll hand deliver the message."

"Good. And for now." She speaks to the two of them. "I want any word of this off the wire. It's my call.

I'll take full responsibility. Let's keep the circle tight. Until further notice."

"Okay." Perez agrees, with a bit of pensiveness. "But what are we looking for?"

Kovach perks up as well.

"We didn't lose Morrison." She stares at both officers and speaks fast. "I saw him. And almost had him. Until he commandeered a vehicle and got away."

"What? Why didn't you say anything?" Perez animates at the thought. "Detective, we gotta move—"

"We are." She speaks over his eagerness. "That's exactly what we're doing. This whole mess out here has turned completely mental. And I've had enough crazy for one day." Her voice drops back down. "So, let's try to move forward. Carefully." Neither officer responds. She continues. "We're looking for a Mercedes coupe. Say. New-ish. With purple vanity plates."

"Purple?" Kovach jumps in. "What's the plate say?"

She thinks for a second. "Ability."

He responds back. "What the hell is that supposed to mean?"

She shrugs. "Not a clue. But it should be easy enough to find. Now the way he was heading, that's close to the I-10 frontage road. If he took the highway, and I'm guessing he did. Then it's one way or the other. Towards Houston or Mexico. It's a coin toss, but…"

"Sounds like a plan." Perez has heard enough. "Let's roll, partner."

"Roger that." Kovach pulls out his car keys. "I'll drive."

"Have a safe trip back to the station." Navarro takes the keys from Kovach and hands them to Perez. "Keep me in the loop. And keep this quiet."

Perez clenches the keys, and the two officers climb inside the squad car. As it pulls away, Roya turns back to the house with a deep sigh and mumbles to herself. "I'll clean up this mess." She follows the sidewalk back towards the front lawn.

"Sacrosanct. It's an inalienable right. One that has existed in this country for two hundred and forty years. You can't ever stop the press. No matter what." On the front porch, Gary Grey stays glued to his cell phone screen and intently records a video. "Here. Look. Can you see? Even more damage. I want to document this entire crime scene." He spins around in a circle. "Alan. Say it. Tell my phone, in your own words, exactly what happened out here today."

"Well." Alan stands on the porch with Grey's phone in his face. "I was filming the body, like you wanted—"

"No." Grey interrupts him. "Not like that. Talk. Be natural. And talk about the officer. The peacekeeper who clearly is nothing more than a big bully at heart. How he frightened you. Hurt you. Assaulted you. And savagely shattered our equipment against the door frame as we went about our duty. As reporters." He moves the phone over the damaged front door frame and brings it back to Alan. "So, let's try again. And tell my phone exactly what he did to you. He wounded you. Didn't he?"

Alan picks up the threads and agrees. "Yeah. He sure did…"

Roya Navarro ignores the on-going spectacle. And walks by the two chattering men like they don't even exist. She steps inside the house as the EMT paramedics zip up the plastic body bag and lift Ron's rigid corpse onto the stretcher.

Chapter Eighteen

Heavy traffic jockeys for position down the I-10 west corridor. A tractor trailer pulls out of the fast lane and cruses under green direction signs. Sonora next exit. Sheffield and Fort Stockton miles ahead.

The Mercedes coupe slows down behind the merging tractor trailer. A phalanx of vehicles flies past dense urban sprawl, and they all move as one down the high-speed highway.

A hypnotic drone hums inside the Mercedes cabin. Tricia stares straight ahead and keeps both hands glued to the wheel. Daniel stays quiet in the passenger seat. His heavy-lidded eyes occasionally shift from the woman to the roadway. Endless traffic flows by.

She gasps in her seat and exhales a whistle of tension. A white police car cruises up next to them. The red-and-blue bubble lights remain still. The word 'Police' in bold letters is stenciled across the vehicle. Tricia goes rigid. Her fingers grip and squeeze the leather steering wheel tight.

"No." Daniel buries his nervousness and stays calm. "Don't apply the brakes. Keep us moving." She doesn't blink; her eyes remain locked straight ahead. Daniel can read the helpful advice written in red letters across the side of the sedan. Call 911. As the cruiser inches past them, they can see the outline of two officers inside.

Tricia shivers and shakes in her seat. Daniel tries to

soothe her erratic thoughts. "They're not looking for us. We're all driving along here. Perfectly normal." He adjusts in his seat. "Another car heading down the highway. That's all it is. You continue to focus on that."

The steady hum of tires droning on the asphalt fill the cabin. Tricia eventually glances over. "Are you gonna let me go?"

He doesn't look over at her. "I will." She doesn't respond. He slightly turns. "As soon as I can. Okay?"

She talks over his question. "Then where are we going?"

"Someplace safe." He thinks before he says anything further. "I don't know." He doesn't ask this time and takes another drink from her coffee thermos. The hot liquid rolls down his throat and the jolt of sugar and caffeine perks him up. "Honestly, I'm not sure where I can go. And I don't know who I can trust."

The cold steel revolver is gripped in his right hand. He tucks it against his thigh and out of sight. "So I'm going to force you to trust me. Do you understand?"

Tricia takes one hand off the wheel and claws in the backseat behind her. "What?" Daniel isn't sure what's happening. "What are you doing?" She keeps one hand on the wheel and the car steady as she continues to reach. "I'm trying to get... I...I need my purse." Daniel looks in the back seat and sees a small bag. "Here, I got it." He grabs the purse and brings it up to the front.

Designer web-striped leather framed by a gold double G motif. He recognizes the logo under the ornate clasp.

His thoughts drift to his bedroom closet. Jude has a Gucci purse, but it was a fake one she bought for dirt cheap from some Riverwalk vendor selling his Chinese wares displayed on a folding tray. She was drawn to it and had to have it. He laughed and told her not to waste the money, but she always wanted a Gucci. He said he would buy her a real one, but she was happy with her knock-off and wore it proudly for the rest of their lazy Sunday. It was a good day.

His mind wanders back to his caustic reality, and he figures this designer bag clutched in his hands must be the real thing.

She sneers at him. "What are you smiling about?"

"Nothing." He shakes away the thoughts of his wife.

She doesn't believe him. "Can I have my purse?"

Daniel doesn't pass it over. He pushes the shiny metal clasp and opens it.

"Sure." She sarcastically spits out. "Be my guest." Her anger rises. "What? Do you think there's something dangerous inside? You're the one with the gun. Not me."

"Uh huh." He holds up her cell phone. "Are you looking for this?" He shakes his head as he slides it in his pants pocket.

She reaches into the open purse and pulls out a tiny case from the small handbag. With shaking fingers, she fumbles out a Virginia Slim cigarette from the case. She clicks the case closed and drops it back into the bag. She reaches in and palms a fancy lighter.

He sees intricate engravings on the lighter as her thumb struggles to strike it, but the heavy weight tumbles from her grasp and falls to the carpeted floorboard.

"Here." Daniel bends down. "Lemme help you." He picks up the elegant lighter and strikes it aflame. Tricia holds the long cigarette with a nervous hand. Daniel grabs her wrist and steadies it as she puffs the tobacco alight. She exhales a big plume of smoke.

Daniel flashes her a crooked grin. She snaps back. "I said, stop smiling at me." He sits back in his seat. "I didn't mean anything by it."

"What?" She takes another long drag. "You think this whole fucked-up experience is funny?" She exhales. "Something to smile about. Huh? Jesus. You really got some nerve."

"Hey, I'm not…" He sighs. "You really shouldn't smoke. That's all."

She barks out a laugh. "Are you for real? Like I want a lecture on smoking from my fucking car jacker." She takes another shaky drag.

He cracks the windows. "My wife still smokes." Air whistles into the cabin, and some smoke drifts out. "She used to try and hide it, but you can always tell." He slightly smiles at the thought. "I'm always on her back to quit. But she doesn't listen to me."

Oh yeah?" She takes another deep drag. "I wonder why she wouldn't listen to you. I mean, you seem so levelheaded."

"Right." He takes the sting. "You can spare me the sarcasm."

"As soon as I saw you panhandling at that intersection." Her voice rises. "I said, now there's a guy who really has his act together." She flicks ash out the window crack.

"Stop it." He leans against the passenger door. "Okay."

"I'm a decent woman." She snaps back. "You're the lowlife." The Mercedes swerves into the next lane. Daniel reacts and grabs the wheel. She sobs in her seat. Her hands flop and drape against the steering wheel. Daniel assists and helps maneuver the Mercedes back into the slow lane. He talks as he works. "I'm sorry. I know that means nothing right now. And I can't explain any of this. And there's no excuse for what's happening to you. I understand that." She calms a bit in her seat, he slows his words as well. "But you don't know me. Other than how we unfortunately met today. And today... Christ, lady. Today my entire life was turned completely upside down. And all I want is my life back." Tricia's breathing hitches. She sniffs back tears and clutches the wheel tight. She keeps the car steady. Daniel watches her. "You got it?"

"Tell me where you want to go." She wipes her eyes with the sleeve of her expensive blouse. "Why are you doing this to me?" She can't stifle the waves of emotion in her voice. "I don't need to know who you are. I really don't care. All I want you to do is give me my life back. And you can give that to me. Right now. Please."

Daniel collapses back and sinks into his seat.

The Mercedes glides further down the I-10. Neither of them says another word. The silence between them is severed by the whistle of wind from the cracked windows and the steady drone of tires on the highway.

The Virginia Slim burns down to the filter. Tricia slips it through the window crack and drops the butt into the ether. Daniel breaks the quiet. "You can take me home. I want to go home."

She glances over at him. He doesn't notice and continues to stare straight out the windshield at the colorful road signs and myriad of vehicles and highway directions. "Okay." She waits a second before she says anything more. "So. Where is your home?"

"The first chance you get." He stays in his daze. "Go ahead and exit the highway. Make a turnaround. Then get us back on the I-10 and head back the way we came. Towards San Antonio."

"Okay." Her tense mood melts a bit, but she's aware of the sudden change and tries not to show any relief. "I can do that. And then where do we go?"

"Do me a favor." Daniel sinks farther into his seat and leans against the passenger door in a funk. "Don't talk to me anymore. Okay." He remembers the wheel gun tucked against his thigh. He slides the revolver into his pants pocket. "Do what I tell you. The better you're able to do that, the faster you can get your life back." His eyes glaze into a vacant stare out the windshield at the vehicles all around him. Only his lips move. "I'll have you back to normal in no time."

Tricia doesn't respond. Her foot hits the gas. The Mercedes coupe picks up speed and heads for the next highway exit.

Chapter Nineteen

A San Marcos police squad car bounces through a pothole and continues down a pockmarked road.

Perez takes it slow and steady at the wheel. His wife and two young boys say he drives like an old man. He always laughs along when they taunt him, but the truth is he's cautious. He controls a car with the idea that at any given moment, every other driver around him is an idiot. It was a bit of wisdom he picked up from his father. And he must admit, in or out of uniform, it's a good rule of thumb. He can hear his wife being playful in his ear. A slight smirk masks her teasing voice as he cushions the brake and comes to a halt at a yellow light.

A panel van in the next lane races through the intersection as the light turns red.

The police car idles at the crossroads. "Did you see that?" Perez leans on the wheel and watches the van speed away. "You feel like protecting and serving, partner? I'll even let you hit the Christmas lights."

He waits for a reaction, but none comes. "Hey, man. I know you're not asking, but I'll give you some advice anyway. Don't freak out about this thing. What's done is done. It won't be so bad."

Kovach sits still as he rides shotgun, his face pale and tense. He finally breaks the quiet. "I saw a gun."

"Yes." Perez watches the light. "Yes, you did." It flickers green. He accelerates forward.

"You know me." Kovach talks over the engine. "I'm not gonna blast a bunch of fuckin' holes through the door for nada." He turns in his seat. "Come on, Charlie. You really think I'm some fly-off-the-handle Okie cowboy?"

Perez shakes his head. "It's not like you. I agree."

"Exactly. And I'm sure as shit not some limp-dick CSO who jumps at every shadow. I know what I saw." He agrees with his personal assessment. "I saw a gun."

"Yeah." Perez agrees with him. "I'm sure you did."

"Hey." Kovach snaps back. "Don't fuckin' patronize me."

"Hey?" He's surprised by the intense reaction. "Damn. Calm down, pal. You wanna remember I'm on your side here." He's about to speak but doesn't respond as they head past a slower truck and steer onto the I-10 highway entrance ramp. "If there's a weapon—" Charlie glances over his shoulder to merge with traffic. "—I'm sure they'll find it."

Kovach utters back. "If?"

"Walter, I was there, man." Perez looks over. "Now, I didn't see Morrison or the guy you shot. Let alone a loose firearm." His tone stays serious "But you approached the scene first. You made the call." Kovach starts to plead his case, but Perez cuts him off. "I mean. That's the way it goes. I'll stand by you, but—"

"I saw a gun." He mumbles under his breath. "I could have planted one easy enough if our fuckin' hall monitor wasn't glued to us the entire time."

"Hey. You best curb that shit." Perez perks up. "We're lucky she was even there. Navarro will play interference with IAD." He merges the cruiser and picks up speed into the fast lane. "SAPD will circle the wagons. Keep 'em off your back."

"Internal Affairs." Kovach dismisses the idea. "Fuck 'em." He watches out the passenger window. "I know what it is. It's a mess. Sure." His tone sharpens. "But it can be cleaned up."

"It can, huh?" Perez mutters as he keeps pace with a pack of traffic. "And how do you plan on doing that?"

"You're gonna help me." Kovach turns in his seat. "I got it all figured out. You and me, we can—"

"You think?" Perez talks over him. "Think again."

He huffs back. "For Christ's sake, you're my partner, and—"

"And" Perez counters, "we're off the clock."

"Oh…" Kovach sits back quiet and fumes in his seat. "You're gonna be that way, huh." His gaze is glued out the passenger window as overhead signs signal the next exit. A tractor trailer cuts off the view.

"Walter, man, you'd do best to get your head on straight." Perez speaks with a soft tone. "Now, we're heading back to the precinct. We'll fill out a stack of fuckin' forms and call it a very long day. Okay?"

They both sit quiet as the highway sounds drone around them. Signs advertise nearby fast food and gas stations. Kovach's eyes bulge. He springs up and leans forward with his hands glued to the passenger window. The single word drips from his lips. "Ability." He bounces in his seat. "That was fuckin' Ability." His crewcut careens against the window. "Holy shit. It's him. It's him, man."

Perez keeps his hands glued to the wheel. "What?"

"Mercedes coupe. Purple plates." Kovach shuffles and shakes. "Right there on the road with us. I swear to fuckin' God. It was him."

"Where?" Perez checks his mirrors and looks at the

pack of vehicles all around them. "I don't see anything."

"Didn't you hear me." He swivels in his seat. "I saw the plate. The purple vanity plate. Clear as fuckin' day. Ability. That's what it said, I swear."

"Okay, okay. I believe you." He turns up the police band radio and grabs the microphone. "I'll call it in."

"What?" Kovach snatches his wrist. "Are you crazy, amigo?" Perez tries to pull away. Kovach keeps his grip. "You wanna let go of my hand?" Kovach doesn't let go. "That lady detective told us to keep it to ourselves. Right? She was real clear about that."

"Yeah." He doesn't like the look in his partner's eyes but goes along with it. "That's what she said. But you saw him."

"Yes, I did. And we can keep that bit of information. To ourselves." Kovach releases his hold. "For a little longer." Perez can feel the burn around his wrist and flexes his hand. "Now, go on and speed up." Kovach bounces in his seat. "We'll bird-dog that son-of-a-bitch."

"Man. We've got our orders." Perez replaces the receiver on the radio. "We can't do it."

"Our orders?" Kovach leans in. "We get Morrison, and I'm clean. Roto-Rooter clean."

"No." Perez shakes that away. "That's not an option, and you know it."

"So, you're…letting him go?" He points out the window. "The fuckin' guy is on the road here with us. Here. Right now. And you're doing jack squat?"

Perez keeps his foot on the accelerator and both hands steady on the wheel. Kovach perks up for a second as Perez glances fast over his shoulder and merges back into the slow lane. He fumes in his seat. Quiet fills the tight cabin until Kovach breaks it. "When we were both back there at the hospital" —a rosy shade of red creeps along his thick neck and seeps into his cratered cheeks— "You heard what Willy Wonka said." He bites his tongue and holds his temper at bay. "And I heard him too." He measures his words as he speaks. "To everyone listening. Find the golden ticket and you win a million bucks."

"Yeah." Perez holds the wheel steady. "I heard him."

Kovach agrees. "Good. Well, that mountain of money just drove on past us down the fuckin' highway. What are we waiting for? Let's go get it."

Perez jumps in. "We can't."

Kovach ignores him. "Because, partner, one million dollars cash, split right down the middle. Man, that is my kind of cutting." The sedan swerves a bit on the road. Perez gets it back under control. Kovach grins like a Cheshire cat. He can see his partner thinking about it. He can't hide the emotions right under his skin. Walter doesn't let up. "Five hundred thousand a piece. What could you and your family do with that kinda dough? Easy money. Dropped right into your lap. I can see the wife's smile from here. Can't you?" Perez can't help but agree. Kovach agrees along with him. "And all we got to do is catch up with him." Perez gives the car some gas. The sedan speeds up. "There you go." Kovach bounces and playfully punches Perez on the shoulder.

He responds by easing his foot back off the accelerator. "Man, we can't be out here chasing shadows." Their squad car slows back down. "What about Detective Navarro? I mean, she's expecting us to tell Air Support—"

Kovach cuts him off. "I saw what I saw. What? You don't believe me? Again?"

"Hey." Perez responds fast. "It's not like that!"

Kovach takes it back. "We can cancel the eye in the sky for now. Hell, we saw the dude right here on the ground. Don't you worry about Missus Detective. Man, she'll be the one—" Kovach leans over and thumps him on the chest. "—to pin the medal on you. Your pretty lady standing there. All smiles, full of pride and shit. Hell, for sure she busts up the marriage bed that night. Give you a third little rug rat. And this one, you'll be able to afford."

Perez hits the gas. The sedan eases into the fast lane and picks up speed down the highway. "Walter. Man, are you sure you saw him?"

Kovach sits up in his seat. "A Mercedes coupe with purple plates and the word 'Ability' written on them. Man, that's the kinda goofy shit thing that when you see it, you see it."

The police cruiser bobs and weaves around vehicles as it races down the I-10.

****

The Mercedes cruises along with highway traffic. Two tractor trailers pass a slower vehicle. Tricia can feel them roar past the car as her fingers wrap around the plush steering wheel. She fiddles with some switches and turns up the air in the luxury automobile.

Daniel stares down at the passenger floorboard.

"Do you mind? I mean…" She clears her dry throat. "Can I ask you a question?" Quiet, other than the steady drone from the tires on the asphalt. She presses on. "What happened to your face?" He still doesn't answer. She waits for a sec and continues. "I mean, you do look pretty beat up."

The quiet returns. He finally offers a response. "I cut

myself shaving." She doesn't reply and keeps her eyes on the road. Green highway directional signs pass overhead. Daniel continues to watch her out of the corner of his eye before he speaks. "Earlier this morning. I was involved in an accident."

She glances over. "If the rest of you looks like your face, you should be in a hospital."

He can see the hospital on the TV in his mind's eye. "You should see the other guy." He can hear Hayden Grant bloviating on Jessica and dead Ron's television. And holding up a blown-up image of his driver's license photo for every criminal cutthroat and desperate jackal to see. He was never fond of that picture. He thought he looked fat.

"It wasn't a guy." Daniel tries to shake the visceral image from his thoughts. "It was a girl. A woman. Politician's wife." He stares at Tricia, his eyes bloodshot red. "That was…. a few hours ago. Jesus. It feels like, forever." Words mumble from his chapped lips. "My wife and me. We had a discussion this morning. I call them an argument, but she likes the word 'discussion' better." Slight cracks emerge on his stoic expression. "And she said to me that I have it all figured out. She didn't mean it. My Jude. She can be sarcastic as hell. Like you."

"Oh my gosh." Tricia tilts her head as a sense of realization rushes over her. "That was you. The thing, the hit and run car crash from this morning. You're the guy they're all talking about on the news."

"I don't care what the news says. Or what people are saying." A well of emotion builds and bubbles up inside him. "They're all lying. I didn't do anything. I was on my way to work. Like every other day." Tricia starts to interrupt him but keeps quiet. "I swear to God." His feelings on the edge spill out like a geyser. "She hit me. Her car ran right smack into me. All I was, was normal. I had a case this morning. It was…" He barks out a laugh. "A DUI. I was running late. My boss was so pissed. Now, he's probably some talking head on the TV." Words trip over themselves as he talks faster. "All I did was take some pills. Tiny little things. To take the edge off. You know. To calm me down. And in a blink—" He snaps his fingers. Hard. "— my life is fucking this."

She holds the Mercedes steady on the highway. "You've got the whole state out looking for you." Her hand goes to the radio knobs and buttons. "Here, listen. They're talking about you all over the local stations." She flips through music and talk radio stations and stops on a local news broadcast.

Daniel turns it off. "I don't need some voice on the radio to tell me my whole world is fucked. It's over. I'm a dead lawyer. At best." He slumps back in his seat. "Won't be long now before I get the chance to see what life is like on the other side."

She holds the Mercedes steady down the highway. The drone of the road fills the cabin. "You killed that poor woman. And all you can do is sit there and whine about yourself." She shakes her head. "And talk about your job? What kind of man are you?"

"That poor woman ran into me." He points to a green road sign. "Here. In two miles. You want to take that exit." He sits back in his comfortable plush seat. She looks over at him, but he doesn't acknowledge it or say anything more. She hits her blinker and merges back into the middle lane.

"Home." Daniel stretches out and relaxes for the

first time in the car. "I'm going home. I never thought I'd ever see it again." He stares out the windshield at the jostling traffic. "Now, I can't wait. Even if it's only for a few minutes. Or seconds. I guess they won't let me gather up my stuff, huh. Well, it's not like I had much left there anyway."

Tricia merges over in the slow lane. The turn-off for Exit 181 approaches in a mile.

"I'm not a murderer. Or a kidnapper. I'm in a deep hole, and I'm trying to climb out with at least some of my hide still intact."

Tricia lets his words sit in the air. Her foot eases off the accelerator. "I'm supposed to believe you?" She hits the blinker as the exit approaches. "A man with a gun in his hand."

Daniel pulls the snub-nosed pistol out of his pocket and drops it to the carpeted floorboard. "You helped me. That's about the best thing that's happened to me all day." He points to the green road sign. "That's my exit. A few more miles to go. And it'll all be over."

The Mercedes glides off the highway and banks down the ramp. "I helped you?" She responds fast. "I really didn't volunteer for any of this." They come to a halt at a stoplight.

"No, you didn't." Daniel turns in his seat. "But I want to thank you anyway."

A pack of cars and trucks idle at the stoplight. A homeless man sits on the median holding a cardboard sign that's too far away to read. Tricia sighs at the wheel and looks over at Daniel. "You're welcome."

The light changes and the group of vehicles inch forward. The Mercedes moves with the pack and drives straight ahead.

****

A San Marcos squad car follows a few lengths back.

"Not too close." Kovach motions for a truck on their bumper to go around them. "You're safe, jackass. No ticket. Go, go. Good."

A FedEx truck bounds on by as it picks up speed and passes them on the state road. The squad car paces along as they both drive further away from the dense highway sprawl.

Perez glued to the wheel. He catches fleeting glimpses of the purple vanity plate and shadows of two figures inside. "There's two of them in there. Morrison and a woman. What do you want to do about her?"

"Nothing." Kovach holds onto the dash and watches out the windshield. "She's worth zilch. We stick with the prize." He turns and looks up and down the road. "We're gonna have to do it out here. Fast and easy."

"You wanna do it out here?" Perez looks over at his eager partner. "Why?"

"Because I know where we are." Kovach points straight ahead. "He's going home. And we need to take him out before he gets there."

"Right. Okay." Perez can still see glimpses of the purple plate in front of them. "Yeah, man. It's on. Tell me when."

Chapter Twenty

Red and blue bubble lights come alive. A piercing siren blasts and whines. The squad car picks up speed down a stretch of ranch road.

Surprised, Tricia looks up at the rearview. Lights flash in the mirror. Daniel turns around inside the Mercedes. "Looks like I won't get to see home after all." The squad car barrels and bounds up behind them. "Might as well." Daniel turns and stares at it out the back window. "Go on and pull us over."

Tricia holds the wheel steady. She isn't sure. Daniel can read her thoughts. "It's fine. Go ahead. My time's up. I'm ready to end this." The squad car stays glued to the Mercedes rear bumper. The siren whoops and a kaleidoscope of light fills the cabin.

"This is good." Daniel points to an approaching construction site. "Right here."

Tricia steers the Mercedes off the asphalt and drives onto packed dirt. The squad car tucks in behind them. Lights strobe. Her pale face is bathed in the colorful lights. Like a straight-A student being sent to the principal's office, she's not used to being pulled over by the police and can't mask her panic. Tricia's dry voice cracks. "What are you going to do?"

"You'll be fine." Daniel pops open the passenger door. "Stay here." He picks up the wheel gun from the floorboard and holds it by the snub-nosed barrel.

He gets out of the vehicle. Tricia stays in the driver's seat and watches his every move.

Daniel holds up his hands as he steps onto the packed dirt. The flashing strobe lights blind him a bit. But he can make out the steel framework of some strip mall coming soon. Pallets of materials placed around the dirt site. A stacked Jenga of jagged metal pylons. Large wheels of pink insulation that look like cotton candy hay bales. Thick tire tracks crisscrossed and cemented in the dried mud.

The construction site was deserted except for the occasional passing vehicle that's glad they're not the ones being stopped by the police.

Daniel slowly steps away from the Mercedes with his hands in the air. Both squad car doors click open. Daniel can make out the outline of two men crouching behind the frames for cover.

"Daniel Morrison." A booming voice calls out. "Stop where you are."

He obliges.

"Drop the weapon." The revolver thuds to the dirt.

"Empty your pockets. Slowly. Turn them out." He drops his wallet and two cell phones to the dirt.

"Hands on your head." Daniel diligently follows each command. "Fall to your knees." His dirty dress pants are dusted with fresh grime from the hardpack as he crouches down to the dirt. A surprised sense of relief washes over him as he comes to the end of the road.

Perez keeps an eagle eye on Daniel from the safety of the open driver's door. "You want the honors?" He calls through the sedan cabin to Kovach, crouched behind the passenger door. "He's all yours. Go ahead and cuff him, partner."

Kovach smiles back. "With pleasure." He slowly walks towards Daniel kneeling in the ground. "God damn. Will you look at that?" Words mutter at his lips. "Out in the middle of fuckin' nowhere. All wrapped up and topped off with a bow." He towers over Daniel. "Who wants to be a millionaire? Hey, I'm talkin' to you, you miserable piece of shit."

Daniel stares at the ground. "I'll go quietly."

"Yeah." Kovach agrees out loud. "I'm sure you will." He uses the heel of his boot to step on the screens of the cell phones in the dirt. They break easy. "You didn't even bother to get rid of your phones? What? Are you a moron. Or maybe too stupid to know any better?" He plants his steel-toed boot in the center of Daniel's back and shoves him face down into the dirt. "Come on. Tell me now." Daniel tries to groan on the hard pack, but the wind is kicked out of him. He stays sprawled out on the ground. Kovach picks up the wheel gun from the dirt and wipes it clean against his bloodstained uniform shirt.

"Kovach." Perez keeps his eye on the road as another car drives by. "Walter. What are you doin', man?" His tension flares like a live wire but he stays put behind the open squad car door.

"I'm securing our prisoner." Kovach stands over Daniel with a wide grin across his face. "All nice and neat." He glances over to Perez. "Get that woman out of the Mercedes, will you?" He follows the question with a swift kick to Daniel's ribcage. Daniel curls up in a fetal position and wheezes from the hard blow.

"It's nice to finally meet you, Mr. Morrison." He crouches down next to him. "You're quite the meal ticket." Daniel doesn't respond as he gasps in pain, and gulps in harsh breaths. "Can you hear me okay?" Kovach grabs a handful of wild hair and pulls him close. "Do I have your attention? Oh, here, wait." He slaps him hard across each cheek. "Let me get all that muck and shit off your face." Kovach drops him to the dirt. "There you go. That's much better, isn't it?" Daniel tries to crawl away. He spits out a blob of dirty phlegm and drools saliva and blood onto the ground.

"Truth is, dead or alive. I still get paid." Kovach paces after him and kicks a cloud of grit into his bloody face. "But if I bring your ass back stone-cold dead—" He kneels down with a grin. "—Well, then. Not only do I get paid, but you get to help me clean up my mess."

"Done. I'm done. Please." Daniel babbles through a mouthful of dirt and blood. "I surrender. I—" Kovach slams his battered face back into the hard pack.

"What is wrong with you?" Tricia bounds out of the Mercedes and shouts out with a sense of entitlement and authority only a rich woman can have. "Have you all lost your damn minds?" She determinedly strides across the ground. "Stop it. I can see what you're doing to him. There's no need to be so rough."

"Ma'am. We need you to remain with your vehicle." Perez gets between Tricia and the scene. "Everything here is under control."

"The hell it is?" Tricia tries to get by Perez, but he keeps her back. "He wants to turn himself in. Why are you being so brutal? Beating on him like that."

"This is police business." Perez continues to shield her. "Please. Get back inside your vehicle." She stands her ground. Perez won't let her pass.

"Here's how you help solve my little problem." Kovach stays crouched next to Daniel sprawled out on the dirt. "You went crazy. All out of control. I couldn't believe it." He wipes down the wheel gun. "You started shooting. Like a mad man. You killed your hostage. You even killed my partner." He pops open the chamber; it's loaded with four live rounds and two spent shells. "I mean. I had no choice." He carefully closes the chamber. "It was either you or me. Now that's a clear-cut case." Daniel sputters out a moan. Kovach pistol-whips him back down. "Goddamn. I'm impressed. You sure are one tough bad-ass, Mr. Morrison." He pulls back the hammer on the revolver.

"Oh, my God. Did you see that? Right there. Clear as day. That animal hit him again. I am a witness." Tricia keeps up her protest. "I won't stand for it. It's police brutality. You can't treat a person like this."

"Please, ma'am." Perez holds her back. "You are in a state of shock and impeding the police. Stay out of the way and let us do our job. The faster we can do that, the faster we can all get out of here."

"Hey, partner." Kovach stays crouched on the ground and calls out. "I didn't think I needed it, but I really learned to like the satellite radio. All those different selections you can choose from."

"Walter?" Perez struggles with Tricia and calls out over his shoulder. "The hell are you talking about?"

"Wanna know my favorite station? 70's on 7. Do you remember this oldies tune?" Kovach flashes a toothy grin. "One is the loneliest number." He aims the snub-nose revolver and fires twice. Two rounds punch into Perez's back. A sheen of blood sprays onto Tricia.

The belch of sharp sound echoes throughout the empty frame of the strip mall construction site.

Officer Charles Perez vomits up more blood. His glassy eyes wide with sudden surprise. He stumbles forward a few steps with shock carved forever on his face. He collapses and falls dead onto the ground.

"That song is so full of shit." Officer Kovach gets up from the hard pack. His boots kick up dust as he peers around the murder scene. "I mean, a million dollars, cut one way. There sure is nothing lonely about that."

Tricia twitches and shakes a silent scream with a mist of wet crimson red all across her face and stained into her Stella McCartney blouse.

Kovach watches her reaction like a curious hunter stalking its prey. He looks down at Daniel, unconscious in the dirt. "How 'bout it, Mr. Morrison." He nudges him with his boot. "Do you want to kill your lady friend, or should I do it?"

Tricia snaps out of her trance and bolts for the Mercedes.

"Run, rabbit, run." Kovach nonchalantly steps over his dead partner and starts after her.

She rips open the passenger door in a blind panic.

"Hey, ma'am." Kovach stops and stares at something on the ground. He crouches and picks up the black and silver fob. He can't help but laugh. "You forgot your fuckin' car keys."

She leans inside the Mercedes, and frantically pulls the glove compartment lid open.

Kovach cocks the snub-nose. He holds it at his side as he looks back and forth down the ranch road. It's all clear. "You're really gonna make me shoot you in the car?" He casually walks towards her vehicle. "Why do you wanna go and mess up a perfectly good Mercedes like that?" He steps up to the open passenger door.

Tricia turns around, sprawled out in the passenger seat. A Colt Cobra .38 Special pistol gripped tight in both hands. One shot thunders out.

Kovach drops to his knees. His eyes glaze over. He falls face-first into the dirt.

Smoke wafts from the barrel. Tricia pants in her seat. The silver-plated pistol shakes still locked tight in her hands.

****

Tension. It was her lot in life for so long she couldn't remember a time when it wasn't constantly swirling around her.

It used to be her long hours stuck at the hospital that gave her so much stress. But her home was an oasis. Her partner was calm and comfortable. Until that tension became all encompassing. From morning 'til night. No matter at work or home. Or with Daniel.

Judy Morrison missed her old life. The strong woman she always was. She was smart and educated. And determined to make the correct decisions in life.

She wasn't in a hurry to meet anybody. Dating was fine. She told Daniel when they were courting that she didn't want a good relationship. Or a great one. She wanted it to be the best they could make it. Face the world, together.

And for years, it worked exactly like that. Until one day that she couldn't even remember it didn't.

Divorce was common among her friends and peers. She watched her best friend Maggie lose her high school sweetheart husband and life-partner to a perky dental assistant who was only a few years older than their daughter. She watched her sister's joy of life slowly melt away from a day-to-day existence in a dead-end marriage. She said they stayed together for the sake of the kids, even as they seemed to live a life constantly at each other's throats.

It wasn't even 50/50 anymore. Divorce and separation were clearing winning. Maybe 80/20? Relationships crumbling under the weight of age and time and bullshit that seemed important but never really was. It was far from the media fantasies they marketed and sold to young girls and innocent women.

Communication was key. Until it wasn't. His temper and her sarcasm never mixed well, especially when combustible subjects came up. They never addressed it head on, never talked about their marriage eroding like the flowing tide, erasing it little by little, until the sand was submerged under a sea of ocean.

She found a marriage counselor and they went once a week, but Daniel made a half-assed attempt, at best.

Maybe self-care was what she needed? Fix herself and then she could do the work with her husband to repair their relationship. She checked websites and read all sorts of articles.

But it was a hallway conversation with a pediatric doctor who pointed her in the right direction. An expensive vacation retreat, a luxury oasis where you could clear the mind and spirit in the middle of the Arizona desert out by Tucson. It was supposed to be ideal for rejuvenation. Which is exactly what she needed.

Daniel was fine with her going away on a girls-trip. He was actually very sweet about it and even helped her pack. She paid the fees and went away for a long weekend with her CEO friend, Cynthia. Wall-to-wall comfort, privacy, relaxation. Ornate artwork, outdoor hammocks. Waterfalls and fire pits.

During a deep Swedish massage session, the Russian masseuse with amazing hands dropped juicy gossip about a tabloid actress and a James Bond actor who were there the previous week.

No phones. No messages. Only sun, seclusion and casual wear. It was all bliss and heaven.

The array of personal pleasures helped make the medicine go down. Professional speakers who were paid handsomely to get to the root of the problem. She attended 90-minute seminars where tears were shed as she bared her heart and soul.

Followed by late nights with good wine flowing and flirtatious banter with a cute waiter who was twenty years her junior but was so polite and looked scrumptious in his black dress pants.

She felt exhilarated and refreshed when she returned home. But it didn't take long for business as usual to wash away all the positivity and mantras.

And she was right back to her marriage falling apart. Where did it all go wrong?

She kept trying to track it down. Thinking of the exact moment when it turned the other way. But for the life of her, she couldn't remember.

Judy sits alone on her living room couch, lost in deep thought, her long legs pulled up to her chin and a burning cigarette forgotten between her fingers.

A swarm of police officers and civilian technicians drift throughout her house. On her nice coffee table, a blast of static amplified from a police band radio. A few tablets and phones plugged into a makeshift charging station. Loose cables run across her carpet. Packs of officers talk amongst themselves or stay glued to their cell phones.

Judy watches the various faces hustle from room to room. She jolts in startled fear as someone slams the front door. A gulp as she swallows her emotions and stays frozen on the couch. Her harsh breaths are shallow as her tired eyes stare at the red runner carpet in front of the couch, now a destroyed wreck blotted in dried mud from dozens of footprints.

She's adrift and alone in a sea of people.

****

"So what's the word here?" Detective Navarro drinks and stomachs the last of her cold coffee and leaves the kitchen with a young police officer. "Any positive hits? Tips?"

"Sure. We've got plenty." The young officer hits it right back. "Stacks of messages from Bible thumpers, New Age weirdos, a few rainbow heads, and some absolutely brilliant insights from your plain brown wackos. Do you want to talk to any of them?"

Navarro doesn't respond back. They continue to stride forward through the house. The officer finds a narrow pathway through a cluster of cops, into a busy living room. He stops and points to Judy sitting on the couch. "She's right over there, Detective."

She thanks the officer as he melts away into the crowd of blue. Navarro takes a few seconds to hide the weight of the day and takes a few steps over to Judy, still lost in her daze.

"Mrs. Morrison. My name is Detective Roya Navarro. I'm with the San Antonio Police Department." She gets no response. Navarro places her empty cup on the cluttered coffee table and takes a seat on the couch next to her. "Do you mind if I speak with you?"

"I don't want to speak to you." Judy doesn't move from her spot. "I've already told officer after officer everything I could possibly know."

Navarro doesn't reply at first. "Careful. You're going to hurt yourself." She gently reaches out and grabs the burning cigarette. The long ash snaps off and scatters to the runner carpet. "Oh, I'm so sorry." Navarro crouches down to clean it up.

Judy snaps a bit out of her haze. "Don't bother."

Navarro glances up at her.

"I really liked that runner." Judy shakes her head. "But it's ruined. I've had an army of people marching back and forth on it. Tracking all manner of shit all over it. All damned day."

Roya nods her agreement and offers sincere sympathy. "I'm sorry to hear that."

Judy pulls out another coffin nail from a crumpled pack. "What do you think? Totally trashing a rug. Is that grounds for a lawsuit?" She lights the cigarette and takes a drag. A fluid plume of smoke shrouds her as she exhales. "Daniel would know the answer to that one."

Navarro stays on her knees and watches the jittery woman huddled into a ball take another shaky drag. "Judy." Her voice is soft and still. "If I may."

Judy looks at her with tired sunken eyes. "If you may, what?"

Navarro waits a second before she speaks. "Let me ask you one question."

"Only one?" Judy sighs and runs a hand down her haggard face. "What is it?"

"Could you show me your bedroom?" The detective offers her a kind smile.

Judy stares back with a puzzled expression. Sparks flicker as she smashes her fresh cigarette into the ashtray. "Sure." Judy gets up off the couch. "Why not." She stumbles a bit to get her circulation back and slowly moves towards the hallway.

Navarro gets up from the stained rug and follows. They both step over cables and dodge various uniforms as they make their way up the narrow staircase.

Judy talks over her shoulder. "My home isn't mine anymore. Feel free to help yourself to whatever. The coffee maker's been going nonstop."

Navarro speaks to her back. "I'm good. Thank you."

Judy gets to the top of the stairs and leaves the chaos behind as she walks into the privacy and comfort of her bedroom. "Hey. What time is it anyway?"

"Umm…" Roya closes the door behind them. "A little after two."

Judy catches her expression in a mirror and turns away fast with a hiss between her teeth like air escaping a punctured tire. "Jesus. What a wreck. I look like hell." She plods over to the bedroom window. "I should have gone into work today. A clinic full of screeching newborns sounds pretty soothing about now." She peers through the slats of the wooden shade. "Look at them all. These news people. There's so many of them. Network. Cable. Satellite trucks." She turns to look back at the detective. "Are they all gonna camp out here forever?"

"Maybe not forever. But I'm sorry to say—" Navarro walks over and leans against the closed closet door. "—they're not going away anytime soon."

Judy stays by the window. Roya tries for sympathy. "I know it's a sad state to see your lawn like that. We've got the walkway roped off and that should keep them off the grass as much as possible."

Judy doesn't reply, she continues to stare through the slats. "It's all such a goddamn circus. I'm sure my neighbors are loving every second of this."

"Mrs. Morrison." Roya comes up behind her. "We could really use your help here." She places a comforting hand on her shoulder.

"Jesus." Judy whips around and shrugs away from her. "How many times do I have to say it?" Her voice rises. "I'll tell you the exact same thing I've been saying all damn day." She pulls her tone back and cobbles her composure together. "I don't know where he is."

Navarro doesn't break close contact. Her tone soft. "Your husband is on the run."

"Yes. Yes, he is." Judy turns away from the window. "From all this. Insanity." She paces around the bedroom. "I've got every type of cop you can imagine stuffed in every nook and cranny of my home, and I still haven't gotten one straight answer all day." Frustration and exasperation drip off of her. "From what I can tell, every bozo in a blue uniform knows next to nothing. Well, I know my husband and I can tell you exactly what he's thinking." She closes the gap and walks up fast to Roya. "Daniel is scared. He is."

"Judy." Navarro doesn't flinch. "I don't want Daniel to get hurt. But the longer he's out there, the more likely that is to happen."

Judy collapses in a heap to the bed like a heavy weight. "I don't know where he is. And I don't know how to find him. What more do you want from me?"

Roya Navarro calmly sits down next to her. "We want you to talk to the press."

Judy snaps back. "Who's we?"

"Well,. the city of San Antonio and multiple municipality divisions and departments." Navarro looks her in the eyes. "But the truth is, I'm the one asking. And I want you to ask Daniel to come home."

"Yeah? Great. That's great." Judy can't help but laugh at the suggestion. "You're an angel and a devil. You sit here and act all sympathetic and kind. When all you really want is to throw me to those wolves outside."

"No. That's not true. Not at all." She shakes her head and answers fast. "We can arrange for one reporter to come inside. We can tape the interview right here. Where you're comfortable. Where you're safe. And keep you far away from all that mess downstairs and outside."

"I don't know." Judy thinks for a second but isn't buying it. "I mean, I feel—"

Navarro pushes further. "I wouldn't ask lightly. But Daniel has to know if he comes here, he's safe. And honestly. I think at this point he'll only believe that if he hears it from you."

"I hate this. All of this. Every little bit. And I hate the fucking press." Judy sits still, the entire chaotic day on her shoulders. "They're the reason why I have a conveyer belt of cops running rampant all over my house. And why my husband is running for his life."

Roya keeps her comforting tone. "If I didn't think it could help bring this whole ugly situation to a peaceful end, I wouldn't ask."

"No. Don't do that." Judy shakes her head. "Don't bullshit me. All you want is…" Her voice cracks. "You want me to help you catch him."

She's fast with a response. "I want you to help save his life."

A dam of emotion wells up, but Judy is adept at keeping it from breaking open.

"Talk to a reporter." Navarro edges a bit further. "And go on the air. That's what I'm asking you. Can you do that for me?"

In a daze, Judy gets up from the bed. "I need to clean up a bit."

"One reporter." Roya speaks to her back. "That's all. And you won't be alone. We'll have an officer in here with you the whole time."

Judy doesn't say anything more. She walks straight to the master bathroom and slams the door shut.

Navarro sighs and stays in the quiet. Until she hears the shower turn on. She walks out of the room and closes the bedroom door behind her.

A group of officers huddles around the living room table. They cluster and hover over the police band radio.

Navarro strides down the stairs and speaks to a SAPD uniform. "Okay, she's on board. We'll go with the press. I want one reporter and one camera and that's it. I can stay by her side and make sure things don't get out of hand."

"Detective." The uniform's face is ghostly pale. "The reports are still coming over the wire. Units are on the way. We're waiting on confirmation, but... You gotta hear this."

She looks at the anxious group all around the radio. "Hear what?"

Chapter Twenty-One

A steady and hypnotic sound in the cabin as tires drone down the roadway.

Daniel's puffy and crusty eyes flutter and peel open. His bruised cheek is flattened, cold and clammy against the passenger window glass. He blinks aware and his eyes jolt open. He springs up in the car seat with a mad panic.

"Hey?" The Mercedes swerves a bit on the road. "Hey. Relax. It's okay." Tricia holds steady at the wheel, and she gets the car back onto the straightaway.

Daniel whips his head all around and immediately regrets it. A wave of intense pain dominated by a sharp headache pierces and slows his movements.

"Try to calm down. Or you're going to hurt yourself more than you already are." She reaches over and pops open the lid of the glove compartment. "Go ahead. I've got a bottle of aspirin in there somewhere. I'm sure you could use a few."

Daniel stares at the Colt .38 Special. The bulky black handgrip and wide silver barrel rests on the Mercedes service manual. He spots a squat white pill bottle under the laminated registration card and reaches over the gun for the aspirin. Tricia holds the wheel but watches his slow movements.

He reacts like he's trying to walk underwater. A full body filled with aches and pain overrides all his faculties.

"The hell happened?" He settles back and sinks like molasses into the plush seat as he fiddles with the child-proof lid. "I don't…understand this. Where are we?"

"We're driving south." Tricia glances at the gun inside the open glove compartment but keeps both hands on the wheel. "Then west. Then south again. I figured it was best to keep us off the I-10 and major roadways." She looks at the flatlands and desolate scrub brush all around. "We're far enough away from the city. On some nothing Ranch Road. Less than an hour from the border I imagine."

A singular pop echoes through the cabin. Daniel manages to open the pill bottle and shakes out a few onto his skin scraped raw hand. He dry-swallows them.

"You don't remember anything?"

"I can remember." He slowly shakes his head and tosses a few more aspirin into his mouth. He mumbles a response. "The police." He slowly moves in his seat and clutches at his side. Raw fingers lift up his dirty dress shirt. "Christ." His battered skin, a colorful patchwork of grime and purplish yellowed bruises. "I think I've got a broken rib." He prods at the tender skin and winces.

She doesn't look over at him. "They tried to kill you." Tricia keeps her unblinking hazy-blue eyes on the straight, flat road. "And then. They tried to kill me." Her hands stay at 10 and 2 on the wheel. "Why do you think they would do that?"

Daniel sits quiet in his seat before he answers. "I don't know."

She slams on the brakes.

The Mercedes fish-tails across the worn asphalt and smoke burns from the locked tires. Centrifugal force throws Daniel violently against the padded dash. He crumbles down to the floorboard and white chalky aspirin pills scatter all inside the cabin.

The vehicle settles to a halt on the faded blacktop.

Tricia claws at the door handle. The driver's door bounces open. She pushes it aside as she careens away from the car. She hobbles a bit on the road and falls to her knees with a deep retch. She gags and dry heaves on the faded yellow line. A rope of saliva stretches from her bottom lip to the sun-bleached tar.

Daniel clicks open the passenger door and stumbles out onto the asphalt. The door-ajar warning sound beeps incessantly and echoes across the desert flatland.

"You…. You don't know?" Tricia wipes at her lips and chin with a wrinkled sleeve. "I've been waiting for you. Desperately wanting you to wake the hell up so you could explain all this craziness to me." She gets to her feet, closes her eyes and lifts her face skywards, her skin warmed from the blazing sun. She speaks to the sky. "This whole time. From the gun right there in my hand. To the dead quiet after at the construction site. To lifting and dragging your dead weight all the way into my car, I've been playing around with it. Over and over."

Daniel moves towards her. She flails and jerks away from his touch.

"Do I call the police? And what am I supposed to say? That I shot a policeman who tried to kill me?" She barks a laugh into the acrid air. "So, what do I do? Run. Yeah, that's it. I'll kidnap the man who kidnapped me. Hightail it out of the city. And let him tell me what the hell is going on here?"

She stands firm on the faded yellow line. The endless desolate road stretches forever in either direction. "At least that's a plan. I can work with it.

Fine." She agrees with herself. "I drive us south. Stay under the speed limit. Take it slow and steady. Remain calm. Get off the main roads. Head away from it all."

She spins and glares at Daniel. "I wait for you to wake up. And wait some more. You finally do that. And then you have the audacity to sit there and say to me, 'I don't know'?" She sprints towards him. "Well, that's not good enough." She closes the gap until she's right up in his face. "You better know something."

Daniel doesn't respond. His wild eyes continue to stare off over her shoulder. "Do you hear that?"

A ray of light glimmers in the distance. Tricia turns around. Sunlight shimmers and reflects off of something down the horizon.

"That's an engine." Daniel stands at her side. "Someone's coming."

A cloud of dust funnels on the road. A Ford F-150 pickup barrels right for them and doesn't slow down.

"Oh my God." Tricia looks to the Mercedes stopped haphazardly on the blacktop; the passenger door propped open. "Is it them?"

He responds fast. "It could be anybody."

She hits it back. "It could be the people trying to kill us. We need my gun."

"Wait." Daniel snatches up her hand. "Don't move."

The Ford truck starts to slow down and a thick dust cloud envelopes it. It cruises straight towards them. Daniel and Tricia hold hands on the faded center line. They stand and watch the truck approach.

A dirty blue pickup, its paint bleached from the harsh sun, bounces on its shocks as it avoids the Mercedes and drives halfway off the road. The driver's side window rolls down.

Tricia tenses up and squeezes Daniel's hand.

An older sunbaked face with a scruffy beard and wiry hair leans out the truck window. "Get your foreign piece of crap off the damn road." He hits the gas and the giant tires spray loose gravel as the truck swerves and corrects back onto the asphalt and drives away.

Daniel can read a fresh bumper sticker that stands out on the dirty chrome. Keep Texas Strong – Vote Hayden Grant for Congress.

He stares at the sticker until it vanishes from view. His legs give out from under him, and he collapses in a heap onto the hot sticky pavement. He contorts on the ground and gulps and gasps a series of deep breaths until he belches a stuttering laugh up to the sun.

"Are you crazy?" Tricia watches him flail on the dirty blacktop like a mental patient off his medication. "What in the hell is wrong with you?"

"You heard the man." Daniel stammers back. "Get off the road. That's good advice. Take it." He yawps into the sky and lays flat on the asphalt. "I'm fucked in every sense of the word, and you want answers. What, exactly do you want to hear from me? I made a mistake and clearly, I'm paying for it. I've got the whole world after me. Why? Money? Fame? The fuck if I know. What? You think I'm lying to you? It's simple. I don't know means that. I don't know." Daniel remains in the center of the road.

"You're having a breakdown? That's how you've decided to handle this? Throw some moody tantrum." Exasperated, Tricia turns away in a huff and heads back towards the Mercedes.

"There you go." Daniel sits up and shields his eyes from the sunlight. He calls to her back. "Do yourself a favor and get far away from me."

"No, you don't get to lose it." She spins around fast and barrels back at him. "Not here and not now. I was having a nice morning. On my way to the HEB. Trying to decide between chicken or beef for dinner." She stands over and shouts down at him. "And you had to go and pick my car. And totally screw with my life." She kicks loose grit and gravel at him. "Why the hell would you go and do something like that to someone like me? Answer me. I'm normal. God damn it. Do you hear me?" Her demeanor is as torn and tattered as her tailored clothes, her upscale mask of makeup wiped away. "Why did you have to drag me down with you?" Her face raw and wild as she pours out all her pent-up frustrations. "I'm normal. You stupid, sick fuck."

She turns away in a fury before she gives in to her desire to really kick and thrash him. She stomps back towards the Mercedes.

Daniel watches her go. "You want normal?" He ignores the constant waves of pain and lifts himself off the ground. "I'm normal." He hobbles towards her and shouts at her back. "I've got a normal house, normal job, three credit cards. Big fuckin' mortgage. My whole life is an utter disaster, and I'm right on the verge of a monster meltdown divorce. What do you think? I think that all sounds pretty fuckin' normal."

He grabs her by the shoulder and forces her to look at him. "Listen to me. This is not my fault. None of it is." His energy spent and his voice hoarse and raspy. "This is being done to me. And now, to you. Please." He sobs and sputters. "You've gotta believe me. And you saw me. I tried to turn myself in. I want this to be over."

Emotions bubble over and he pleads with her.

"You're the only person in this whole fucked-up situation who is actually helping me. I'm begging you. Let me do whatever I can to make things right."

Desert stillness and quiet as she stares back at him. A persistent buzz. An annoying insect bombards and flies around them. She swats it away and finally responds. "And how do you plan on doing that?"

He thinks for a second and offers her a defeated shrug. "Honestly, I haven't quite figured that part out yet." Rapid-fire, he stammers at her. "We can do this together. I'm asking you to trust me. Which I understand is asking a lot." He realizes he still has a grip on her arms. He drops his hold and turns away, pacing around the asphalt. "This morning, it was just another day. Now, I'm a dead man walking. It's all so fucking mental." Daniel stops and stands on the empty road with the weight of the world on his shoulders.

"Tell me everything." Tricia takes a step towards him. "From the crack of dawn to the moment you jumped into my car. I want to hear it all."

Surprised, he looks at her but can't read her poker face. "I'll tell you." He steps close and shakes his head. "Whatever you want to know."

"Okay." She heads for the Mercedes and talks over her shoulder. "Then let's get going." She opens the door and settles back inside. "If we're a target, I'd rather be a moving one." She closes the door, and the car catches to life and purrs on the asphalt.

Daniel looks up and down the empty blacktop. The blazing sun torments overhead and the cloudy big blue sky seems to extend forever.

He climbs inside and closes the passenger door. The Mercedes drives off down the desolate road.

****

Spires of steel outline the growing structures of the strip mall construction site.

A worn wooden sign shows an architect's dream of the finished buildings, framed with leafy green trees and pristine pavement: Coming Soon. Commercial pad sites For Sale.

Four San Antonio police cruisers are parked in the dried mud alongside pallets of bricks and bags of cement.

Caution—Do Not Cross, yellow tape extends across cracked and dried ground and encircles the San Marcos police cruiser.

A forensic photographer hovers around the vehicle and lines up his shots. He snaps a bevy of pictures from different angles.

"Evers, you make sure you document every inch. As far as I'm concerned, this whole dirt mound is a crime scene." Sergeant Hector Torres walks the area with two patrol officers. He crouches down next to some tire tracks in the mud. "Let's get a casting of these tracks." He looks at one of the patrol officers. "They look a lot fresher than anything else out here."

The patrolman places a plastic flag into the mud next to the track. Sergeant Torres continues to scope out the site.

Detective Navarro ducks under the yellow plastic tape. The forensic teams hover around the police car. She's careful where she steps as she heads for them. "Sergeant Torres." He turns with a nod of recognition and offers his hand. "Roya." They shake.

She takes a moment to survey the grisly field. "Was it Morrison?"

Torres agrees. "We've got his phone. Busted all to

hell, but we'll get what we can off of it. And…we've got an eyewitness."

She perks up. Torres motions towards the patchwork metal frame. "Drifter. Camped out in the construction site. Made a nest in a pile of insulation about two hundred yards from here." The sergeant pulls a small notepad from his chest pocket and flips back a few pages. "He stayed hidden when the squad car pulled in. But claims he heard multiple gunshots. And saw a fancy car leave the scene. Going that way. No driver description. No license plate number. Only letters. Started with an *A*. You want to talk to him?"

Navarro watches the forensic team at work. "Is there more information to get from him?"

"He's bone skinny. No teeth. Covered in sores." Torres puts away his note pad. "Probably on day infinity of a hardcore meth addiction. He's in the back of the ambulance hydrating on an IV drip if you want to pick his brain."

"It can wait." Navarro shakes her head. "What's the word on Perez and Kovach?"

"Homicides. Bexar County Medical Examiner has them."

Navarro walks the scene. She avoids a cluster of plastic evidence markers and stands close to a patch of dried blood in the mud. "Hector, what in the hell happened out here?"

"Well, the way we figure." Torres moves towards a set of spray-painted outline markers. "Lights flashing and they pull Morrison over. He comes out, guns blazing." He points over towards Navarro. "Officer Perez goes down, right next to where you are. Wounds were through and through."

Torres walks around a plastic flag and steps over to a second outline highlighted by dark blood stains soaked in the mud. "There were deep powder burns on Kovach's shirt. Had to have been a close-range hit, right about here." He points to the center of his sternum. "They were both pronounced dead at the scene."

Navarro scans the deserted site. "It's a pretty quiet place." Empty fields stretch off on either side, an occasional car drives by on the ranch road. A few gawkers slow down to take in all the activity. "Did they call it in? Call for back-up? Let anybody know they were on top of Morrison?"

"No idea." Torres motions over to a group of squad cars. "You can check in with San Marcos PD. There was a Homicide Sergeant out here a while ago." He calls out to the photographer. "Evers, bodies, blood splatter and evidence. I want all those photo files within the hour." Officer Evers looks up from his camera long enough to wave an affirmative as he continues to document the crime scene.

Navarro paces with Torres. "There's not so much as a traffic ticket on him before this morning. Really. I checked and double-checked."

Torres glances over. "So what?"

Navarro continues. "So, I mean, we're saying, in a few hours, the man goes from a clean slate to hit and run, a kidnapping, to the cold-blooded murder of two cops. It doesn't add up."

Torres stops in his tracks and turns on her. "Do you know how many more Daniel Morrisons there are in the city proper and surrounding counties?"

Navarro shrugs and waits for the answer.

"Four. One got his house fire-bombed. One left

town. They tell me his phone keeps pinging away with death threats. And two who pulled short straws and are the lucky guests of the M.E., currently residing on the slab down at the morgue due to some trigger-happy neighbors." He wipes the tension from his face and shakes his head. "There is nothing about this whole damned day that adds up."

"How about his hostage?" Torres heads towards the pack of San Antonio squad cars, unmarked vehicles and an ambulance as Navarro keeps pace. "Talk to me, Hector. What did her do with her?"

"Roya, are you serious? I don't have time to play 'what if's.'" He tries to hide his growing annoyance. "Now, if you'll excuse me."

"Think about it." Navarro doesn't let it go. "The woman he grabbed. Tricia Kelley. Did she sit around and watch while he turned this place into a death trap?"

"Maybe he tied her up?" Torres shakes her off. "Or tossed her into the trunk. Who cares? He's a cop killer now." Torres walks away but stops. "Hey." He turns back around. "That million-dollar reward is still payable when he's dead, right? Cause that's the only way this motherfucker is ending up."

She mutters to herself. "Thanks for your input, Sergeant." The weary detective walks away from the crime scene and ducks under a line of yellow tape.

Chapter Twenty-Two

A pulsating press pool stakes their claim all along the trampled lawn and walkway of the Morrison home.

Neighbors are bored with the spectacle. They're more concerned with a fleet of vehicles and vans parked up and down South Guadalupe Street. The sounds of a classic rock tune play from someone's car speakers. The song drifts across the chaotic lawn.

Reporters from local stations record their updates. Newsmen and women primp and preen in front of various camera lens. One reporter motions for a retake. He shakes it off and puts on his serious face as he starts to report again.

The front lawn of the Morrison house is roped off, but it's ignored. Various uniforms and civilians treat the yellow tape as an annoying obstacle more than anything else. The circus atmosphere continues, all focused on this square of green lawn and cookie-cutter house in the middle of suburbia.

The front door cracks open. Abrupt chaos funnels towards it with a mash of dueling microphones and clicking cameras. "All right. That's enough." A broad-shouldered uniformed police officer slips out and guards the open door as a baby-faced Officer Haxton stands at his shoulder. He raises his hands to try and placate the mob. "Let's have some order here." No one heeds the warning, and a jumble of questions are shouted out.

"What is the holdup? We're due for an update?"

"Do you have any further details on Daniel Morrison's whereabouts?"

"We want to hear from a police liaison."

"Is this cowering? Why are you all hiding inside there? The press has a right to know."

"Any comment on the two dead police officers found at a nearby construction site? Was it Morrison?"

"No comment." Officer Haxton ignores the barrage of shouts and microphones. "No comment. At this time. We will update you all shortly." He scans the undulating crowd and finds who he's looking for. "Grey. KTXU. Gary Grey. Let's go."

Gary Grey moves through the crowd of reporters with Alan his camera man in tow. He flashes a pearly white smile as he elbows his way forward. Envious reporters and news people pepper him with questions.

"Express lane to the front row."

"What the hell is this about, Grey?"

"Whose ass did you kiss to get on the VIP list?"

"You fuckin' hack."

That stops Grey in his tracks, right at the edge of the front porch. "Awe. Don't be jealous. It's called doin' my job." He drags Alan through the throng and pushes him onto the porch. The officer allows him and his camera inside. Grey ignores the crowd and speaks to the snide reporter. "Hey, Manny, do what you do best, those hard-hitting interviews from the Poteet Strawberry Festival. Me? I've got a date with the wife."

Manny spits back. "Go fuck yourself, Grey."

He ignores the crass comment as he waves to the crowd of reporters and makes his way up on the porch. "Officer Haxton. Nice to see you again. Appreciate the assist." He allows Grey to pass and steps inside as well. Another officer closes the front door fast on the mash of bodies jousting with cameras and microphones.

Alan and Grey stand inside the foyer. Alan preps his camera as Grey checks the place out. "Real nice. A house full of cops. That'll grow hair on a duck. Okay, young squire." He claps a hand on Officer Haxton's shoulder. "Let's protect and serve. Lead the way."

He doesn't move. "Are you forgetting something?"

Grey thinks for a second and returns a smile. "Of course. Coin of the realm. Here you go." He passes over a folded wad of bills. "Don't spend it all in one place. You little scamp."

The officer still blocks their way. "That got you in. But it's gonna take more to get you down the hall."

"What?" Grey looks to Alan and back at the officer. "Hey, come on now. We had a deal."

"That's right." Officer Haxton agrees with him. "The key word there is *had*." He looks over his shoulder. No one in earshot. "So, what's it gonna be? Do we move on in, or do I send you back outside?"

"You cleaned me out." Grey shrugs. "I gave you what I've got. And unless there's an ATM machine in this cramped hallway. What do you want from me?"

"Fine." Officer Haxton reaches for the front door. "You're both back outside."

"Wait." Grey stops him. "I'm sure we can make this work." He turns to his camera man. "Alan. How much cash do you have on you?"

"I don't know." He fumbles around in his cargo short pockets and pulls out a Velcro wallet. "Maybe a few bucks—"

Grey snatches all the cash from his wallet and holds

it out. Haxton grabs the bills and makes them disappear.

"You know, I usually get dinner and a movie before I get fucked like that." Grey claps Officer Haxton on the shoulder. "You'll be the chief of police in no time, son."

He steps out of the way. Alan moves down the hall with his camera. Grey starts to follow. Haxton stops him. "Be gentle, Grey. That's word from up high."

"Not a single worry to be had." He grins back like a Cheshire cat. "I'm as harmless as a baby kitten. You all can breathe easy."

Grey catches up with Alan as they move inside the house. Alan whines. "That was all the cash I had 'til payday, boss. What am I supposed to do until then?"

"Don't worry about it." Grey claps him on the shoulder. "Pocket change for what will be an award-winning interview. If that cop wanted his dick sucked, you'd be down on your knees 'til it's done." He points to the carpeted stairwell. "There we go. Second floor. Our destiny awaits."

Alan lugs the camera equipment as they head up the stairs towards the master bedroom.

****

The Mercedes cruises down the desolate two-lane road. An occasional vehicle drives past, heading the other direction. The barren landscape of scrub-covered hills seems to stretch forever. Windows are cracked, the drone of the tires on the road overpowered by the rush of air into the cabin.

Daniel passively stares out at the endless solitude.

"Hey." Tricia at the wheel. She smokes and taps the ash outside. It sparks and vanishes between the thin crack in the glass. "We're getting low on gas."

Daniel glances over at the control panel. Two digital

dashes are left on the meter. "I guess we better fill it up then."

She adds in, "You lost my phone. Back there at that, mess. And I need to make a call."

"Well." He looks over and shrugs in his seat. "Dead or alive, you still get paid."

She snaps back. "I'm not turning you in. I have to talk to my boyfriend. And tell him…something." Her voice sharpens. "I had a life, you know. Before you blew it all apart."

He ignores her edge and asks a matter of fact. "What's his name?"

She isn't sure she wants to say anything, but finally does. "Bernhard."

"Bernhard?" Daniel grunts. "Is he German?"

"No. Austrian. From Salzburg."

They drive in silence. Until Daniel breaks it. "So, what does he do?"

"Not that it's any of your business. But he's with Whitley Penn out of Fort Worth. One of the top public accounting firms in the country."

"You're dating an accountant." Daniel shows some surprise. "I wouldn't have guessed that."

She's fast with her response. "He's a nice man, stable, dependable. Bernhard, he made me carry the gun in my car. He travels a lot and was comfortable, you know, knowing I was safe, protected." Her warm thoughts melt away. "I shot and killed all the paper targets down at the range. When I pulled the trigger today, I actually understood what all that practice meant." Her hands grip the wheel, and she keeps the car steady. "So, I wouldn't hesitate."

"Hey." Daniel turns to her. "Are you okay?"

She doesn't answer him and instead asks another question. "Have you figured out what we're doing?"

He stares out at the craggy sunbaked land. A paint-flaked sign along the side of the road rapidly approaches.

Plateau Truck Stop – 5 miles. Food, Gas, Diesel, Showers. Next Gas – Pablo De Luna, Mexico.

He careens in his seat as the sign passes and settles back. "There you go. Plateau. Five miles. We can gas up. You can make your call." He gets comfortable. "And that's about all I've got figured out at the moment."

Tricia kills the quiet and turns on the radio. She fiddles with the scanning buttons. Blasts of static. Brash Tejano horns. She turns down the volume a bit. "What about your wife, Judy? You should call her."

"No." Daniel stares out at the vast flat landscape. He talks to the window. "I wouldn't even know what to say."

Tricia continues to scan the radio. Oldies doo-wop. A perky commercial. A warbling auto-tuned voice. A stern news reporter. Static. A steady Ranchera beat.

"Wait a sec." Daniel sits up in his seat. "I know that voice. Go back."

Tricia stops scanning the radio. "What?"

"On the dial. The button. Make it go backwards."

Tricia switches buttons. The Latin singer fills the cabin. A blast of static. And a deep stern voice. "—reports are coming in that imply over a kilo of illegal narcotics were found in the wheel-well of your husband's Bronco. Do you have any response for that, Mrs. Morrison?"

A woman's bewildered voice comes through the stereo speakers. "I…I don't…I think. That's not true."

Daniel goes rigid in his car seat. He turns up the dial.

"It's not true, you say?" Gary Grey's silky-smooth

tones are even louder inside the Mercedes cabin. "Well, that is a puzzling predicament. Perhaps rumors, innuendo. At best, we can confirm that a number of pills were found scattered throughout your car's interior. Will you admit to us, here and now, that is a true statement."

"That…" Judy stammers her response. "That's what I've been told, yes, but—"

He cuts her off. "And is it also true that your husband has been battling his addictions for quite some time."

She takes a second before she responds. "I'm not sure what—"

He cuts her off again. "That's a very straightforward question, Mrs. Morrison. You should be able to answer yes or no. So, which is it?"

"Yes…" Her defeated voice deflates a bit further. "Yes, but—"

"Mrs. Morrison. Please excuse my forwardness, but perhaps the problem is, you didn't know your husband as well as you think."

****

A hundred miles away from the moving Mercedes. Tucked inside the Morrison master bedroom, Gary Grey sits on a fold-out chair, a jackal on the hunt, toying with his prey.

Judy Morrison sits on another fold-out chair directly across from him, frozen like a deer in the headlights. A fold-out table stands between them. Alan's camera lens looms above her. Her tired bloodshot eyes occasionally drift up towards the imposing bulky camera.

"Addiction is a breeding ground for lies." Grey guides her back towards his shark-like grin. "I would like to remind you that an innocent woman has died here today. The wife of a very prominent and well-respected citizen. Mrs. Morrison, what would you like to say to him, right now?"

"I'm sorry." She glances from the looming lens and back to Grey. "Say to whom?"

Grey leans back in his folding chair. "Congressional candidate Hayden Grant. I'm sure you've seen the commercials. And I'm sure he's out there. Watching or listening to us have our little chat. Here's your chance. Go ahead. What would you like to say to him?"

"Well…" She's caught off guard. "I… I—"

Grey likes her off-guard. "Well, I'm sure you feel horrible. As we all do. Now, let's talk about your husband, the murderer. Shall we? Let's dig down deep." He savors the moment. "We all know he's out there. Somewhere. Daniel Morrison. A brutal monster. A drug taker. A drug dealer, perhaps. A—"

"I'm sorry. I can't…" Judy jumps over his speechifying. "These things you're saying. I don't believe any of that for a—"

"A few hours ago, I was at your sister-in-law's home." Grey leans forward and talks over her. "She's in mourning, completely devastated, with her dutiful husband, sprawled out dead on their tile floor, another innocent victim of this endless rampage. I'm sorry, you say. Well, I'm sorry to be the one to tell you." He leans back, his tone soothes out. "Something has clearly snapped in your husband. A major malfunction turned the man you know into the monster we can clearly see. Except for you. Ms. Morrison. And I don't understand why. Enlighten us. How do you explain that?"

"No. That's not true. None of it is." The camera zooms in tight. She shakes her pale and tired face, on the verge of a torrent of tears. "Never. He wouldn't have. He's a good—"

"Good. I'm sure he is." Grey continues to walk all over her. "He's very good at what he's doing. That much is obvious. But before today, before he snapped. How was he?"

She answers fast. "He was…no, I mean…he is. Daniel is a normal husband. What you're saying. My Daniel would never—"

"I can see you're upset." Grey leans forward. "But that's no reason to lie. On camera. Please play straight with us. We expect the truth. Now, your neighbors tell us, they've heard some horrible shouting, emanating from this very room, I'm sure." He holds up his hand to the camera and counts it out. "Not once, not twice, but a number of times. Any number of times. Would you care to comment?"

"Arguments. Sure. We've had arguments." She stammers her response. "Like any other married couple. Maybe they were a little loud sometimes, but—"

"Does he hit you?" He oozes fake compassion as he leans forward and takes her clammy hand. "You can be honest with us. We're here to help you. Has that violent temper we've all heard about today. Reared its ugly head in the past?"

"No, no." She's lost in the fog of his words. "That's not right. Daniel is…he is a kind and considerate—"

"That's enough." She startles as Grey slams his hand down on the fold out desk. The camera zooms in tight on him. "Let's be real here. You knew, Mrs. Morrison. You knew he had a problem. And you didn't say anything. Not one word. Now, wouldn't you say that makes you responsible as well."

"What?" She blanches at the thought. "No, I—"

He steamrolls over her. "Sure. You weren't driving the car. You didn't pull the trigger. But you let him loose. Didn't you? Please. Speak up for yourself."

"I have nothing…" Judy's voice drops to a hush. "I don't want to talk anymore."

"I have all the details, right here." Grey drops some loose papers on the flimsy desk. "A police report, dated only two months ago. San Antonio's finest were sent out, to this very house on a domestic disturbance call. Weren't they?"

"That…" She glances at the pages and shakes her head. "That was nothing. One of our neighbors overreacted and—"

"Overreacted?" His voice rises a few octaves as he plays for the camera. "All the signs were there. And you could see them. You made the call. That was your cry for help. Any one of our audience members would do the exact same thing. You stood up for yourself, against this monster. Bravo. But you sent the police on their merry way. Why?" His voice drops to a hushed tone. "Did he threaten you? Put his hands on you? Be honest. He hurt you, didn't he?"

Judy tries to hold back, but her emotions overpower her words. She breaks down into a spastic sob.

"Okay, Grey." Officer Haxton steps forward in the cramped bedroom. "I think we're about all done here. Wrap it up."

Grey ignores the bribed officer and presses on through Judy's flowing tears and tattered emotions. "What would you like to say, Mrs. Morrison, to the loving husband who is grieving for his wife at this very minute?" Judy stands up on shaky legs. Alan keeps the camera on her. Grey doesn't let up. "How do you feel? Right now. Tell us. How do you feel?"

"Daniel," Judy blurts out the words through her tears, "I'm sorry. Please come home."

Officer Haxton comes to her aid and escorts her into the master bathroom. The door closes behind them.

Alan swings the camera back to Gary Grey. He sits alone on his fold out chair. As he collects the scattered papers from the table, he talks to the camera in his serious reporter mode.

"I'm sorry, Daniel. Well, it's a little late for that now, isn't it? Judy Morrison, this poor brainwashed housewife here may not see it, but we sure can. Daniel Morrison, hear me loud and clear. You can run, but you cannot hide. Your time has come. And the bell, it tolls for thee. This has been Gary Grey. KTXU News, San Antonio. Live, on the scene."

****

A woman's anchor voice comes through the Mercedes stereo speakers. "That was our own Gary Grey with quite the interview live from the Morrison household. This is a tragic story reverberating all across central Texas, with a number of new skeletons seeming to parade out of the closet. Not to make light of this morning's tragedy, but I think—"

Tricia switches off the car radio. Silence fills the cabin. Until Daniel slams his fists against the padded dashboard. He hits harder and harder. Tricia stays glued to the steering wheel as she watches Daniel rage in the passenger seat. "Stop it. Can you calm down? Calm down. Please."

"Did you hear him?" Daniel shakes in his seat and points to the radio. "All that, bullshit. That was my wife, and he…ohhh. That's it. That's so fucking it."

"We're almost to the truck stop." Tricia punches the accelerator. The car picks up speed. A tense cloud hangs inside the cozy confines. Daniel watches as Tricia tightens her grip on the leather steering wheel. Her hands twist and flex.

"You don't believe any of that nonsense. Do you?"

"I was very clear with you. And I told you to tell me the truth. All of it." She keeps a soft tone, even though her body is a live wire. "You gave me the bits about the accident and the pills and divorcing your wife. But it sounds like that was all the tip of the iceberg."

"Wait a minute." Daniel can't believe what he's hearing. "Are you serious? That cocksucker on the radio straight-up manipulated her. He knew what he wanted to hear, and he prodded Jude along until he got there. It's a cheap trick. Lawyers do it all the time."

She shakes him off. "But why would he make up those things? Your brother-in-law? He's dead?"

"Look, I didn't…" He stammers back. "I know, I didn't tell you anything about that. Ron, I… I didn't hurt him. It wasn't me."

"Right." She talks over him. "And the narcotics in your trunk. And those police reports for assault?"

"Wait a second." He gets animated. "That narcotics in the trunk thing is a fucking lie."

She calmly talks back. "You said you had drugs in your car—"

"Yes, I did. I admit that. But I only had a small tin of pills. That's all. And assault? What? I never… I didn't hurt anybody. Jude and I had an argument. And we got a little loud one night. So, what does that have to do—"

"Answer the question." She cuts to it. "Were the

police at your home or not?"

"I'm…" he stammers back. "I'm not a violent man. I never—"

"Did the police go to your house?" She waits for his response. He doesn't give her one.

"Get me to a phone." He turns away from her and speaks to his reflection in the passenger window. "We need to have a little talk."

She keeps the wheel steady. "Who do you plan on talking to?"

He snaps back. "That lying fuck, weasel reporter. Who else do you think?"

"Okay." Her voice is soft. "How about your wife?"

"Jude." He shakes his head and burns in his seat. "Jesus Christ, I'm gonna kill that fuckin' guy."

"You'll what?" Tricia keeps her eyes on the road.

Daniel winces at his last comment. "It's not…" He starts to say more but decides to keep his mouth shut.

Two rusty poles climb into the sky. A broken Exxon sign hangs high overhead. The plain, flat sun-blasted buildings of the truck stop loom in the distance.

Tricia pulls the Mercedes off the road and steers onto a stretch of dirt road. A grimy dust cloud engulfs the car.

Chapter Twenty-Three

The vast southern flatlands extend forever in every direction. Texas big blue-sky country disappears into the horizon while a harsh midday sun turns the cloud cover into a streaked kaleidoscope of burnt orange and umber.

Like an out-of-place modern oasis in the center of the barren desert, a faded sign for the Plateau Truck and Auto Center towers over a small cluster of sun-bleached buildings topped with rusty red metal roofs. A few round windows cut into the dirty white stucco give the main old building a New Mexico adobe look and style.

Four gas pumps that were new when a Cadillac had fins stand sentry off to the side, shaded under a faded red awning. A dusty Peterbilt work-horse truck with an extended cab sits parked next to one of two available diesel pumps. The old awning is a bit taller to accommodate the parade of long-haul trucks and transports that come through.

Two work worn pick-up trucks and an old sedan that has seen better days sit parked next to the main adobe building. A large profile picture of a faded Indian chief painted on the side of one building, the intricate facial details and bright colors worn down by weather and time.

A large dust cloud rapidly approaches from the ranch road.

The Mercedes slows down as it closes in on the buildings. Even covered in dust and dirt, it looks out of place among the assorted parked vehicles. It eases up next to a gas pump and comes to a halt.

Tricia kills the engine and climbs out of the car. She turns her face up to the fleeting sun and feels the warmth.

Daniel pops out of the passenger side. "Hey." Tricia turns back, the Mercedes in between them. "Are you okay?" Daniel asks in a hushed tone.

"Yes. I'm fine." She responds fast. "Could you fill up the car? I'll pay for it inside. I'll make my call. And get us an old-fashioned map. Maybe we can figure out where we're going."

She turns away from him. He calls out again. "Hey."

Her shoes scuff in the dirt. "What?"

He leaves the gas pumps and steps up close to her. "Don't you think you might need some sunglasses? A hat, maybe? So you can cover yourself up."

She chuckles a bit. "For what?"

He looks around. "Well, the people inside. Security cameras. Trust me. You don't want your face on TV. Any more than it already is, I mean."

"I won't make any new friends." Tricia looks around at the dust covered everything. "Besides, you really think a place like this has cameras. What's the worst that can happen? They try to kill us again?" She heads away from the pumps, towards the main adobe building.

"That's not funny." He calls out to her back. "You shouldn't talk like that."

She whips over her shoulder. "It was just a joke." Tricia faces the building with a steady stride in her step. The slit of a smile fades fast into a determined stare as she grabs the handle on the smudged glass door and heads inside.

Daniel steps to the rear of the car. He unscrews the

Mercedes gas cap and waits by the pump. The desert is quiet, other than the hum of florescent lights under the awning that attracts an endless swarm of insects. He takes in his surroundings and glances around the empty station. He lingers on the mural of the Indian chief. His eyes don't stay on the faded war paint, but on the two doors flanking it and the dusty Verizon pay phone enclosure. Daniel leaves the gas cap hanging and walks away from the pumps, towards the mural.

A layer of dust covers the old pay phone. The Verizon advertisement faded and peeling away from the metal enclosure. Daniel runs his fingers along the rusty wire cord and grabs the greasy black handset. He wipes the handset on his dirty shirt and places the receiver to his ear. He fiddles with the tarnished cut-off button until he hears a dial tone on the line.

He presses 00 on the worn keypad. Muted clicks tumble in his ear. Until it connects. He listens for a few seconds. "I want a person." Daniel speaks slowly into the phone. "A real person. I want to speak to an operator."

"This is Verizon Communications." A tinny pre-recorded message plays through the receiver. "To place a call, please dial the number you are calling. For U.S. Directory, press one. For other requests, please say, information, credit or operator."

Daniel talks over the recorded message. "Operator. Information. Operator." Muted clicks tumble in his ear. He rests against the scarred and scratched metal lip of the enclosure and stares out at the endless desert and scrub.

Away from his line of sight, a bell jangles over the door to the adobe. A snippet of country music wafts in the air before it's cut off as the door seals closed. Daniel perks up as he hears boots slowly scuff through the dirt, closing in on the phone enclosure.

A flat voice from an actual person comes through the receiver and gets his attention. "Thank you for calling Verizon communications directory services. How may I help you today?"

"Yes, operator." Daniel clears his throat. "I need a...it's a number out of San Antonio. For, uhm, KTXU. It's a television station."

"Please hold." More digital clicks tumble until the flat voice returns back on the line. "I have a listing for a KTXU-TV at 5400 Fredericksburg Road in San Antonio. Would you like the number?"

"No, that's okay." He leans against the metal lip and faces back towards the gas pumps and the dust-covered Mercedes. "Could you call them collect. Say it's from Daniel Morrison. I'm sure they'll accept the charges."

"Daniel Morrison. One second. Please hold." Digital clicks sound through the receiver. Daniel leans against the enclosure and waits for the call to connect.

****

A few minutes earlier, Tricia enters the main adobe building in a hurry. The smudged glass door seals closed behind her.

Twangs and strings of a popular country song waft overhead through cheap speakers. Ice cold air from an industrial-sized air conditioner chills the sweat on her furrowed brow. She almost runs smack into a shelf stacked with an army of cheap Virgin Mary statues. Plastic Jesus holds a crooked wooden staff and stands with his flock of little lambs. His painted skin appears whiter than the usual Middle Eastern olive complexion.

Tricia's wild and wide eyes take in the cramped gas station. A maze of glass booths showcases rows of kiddie cowboy boots and colorful tacky tourist trinkets. Another counter is stuffed full of leather purses dripping with turquoise buttons and baubles. She can hear voices towards the front of the adobe. She follows along a wall made up of velvet paintings of Frida Kahlo in a number of poses. An adjacent wall is full of Day of the Dead painted skulls and skeleton statues and artwork.

Tricia heads past stacked cases of Lone Star beer and sleeves of RC colas and a pyramid of sodas. A leaning tower of water teeters on a splintered pallet, until she can finally see the register. She spots a large man in a faded red Beech-Nut cap and Budweiser beer belly, framed by packs of cigarettes and a rack of cigars and chew. Tricia strides on past a few square tables with dirty white countertops.

A stocky trucker kicks back at one table, lost in a close conversation with Lizzy, a woman in a frayed waitress uniform. Her fake nails are too long, and her make-up is too thick, but the trucker doesn't seem to mind. His coffee gets cold as he teases and flirts with her.

Joe Steve, a greasy-spoon short order cook, flips a hockey-puck burger on the crackling grill as he whistles along with the country song playing over the speakers. He slides a hot plate of crispy fries up on the counter under a glowing heat lamp. "Lizzy. Order up." His free hand dings a bell. He dings the bell again.

She ignores the two bells and the hot order of fries as she continues to lean in closer against the tabletop and smiles and flirts with the long-haul trucker.

Tricia finally steps up to the register. She stands over the spread of lotto tickets under glass and stares into the broad but paper-thin tourist smile of a heavy man in a sweat-stained cap. A crooked pin attached to his tee-shirt states a name, Hap.

"How can I help ya' there, miss." Hap turns up the wattage of his smile even brighter.

Tricia doesn't smile back at all. "Do you have a telephone?"

"Sure do." Hap shakes his head. "Out by our old chief." He points over her shoulder. "You wanna go 'round the back. Next to the facilities."

"Umm. No. That's not gonna work. No." She shakes her head with worry. Nerves in her hands and face twitch and jolt. "It's an emergency. Please. Do you, I mean, do you have another phone handy? Maybe your cell phone that I can use? Anything."

"Yes, ma'am." Hap hitches his belt under his belly and leans into the worn countertop. "Sure thing. I can help you. Any way that I can. But…" His voice drops low. "Are you all right? It's none of my business and shouldn't be my concern. But. You do look shook up."

She sighs and snaps back at him. "Do you have a phone, or not?"

"Yes. We sure do." He keeps his thin smile. "We've got one in the kitchen. Come on 'round the side. Joe Steve will let you on in." Hap comes out from behind the register. He keeps a leery eye on her as Tricia looks all around, tense and impatient.

"Pick up, Lizzy." Joe pounds on the order bell. "Pick up, pick up, pick up." Sharp dings ring out again and again. "One gosh darn order sitting here on the counter, and you still move like molasses."

Hap steps up to the counter. "I'll take the food on over, Joe. Do me a solid, will ya?" He points his chin at Tricia. "Help this here little lady find our phone."

Joe fixes a wary gaze on Tricia as he lets her back

into his domain. He cocks a thumb at a lime-green handset on the wall. She zeroes in right towards it with a sigh of relief and picks up the handset. Joe Steve's lazy eyes widen as he watches her punch in 911 and cradle the receiver tight against her shoulder.

Hap walks the food over and places it on the Formica tabletop next to the mug of cold coffee. The trucker barely notices. He's much more interested in his callused hand caressing Lizzy's stocking knee. "You were letting my fries get cold, darlin'."

"I was waiting for you to answer my question." Lizzy smiles back. "Are you still gonna take me to the Horseshoe tonight? I'm in the mood to dance."

Trucker smiles wide. "I can see that." His hand moves off her knee and inches on up her thigh. "Sure do got the legs for it."

"It's the damndest thing." Hap breaks their mood and whispers in a low raspy voice. "All strung out, herkie jerky and wild-eyed like she's been on a tear huffing paint or somethin'."

Lizzy turns away from her trucker. "What are you on about, Hap?"

"That young city girl who came in." He cocks his head towards the grill. "She's over by the grill using our phone. What'cha all make of her?"

Trucker shrugs. "Nice rack." He grins even wider. Lizzy guffaws and swats at him.

"Pretty little thing. All wound up like that." Hap shakes his head. "She's got herself in a right panic."

Lizzy dismisses it. "I didn't see nothing."

"Somethin' ain't okay." Hap makes up his mind. "I'm gonna take a look around outside."

"Yeah." Trucker is more than happy to see him go.

"You go do that." He playfully paws at Lizzy. "Darlin', if you wanna go dancing at the Horseshoe so bad, then we better get some practice in."

"Hold on, cowboy." She chuckles and laughs as he tries to pull her onto his lap. "We don't need that kinda practice. Yet." She holds his roaming hands at bay but still keeps them hovering close to her ample hips.

Hap glances towards the grill as he heads for the back door.

****

A couple hundred miles away, deep in the heart of San Antonio rush hour traffic, Gary Grey kicks back in the passenger seat of the news van.

"After today, I better start getting used to the idea. There's no doubt, I earned it."

Alan holds steady at the wheel. He looks over his shoulder and picks his moment. He weaves the van around a slow-moving tractor trailer as Grey keeps talking. "Time for the big leagues. I'm hungry, ready and I want it. Trust me, I've been out there enough."

Alan watches the road and offers a well-placed "Uh huh" into the conversation.

Grey continues. "I'll be honest. Most of the district is a third world shithole. It's one-part Georgetown with pretty monuments and three-parts gangland war zone. Know what I'm saying? Have you ever been?"

"Actually—" Alan merges the van back into the slow lane. "—Yeah. I went to Washington, D.C. once when I was a kid. On a holiday weekend school trip."

"Where's Bob Woodward live?" Grey smiles at the thought. "That's where I'm going. I'll move in right next door. We'd become fast friends. Hey, Bob. How's it going? Those rose bushes are looking mighty fine. Let's grab a drink later. Your treat." He chuckles to himself as his cell phone pulses and rings. He answers it on speaker. "This is Grey. Talk to me."

A woman's voice fills the cabin of the news van. "Gary. It's the station switchboard again. And I've got another Morrison on the line for you."

Alan merges the van into the slow lane and gets ready to take an exit. Grey laughs as he cradles his phone in his palm. "Ha. How many is that in the last hour? Twenty-three? Tell him to take a number. You can take a message."

"I already tried to take a message." The switchboard voice is annoyed and persistent. "This one is ready to blow a gasket. He says he'll talk. But he'll only talk to you. What do you want me to do?"

Alan takes the highway exit ramp.

"Listen to this." Grey nudges him. "I love poking the crazies." He speaks into his phone. "Fine. Go ahead and transfer him over."

The relieved switchboard voice replies. "Okay, Mr. Morrison. You're on with Gary Grey." Clicks skitter through the cell phone speaker.

"You there? Hell-ooo." Gary gets comfortable again in his seat. "Listen, Mr. Loony Tunes. I sure do like a prank call as much as the next guy, but it's been a real long day and I—"

"I don't want to hear about your day." Daniel's calm and stern voice fills the cabin of the news van. "I know my wife smokes when she's nervous. I'll bet she was a chimney around an asshole like you."

"Yeah, you didn't like the interview." Grey takes the insult in stride. "Everyone's a critic. Next time, you go right on ahead and change the channel. Now if you'll excuse me, I've got—"

Daniel's voice cuts him off. "The drugs in my Bronco were blue and barrel-shaped pills. What else do you want to hear? My birthday? Mother's maiden name? I want an interview."

Grey takes the call off speaker. He shoves a startled Alan. "Pull over."

Alan holds the wheel. "But, boss, we're almost at the station."

"Right the fuck now, Cornball. Pull this van over." Grey doesn't let up. "I don't want to lose this signal."

Alan changes lanes and turns into a Taco Cabana parking lot. Grey returns to his cell phone, cradled against his ear. "Sorry about that. Daniel. It's really you, isn't it? You're Daniel Morrison."

After a few seconds, his stern voice filters through. "What do you think?"

"I think we need to talk." Grey holds the phone tight against his ear. "Can you hear me clearly? Where are you at, pal?"

Daniel's clear voice snorts at the fake gesture of friendship. "You got a pen?"

****

Daniel leans against the dusty Verizon phone enclosure. He stares at the worn down and paint-peeled Indian-chief mural as he speaks into the handset receiver. "A place called the Plateau Truck Stop. Out in the middle of nowhere. We've been on ranch roads for a while, but I did see a sign for El Indio. I think." He looks around at the old gas pumps and faded red awnings. "I'd say we're a handful of miles from the Mexico border."

"Jesus, pal." Grey's surprised voice filters through the handset. "How'd you get so far?"

"You're the reporter." Daniel shifts his scuffed dress shoes around in the dirt. "You figure it out. Can you find the place?"

"Plateau Truck Stop. El Indio." Grey's voice filters through the receiver. "Sure. No problem. Oh, wow. I can smell the Pulitzer from here."

"No, that's from the crap you're always spewing." Daniel's anger wells up. He grips the black handset tight in his fist. "Bring your camera. Bring your microphone. I'm tired. And I'm done running." Daniel slides his right shoe in the dirt. "I'm drawing a line in the sand. Right here. Get your ass on down here and cross it."

"Pal, I am on it." Grey's excitement comes through the receiver. "You hold tight, Morris—"

Daniel slams the black handset hard into the cradle and disconnects the call. He stands by the phone enclosure and breathes heavy until he's able to get his composure back. The desert peace and quiet settles all around him. "Hope you're happy." He talks to himself in a low rasp. "There's no going back now."

The sun hangs low. A fiery orange glow burns like wildfire across the big Texas sky. His shoes kick up a cloud of dirt as Daniel starts back for the Mercedes.

The long lights under the awnings flicker and pop on. Overhead rows of fluorescent tubes shine pools of blue light down onto the sets of gas pumps.

The dirty Mercedes and the single Peterbilt semi-truck parked next to a diesel pump shine under the red awnings and intense lights.

Daniel slowly returns to the open gas cap hanging from the rear of the Mercedes. He wipes sweat and grime off his forehead as he grabs the handle and hose from the gas pump and lowers the trigger lever. He inserts the chrome nozzle into the Mercedes and begins to pump the gas. Numbers spin on their dials. The cost and weight in gallons continue to flip. A sharp ding rings out every time the meter passes another gallon.

Overhead, waves of insects dance and dart all along the florescent tubes.

Lost in the continuous hum of the gas pump and desert silence, Daniel's tired eyelids droop.

A thunderous boom kills the quiet. The Mercedes passenger's and driver's windows blow out in a spray and shower of safety glass.

Daniel reacts with sudden shock. He instantly drops to the dirt. His arm snags around the gas pump hose. The gas nozzle pops out of the Mercedes and spews an oily fountain of noxious fluid as it hits the ground.

Chapter Twenty-Four

In a dark, plush office, surrounded by polished brass and wood. John Smith sits stoic in a large leather-bound desk chair, a cell phone to his ear. His expression never changes as he listens to continuous chatter from the voice on the other end. "Yes, Mr. Grey. I do understand. Your information is very much appreciated." He responds with an even keeled tone as unknowing as his usual poker face. "I agree as well. It is an urgent matter. Yes, I can do that."

John stretches across the thick wooden desk and picks up an ink pen from the leather blotter, along with a slip of paper from a letter rack. "I'm ready. Go ahead." He starts to scribble.

A black and white photo adorned in a gold frame, Hayden Grant in his element on the political stump, stares back at him. Loopy cursive letters fill the paper: El Indio. Border town. Plateau Truck Stop.

"That should be more than enough. This is an unexpected boon. I'm certain he will be pleased." John stares at the paper and returns to the phone call. "Yes, I will speak with him immediately. Time is of the essence. Have the local or state police been notified?" He draws out a large question mark on the note.

"Of course. You can count on our discretion." He shakes his head to no one in the quiet office. "Can we rely on yours as well? Good. Yes. We will be in touch.

Thank you."

John hangs up the phone and doesn't move from the desk. The chair creaks and pops under his weight as he reaches across the wide wooden surface and starts up a cherrywood antique metronome next to the picture frame. The pendulum rod continuously clicks back and forth; the soothing sound dominates the quiet and echoes off the wooden shelves and walls.

Shaded dome lights illuminate various framed awards and pictures of Hayden Grant with an assortment of rich benefactors. A group of happy guys on a fishing charter. Arms around shoulders and all smiles on the 18th hole at the club. And Hayden working the stage during the heat of the campaign trail.

One wall is dominated by an old campaign sign from Grant's first political foray. Bold lettering in red, white, and blue: "Our Texarkana Schools Need A Man Like Hayden Grant." The worn yard sign is covered in faded signatures and scribbled congratulatory messages.

John stands up from the desk and slowly steps over to one particular framed painting on the wall. He stares at a portrait of Hayden Grant dressed in an expensive suit, standing next to his deceased wife, Claudia. She's seated on a plush velvet lounge; adorned in a silky dress with a string of cultured pearls around her lean neck.

John steps in close and studies the painting from the frame down to the individual brush strokes and colorful swirls and deep valleys of oil paint dried on the canvas. He abruptly reaches over and stops the swinging metronome pendulum in mid click then strides out of the office and heads down a hall.

A loud TV masks the sound of his polished shoes across the tile floor as he steps through an open archway and into a large bedroom suite. On a giant flat-screen TV, raw footage from a new campaign commercial plays continuously. The digital crackle of a sound check. The image is fuzzy on the screen until it focuses clear and steady. Hands hold a clapboard that fills the screen. An unseen voice chimes in. "Grant for Congress. Traffic in Texas ad. Take nine." The clapper slaps and gets out of the way.

On the screen, Hayden Grant stands at the edge of a busy highway overpass. He walks towards the camera, dressed in a plaid shirt, ten-gallon hat and cowboy boots right out of the box. "You can walk faster than you can drive on most roads here in Texas. Hi, I'm Hayden Grant. And my plan adds billions for new road construction without raising taxes, fees, or tolls. We pay for it all, by… For fucks sake. Line. What's my goddamned line."

"Cut." An unseen voice calls out. "Everybody. Back to one." The screen goes black and turns over to another set-up. The clapper fills the screen as the focus goes in and out.

"Sir." John turns down the TV. "Sir. Are you in here?"

"Yep," a voice calls out from deep in the master closet. "Come on back, John." Hayden stands in a massive closet in front of rows of shirts and suits. The top and bottom racks are overflowing. "No matter how many of these blasted things I've got to attend"—his hair is still wet, and a damp towel is wrapped around his waist as he flips through possibilities— "I still hate the rubber chicken dinner circuit."

He inspects two light-blue shirts and shoves them aside for the next one in line, an Eton white signature twill with French cuffs. He takes it off the hanger and slips it on. "It's like an endless bad dream." His pale gut sticks out from the bottom of the starched white dress shirt as he fumbles with the pearl buttons in front of a full-length mirror. "Whose ass am I kissing tonight? The Pachyderm Club or those old shrews at the Yellow Rose of Texas?"

"It's actually the Conservative Christian Research Institute." John stands at his shoulder as he buttons up his dress shirt. "Sir. I have news."

"I told that Hebe tailor." Hayden sucks in his gut as he works on the buttons. "He's making my shirts too damn tight." He swings around on John. "I mean, look at me. This is fuckin' ridiculous." Hayden tears the shirt off his back. Mother-of-pearl buttons ricochet across the tile.

"Sir." John clears his throat as Hayden flips through more possibilities along the rack. "I have good news."

"Did you check out the new commercial? Pretty sweet, huh?" Hayden rummages down the line. "Number crunchers say it'll help me with the Latino vote." He selects another crisp white shirt and rips off the dry-cleaning bag. It drifts to the floor. "I didn't know Mexicans gave one tin shit about road construction. Guess you learn something new every day."

He checks out his reflection in the mirror. "Here we go." He buttons up the new shirt. "Yeah. That's much better." John watches and waits. He finally breaks his silence. "Sir. We have a solid lead on Daniel Morrison."

"Who?" Hayden steps over to an elaborate tie rack and spins it around. "Hmm. Nothing too fancy for these dinosaurs. Basic red or basic blue. What do you think?"

John doesn't answer his question. "This morning. The hit and run driver. He murdered Claudia in cold blood. He's public enemy number one throughout the entire state. And I know right where he is."

"Oh. Him. Right." Hayden selects a blue tie and drapes it around his neck. "Well…" He fiddles with the tie. "I'm certain some God-fearin' patriot will fix that problem for us. Hell, it gave us a boost with the press. Right when we needed one. They say I'm up in the daily polls, by plus seven. Numbers don't lie. You can't beat that kinda spread." He stops tying the tie. "How much did I offer again?"

John stands stoic. "A million dollars."

"Jesus." Hayden goes back to the mirror and works on his Windsor knot. "I should learn when to keep my big trap shut." He looks at John through the mirror. "That's your job, you know. You're supposed to watch out for me." John doesn't respond. Hayden returns to his reflection. "We don't actually have to pay any of that out. Do we?"

John still doesn't respond. Frustrated, Hayden undoes the blue tie and starts over. "Go ahead and talk to Legal. See if they can find enough red tape to unstick me. And let's get some loyal foot soldiers out on the talk radio. Say, I never meant to say it that way. The liberals are twisting my words. Here we go again. False flag. All that bullshit."

"Sir." John's solid oak exterior breaks open a bit. "But, what about Claudia?" His emotional cracks start to widen.

Hayden takes off his damp towel and hands it to John. "Hand me my slacks, will ya'? And those black Ferragamo shoes."

"Claudia. I mean…" John holds the wet towel at his side. "She's gone. She died this morning." John sputters out a sob that he swallows back.

"Hey? Christ, take it easy." Hayden shows surprise. "Wow. I didn't think Mormons were allowed to cry. Least out in public." He stands in the closet half naked and stares at his body man as John's fault lines of feeling run rampant and open up. "John." He goes for compassion. "Listen to me. It is a tragedy. Worthy of our flag flying at half-mast. And I will weep. Copious tears for her. At the appropriate time. Inside a big church with all those lights and cameras on me. But until then—" Hayden flashes a toothy smile. "—Good riddance to that cheating bitch." He impatiently waits. "So." He thumps John on his broad chest. "Where are my pants?"

John drops the damp towel and pulls himself together. He grabs them off the rack and holds them out.

"What the hell's gotten into you, John?" Hayden snatches the pressed slacks from him. "Since when do you give a cuck's limp-dick about women?"

John wipes away his tears as Hayden climbs into his dark dress pants and tucks in his white shirt all around his girth.

"Let me tell you something about my dearly departed wife. Or Number Three as I liked to call her." He sucks in his gut to button up the slacks. "Claudia was a high-class whore. There wasn't much that woman was ever good at. Except for being down on her knees. And between you and me, she wasn't very good at that, either." He finds a black leather belt and slips it on. "She was a walking pharmacy with a champagne bottle glued to her hand. I'd say she spent most of her waking hours in a fugue state. Either drunk or stoned."

Hayden picks a set of polished black Italian loafers from a cubbyhole and drops them to the floor. "Let's face it. She was no good to anybody. Alive." He uses a long shoehorn to slip into them. "And when fate came wrapped up in a bow this morning, I seized the opportunity. She's more useful to me now than as some drug-addled diva."

Hayden grimaces as he toys with the large Windsor knot at his neck. He loosens it and tightens it again. "Life goes on. I've got Monica waiting in the wings. She's been promoted. Up from the secretary pool into wife number four. And four's my lucky number." He chuckles to himself. "She'll make a fine Mrs. Hayden Grant." He checks out his reflection in the full-length mirror. "Besides, we've got bigger fish to fry, my friend. We're up in the polls with enough cushion to breathe. We're on the home stretch of this shit-slog campaign. And we're on a glide path straight into Congress. Washington, D.C., here we come." He looks at John in the mirror. "Now doesn't all that good news make you feel better?"

John stands in the closet but his mind is miles away. "I loved her."

"I love it too. Clear skies ahead." Hayden goes back to fiddling with his neckline in the mirror. "God damn it." He tugs and strips the blue tie off his neck and drops it to the floor. He grabs the red one off the rack. "I don't want a tie knot fatter than my dick." He adjusts the red tie under his collar and begins again. "End up looking like some pimped out, megachurch preacher."

"I said, I loved her." John watches his boss, his voice at a whisper, quiet and distant. "And we were going to be together. Forever." John stares down at his polished shoes. "We talked all the time. And this morning happened to be for the last time. I was there. On the phone with her. I heard it all. I heard her die."

Hayden remains focused on his tie and the mirror. "Uh huh. Who were you on the phone with?" His hands continue to juggle and smooth and loop the silk material around and over.

"She was mine." John crouches down to the tile and picks up the discarded blue tie. "And we belonged together." John stands up and slips the blue tie around Hayden's neck and pulls tight.

He sputters out a gasp of surprise as the silk cuts into his windpipe. Hayden's eyes balloon and bulge out. In a panicked wheeze, hands claw and grab at his neckline as John jerks and tightens his grip. "You never cared about her. She was never yours." Solid knots of muscles in his arms flex, and he holds Hayden against his barrel chest and keeps him lifted off the tile. Drool runs down his chin as Hayden's lips flap like a dying fish. The color in his face turns shades of red and blue. His Ferragamo shoes lifted off the ground, his feet flailing and kicking. One shoe falls off. His sock rubs against mirrored glass. "She loved me. She never loved you." John doesn't let up; he twists the silk tie even tighter. "I wanted her. And she was *mine*." He grunts the last word and pulls up on the silk garrote. An audible snap as Hayden's neck breaks.

The panic saps out of him. His bugged-out eyes go to glass. Clawed hands drop from his neck and hang in the air. Life depletes and drains from him until he falls completely limp in John's oak arms. John lowers him down to the tile. He never blinks as he watches Hayden and waits for any sign of sudden movement. Dead eyes stare back. John releases his hold on the silk collar. Hayden's lifeless body falls flat.

John slides down and sits on the floor next to the

dead body and stares at his haggard expression in the full-length mirror. His pulse rate slows as he gets his breathing under control.

The TV commercial blares on the flat screen TV. Hayden in his new shirt and boots walks away from the overpass. "Hi, I'm Hayden Grant. And my plan adds billions for new roads and bridges. Wait, wait. My bad. I screwed it up." On the screen, Hayden kicks his new steel toes in the dirt. "I said, bridges. What the fuck? It's road construction. I got this. I do."

"Back to one." An unseen voice shouts commands to an unseen crew. "Hustle, people. Come on. Watch the chatter. Let's go." The screen goes blank until the clapper board fills the picture. "Quiet. Sound. Speed." An unseen voice calls out. "Grant for Congress. Traffic in Texas commercial. Take seventeen."

John completely turns down the volume on the TV. He watches Hayden pantomime on the TV screen as he picks up a house phone on the desk and dials a set of numbers. "Field department. This is John Smith. I've got word from the boss. And it needs to get to your director, immediately. Yes. Tell me when you're ready."

He waits for the voice on the other end of the line. "The boss will not be attending the Christian coalition dinner tonight." He listens and shuts the voice down. "No. You are not in a position to ask me anything. Your director's name is Randy Rowe. If I have to ask you for your name, you're fired. Understand?" John waits for the voice and continues. "Good. Tell Randy he needs a surrogate speaker for the dinner tonight. The boss is entertaining guests. Do not disturb. And he will be unavailable for the entire evening."

John watches Hayden on the TV screen. He walks

and stumbles. It goes black, and the clapper fills the frame again. He returns to the phone. "Read it back to me." John listens to the voice on the other end of the phone. "Good. Now take that message to Randy. Not an assistant. Not a secretary. To him. Directly. If he needs me, he can call me."

John doesn't wait for a response and hangs up the phone. He stares at the open closet door and dials another number. "Helipad. This is John Smith. Gas up the machine." John watches Hayden silently rant and throw a tantrum on the TV. His angry red face fills the screen until it cuts to black and is replaced by the clapper board. "Yes. It's a priority one trip. On orders from the boss."

John carries the phone over to the master closet and closes the door. He sees Hayden's pasty legs sprawled out on the floor before the closet door seals shut. The voice on the phone gets his attention "Destination? El Indio. I'm leaving as soon as possible."

John hangs up the phone and watches a silent Hayden on the TV screen walk and gesture next to a busy highway overpass.

Chapter Twenty-Five

A scattering of colors bleed together as dusk settles. The shroud of the moon drifts through the cloud cover, high in the kaleidoscope sky. Night creeps across the desert ever slowly.

Daniel crawls through the pebbles of safety glass scattered on the ground. He scurries for safety behind the dirty Mercedes. Gasoline seeps from the nozzle and soaks into the hardpack. The pungent smell overpowers.

A shotgun racks, the spent shell tumbles to the dirt by the pumps. "Morrison." A gruff voice calls out. "I'm locked and loaded. And I got somethin' for ya'. Come on out and save yourself a lot of pain."

Daniel peeks under the Mercedes. A pair of scuffed work boots inch forward. He opens the passenger door and leans inside the car.

"I see you down there." the voice calls out, hackles of fear masked by a Texas bravado. "You give up, right now. Or else I put you down. What's it gonna be, boy?"

The smudged glass door bangs open. "Go on and shoot him again, Hap." Her shrill voice loud and breathless, Lizzy leans out, not quite comfortable enough to leave the safety of the gas station. "That man is a walkin' scratch-off. Between you, me and Joe. How much is one million split three ways?"

"Four ways, darlin'." The trucker shoves Lizzy out of the way. "Don't cut me out of the play, I want a piece of this too." He jogs for his Peterbilt truck parked at the Diesel pumps. "Hold on, Hap." A detailed design with the words Lucky 13 stenciled across the driver's door. It clicks and creaks open. "Lemme get my widow-maker."

"Leave him alone." Tricia shoves her way out of the building. "Please, there's no reason for this. Don't hurt him. Wait for the police to arrive."

"Jesus, lady." Joe Steve grabs her around the waist and pulls her back. "Stop fussin' about. This ain't your problem anymore." Tricia struggles but can't shake his arm-bar grip. "Let us take care of business." He tries to calm her down. "You get back inside where it's safe."

"Get your hands off of me." Tricia fights against him. "Let go. Leave me alone."

The driver's door slams shut on the Peterbilt truck. "Hey, Hap." The trucker jogs over with a large revolver in a calloused hand. He hitches his belt and catches his breath. "We do it together and bird-dog this sumbitch."

"I don't see him moving around." Hap holds the shotgun in shaky hands. "Maybe I got him good? Could be he's bleeding out?"

"I got a plan. I'll rush him fast." The trucker bounces in place and is ready to bolt. "You back me up."

"Daniel." Tricia breaks free from Joe Steve and shouts out. "It's all over. Police are on the way. I had to. I had to stop this."

"Damn it, woman." Joe grabs her again and drags her back towards the safety of the station. "Will you keep your big yappers shut."

"Hap. We need to do this." The trucker is as anxious as a player rounding first base and heading for second. "Sheriff from Eagle Pass or the border boys. Someone's gettin' here soon. The TV said, dead or alive. So, let's put him down like a dog. Collect that cash re-ward."

"Yeah. We can do it." Hap finds his courage with the heavy shotgun tight in his meaty hands. "I'm gonna blow him apart." He starts forward towards the florescent-lit Mercedes.

Two gunshots ring out into the darkening sky. Hap and the trucker hit the dirt and scurry for safety. Daniel shouts out. "Stay the fuck away from me." He pants and tries to reel in his blind panic with his back stuck against the front tire. He holds Tricia's snub-nosed wheel gun out and up, gripped firmly in both hands.

A rain of gunfire punches into the Mercedes. Rounds of buckshot peppers the hood, and the revolver unloads along-side the car. The steady sound deafening. Daniel curls up in a ball and stays put against the tire and waits for the barrage to subside.

It finally settles quiet. Daniel works up the nerve to take a peek around the car. A single shot shatters the Mercedes front headlight. Daniel jerks back against the tire. A wave of anxious emotions wash over him. He tries to pull away from the brink and catches up with his frantic panic. He's suddenly aware of the sharp smell of gasoline. He stares at the discarded hose. The fuel runs from the lip of the silver nozzle and soaks into the dirt. He scoots over to the edge of his safety and swallows back nausea and fear as he times the movement. Daniel reaches for the nozzle. A gunshot hits close. He snaps his hand back and retreats behind the front tire.

"Want some more?" Hap's voice rings out. "Or are you all finished, Morrison."

Daniel carefully slides away from the tire and gets down completely into the dirt. He gags at the smell of gas seeped into the ground as he lays prone and peers under the Mercedes chassis. A set of worn work boots inch closer. Daniel steadies his breath and tension. "I see you." A whisper hisses between his teeth. "I got you." He aims the wheel gun and fires.

The bullet hits Hap in the shin. He screams in pain as he drops the heavy shotgun. "He shot me." His bulk collapses and quivers on the ground, right at the lip of the covered gas pumps. "He did. Oh, my Lord. Hurts. It hurts." Blood flows into the hardpack, staining it black. "God, I can feel it. My whole leg is burnin'." Hap carefully cradles his wounded leg and rolls around in the blood and grit. "Help me. Help. Me."

The trucker kicks up a dust cloud as he takes off for his Peterbilt.

Daniel stands up from behind the Mercedes. The snub-nosed pistol swings and aims at any movement around the station.

Joe Steve holds onto Tricia and uses her as a shield.

Lizzy dives back inside the station for safety. The smudged door seals tight. She peeks through the decal-covered windows.

"You dirty shit-kicker, puss-fuck. You shot me?" Hap wobbles and rolls around, moaning and clutching at his bloody shin. "Oh, it hurts. It fuckin' hurts."

Daniel tracks the pistol from person to person. His eyes wild. "You all done?" Daniel shouts out into the evening sky. "Anybody else wanna play with me?"

Headlights illuminate the faded Indian chief mural. The Peterbilt's engine turns over. It sputters and dies out. The headlights flicker on the mural as the semi-truck cranks over and starts up again.

Daniel drops the pistol down to his side. "Oh, fuck." He turns back for the Mercedes.

The Peterbilt truck engine catches. Exhaust blows from the dual silver stacks. The accelerator guns as the Lucky 13 truck lurches away from the diesel pump.

Tricia shakes free from Joe and sprints towards the Mercedes. She shouts out. "Daniel." An arm grabs her legs, and she tumbles to the hard ground. "Get back here, girly." Hap leaves a black blood trail in the dirt as he snatches her ankle. "You ain't goin' anywhere."

The Peterbilt truck trundles along and shifts gears as it starts to swing around and turns back towards the gas pumps. Exhaust belches from the dual stacks as it picks up speed. It heads straight for the Mercedes.

Daniel leaps into the car and punches the starter button. The engine doesn't turn over. He searches for the key fob. He sees Tricia struggling in the dirt. Hap claws at her as he holds onto her calf and pulls himself forward. Daniel shouts through the blown-out passenger window. "Keys. Gimme the keys."

Tricia kicks and flails and connects with his wounded leg. Hap screams out as she digs in her pocket and flings the key fob like a skipping stone across a still pond. It lands in the dirt at the base of the passenger door.

Tricia crawls for the dropped shotgun. "Stop that bitch." Joe Steve leaves the station doorway and shouts out. "She's goin' for your gun, Hap."

The Peterbilt semi-truck barrels straight for the Mercedes. Headlights illuminate the car's interior and Daniel's round saucer eyes and pale scared face. In a blind panic, Daniel mutters a pleading prayer and punches the starter button over and over. The dashboard lights suddenly pop on. The car comes to life. He drops the shifter to Drive and stomps on the gas.

The Mercedes lurches away from the pumps as the

Peterbilt misses the rear bumper by inches. The Lucky 13 truck slams into the line of gas pumps and rolls over them like they were papier-mâché. Metal crunches as the faded red aluminum awning collapses. From the remains of the exposed pumps, gas spurts into the air like a fountain. A rainbow of oily colors in the flood of slick fuel as it rains down on the dry desert hardpack.

Inside the Mercedes, a sharp chime signals over and over as a calm electronic voice utters a computerized caution. "Warning. No key detected. Warning. System error." Daniel frantically shakes the steering wheel and keeps his foot on the accelerator as the engine automatically cuts off, and the vehicle drifts to a stop.

"Get away from me." Tricia holds the shotgun on Hap and Joe Steve. "You. Stay back or I swear to God I will unload this right into your gut." Hap groans on the ground. "Ha. Little ladies," Joe spits back, "don't have the stones to pull the trigger." He inches closer. Tricia swings the barrel square on him. "I will fuck you up with this if you move one more time." Her hands shake.

The Peterbilt belches exhaust as it drives away from the station and the soft glow of lights. Gears shift on the massive Lucky 13 machine as it drives up a small hill.

Daniel stumbles out of the dead Mercedes. He watches the big truck trundle and bounce away into the dark desert. Red brake lights flash in the dark as the beast shifts and starts to turn back around. Daniel falls onto the hard ground and propels forward on his knees as he scrambles in a blind search for the lost key fob. Half of the awning turned into a pile of metal debris as a rain of slick fuel continues to fountain and fall from the sky. The florescent lights that still work flicker and strobe.

Daniel slips and slides in the wet mud and gasoline

mix as the oily rain soaks into his matted hair and drips and streaks down his dirty skin. In his frenzied fear, he looks like the Indian chief mural, covered in oily black war paint.

"Don't you move." Daniel glances over at the sound of her voice. He sees Tricia hold a man in cooking whites at bay with a shotgun clutched in her hands. The heavy man he shot in the shin cowers on the ground. He can hear the anxiety and alarm in her shaky voice. "Tricia." Her name mumbles from his lips. A weak and weary Daniel starts for her when he stops. There on the ground, drops of fuel fall along the small silver Mercedes logo. It shines under the strobe lights and looks like an alien relic stuck in the wet desert earth. With a white toothy smile through his muddy and oil-streaked face, Daniel scoops up the missing key fob. "Tricia," he shouts out into the night sky. "Time to go."

She turns towards the voice. Joe Steve picks his moment and grabs ahold of the steel shotgun barrel. "Gimme that, woman." He tugs and tries to wrestle it away from her. Tricia pulls the trigger. An explosive kick as the weapon fires blind into the earth. The shotgun is ripped from her loose grasp. The steel barrel scalds and burns the flesh off of Joe's hand. He drops to the ground with a howl of pain and a broken wrist, the pearly white bone exposed through his hairy flesh.

Tricia shakes her sore hands and seizes the moment as she slips and stumbles for the Mercedes.

The Lucky 13 semi banks hard and steers into a straightaway. It grinds and growls in the dark as it picks up speed. Headlights shine sharp in the dark and illuminate the Mercedes.

Tricia clamors for the car and pops open the door.

She dives into the passenger seat.

Daniel sits behind the wheel. The dashboard all lit up, the glow shows his face and clothes covered in oil and mud. "Go!" Tricia shouts out in a panic. Daniel doesn't react. The car idles in place and stays put.

The Lucky 13 semi shifts into a higher gear and picks up speed. It barrels for the still Mercedes.

"What the hell are you doing?" Her voice is shrill and frantic. "You do know—" Daniel holds her open purse in his dirty lap. His voice is crisp and calm. "—You got us into this mess." He turns to look at the headlights through the blown-out driver's window. The roar from the truck grows deafening, and the headlights get brighter with every passing second. Tricia wallows in fright. "Well." Daniel waits. "Don't you have anything to say?"

The semi crushes the downed awning like a beer can and rolls through the gasoline fountain. Wipers whisk away the gasoline from the large windshield. The headlights brighten the Mercedes interior. The truck roars, the steel grill yards away from the Mercedes cabin.

"Daniel." In shock, Tricia pleads. "Please." He shakes his head in the driver's seat. "That's good enough." Daniel holds up her heavy elegant cigarette lighter. He strikes it aflame. The long flame flickers in the light of his wild eyes.

He tosses it out the shattered driver's window and punches the gas. The Mercedes fishtails in the mud. The lighter drops to the ground and lands in a puddle of liquid. It ignites a small ball of flame and explodes.

A huge fireball engulfs the raging Lucky 13 semi-truck. The gas pump fountains erupt and turn into glowing torches of fire and fury.

The round windows of the gas station shatter and implode. Anything not nailed down is blown to pieces. Hunks of metal and fiery debris rain down on the gas station remnants. Under a wall of flame, the Indian chief mural bubbles and melts off the brick in colorful streams.

Concussion explosions erupt and hit as the underground fuel tanks catch and burst through the desert hardpack in hellacious fire and crash back down to the desert in balls of twisted metal.

The Lucky 13 semi-truck rolls along. Rows of tires glow on fire, they leave a trail of melted rubber behind them. Flames flicker all along the steel grill and undercarriage. The detailed design and Lucky 13 paint on the driver's door melts off the fuselage.

The truck continues to bounce and roll along, until it finally comes to a halt. The scarred and burnt machine detonates in another explosion of fury and melted metal.

The bashed and beaten Mercedes limps away from the carnage and devastation. It leaves the oasis truck stop behind in a sea of fire.

Chapter Twenty-Six

The Airbus EC 120 light patrol helicopter flies about a mile above the desert. The main rotor and tail rotor hum a quiet whisper in the night sky. Stars twinkle above. Moonlight shines on the shadowed hills and scrub far below. The black and white colors cover the fuselage, augmented by a stark image of a wild eagle with razor sharp talons swooping down to capture its prey. The registration number, N573AJ, stenciled along the tail. Towards the front of the aircraft, a black and white logo: San Antonio Police – Protecting the Alamo City.

Two officers from the SAPD's E.A.G.L.E. unit sits in the cockpit. Decked out in black reflector helmets and flight suits decorated with identifying patches, Officer Sal "Skip" Moreno is at the control stick and his co-pilot, Officer Betty "Boop" Reyes in the seat next to him. Reyes monitors the various cameras that dot the aircraft. She switches over to the thermal camera and keys her microphone. "Detective Navarro, you may want to take a look at this."

"How do you work this damn thing?" Navarro sits in the back of the helicopter, the visor up on her flight helmet. "The hell?" She takes a second to remember how to use the microphone. "Test, test. I'm good, I'm on. What do you got?"

"Right here." Reyes motions to her main screen. "We're showing a pretty large spike on the thermal imaging camera."

Navarro scoots up in her seat and checks out the multi-colored screen. "Okay." She can't make heads or tails of it. "Which one of these blobs am I supposed to be looking at?"

Reyes chuckles over the microphone. "These pixels here are picking up pockets of desert heat. But this sliver here. Is something else." A small line of orange and red is sharper than other yellow blobs on the screen.

Navarro fiddles with her mic. "What is it?"

"I'd say." Reyes flips through some screens. "There's a pretty big wildfire out there. Maybe seven to ten miles, southeast."

Navarro can't make out anything on the thermal screen. "The cameras on this bird can see that far away?"

"Oh yeah." Skip Moreno speaks up from behind the stick. "You don't wanna know how sensitive some of these peepers are."

Navarro looks out the window at desert darkness in every direction. She returns to the microphone. "Could it be a brush fire?"

"Maybe." Reyes turns in her seat. "But this baby came on real hot and heavy. One minute there's nothing out there. Now, it's showing me an inferno." She switches through images trying to capture more detail.

Skip Moreno keys his microphone. "What do you want to do, Detective? It's your ride."

Navarro studies the thermal camera. "How close is it to the coordinates of the Plateau truck stop?"

"Gimme a sec." Reyes checks and doublechecks. "Wow. Dead center. Right on top of it."

"Goddamn it. Morrison." Navarro mumbles under her breath but it's picked up and echoes through the cabin. Skip smiles under his visor. "You really think this is your man?"

"Nothing surprises me today." Navarro touches the thermal camera screen. "Let's go check it out."

"Roger that." Skip shifts a lever and lifts up on the collective. The light helicopter banks downwards and picks up speed, on a southwest course heading.

Reyes checks the clock. "ETA. Ten minutes."

"Hey, Detective." Skip's voice is chipper over the microphone. "Can you still trade him in for the cash if your guy's burnt to a crisp?"

Navarro starts to speak but doesn't answer him. She lowers her mic and sits back in her seat. The rotors whisper high in the night sky.

****

The collection of truck stop buildings burns fierce, the decimated gas pumps and awnings turned to twisted metal and black ash. The husk of the Lucky 13 semi-truck smolders to cinders, leaving a burnt-out shell.

High desert winds blow all throughout the mangled debris and destroyed grounds. Tumbleweeds and twisted brush around the rubble of the gas station spark with glowing red embers and go up in flames.

Fire climbs the two worn wooden beams of the towering road sign for the Plateau Truck and Auto Center. The support structure weakens and breaks with a snap. The large sign teeters and crashes to the bubbling asphalt with a shower of sparks as fresh fire claims it.

A spotlight shines on the fallen sign.

High winds increase to a roar from spinning rotors as a black helicopter descends and circles overhead. Flames kick and sputter out under the steady wash from the rotors. The shiny spotlight scans and drifts across scattered metal and debris.

From one of the burning buildings, another concussion explosion from the remains of the truck stop diner ignites and belches a ball of flame high into the night sky.

The black Bell 222 helicopter descends and circles the destroyed truck stop like a sleek shark moving through the water.

A figure stumbles through the wreckage and plods across the barren hellscape. Two arms frantically wave into the sky. The harsh spotlight drifts and settles over the figure. Lizzy squints under the intense light as her hair blows in a wild mane. Her waitress outfit is covered in blackened soot and ash. She desperately signals the sleek bird as it circles and descends.

Under the waves of air from the thundering dual rotors, dust devils spin across the coarse sand and scarred hardpack. Small brush fires are extinguished. Lizzy jumps up and down as she gestures to the aircraft.

The Bell helicopter drifts and settles on a patch of asphalt road close to the fallen truck stop sign.

"Oh, thank God. Thank the Lord." Lizzy staggers towards it with a grateful sense of euphoria shining through her dirty face. "You came for us. They're all dead. My God, they're all gone." She shields her face from the blowing grit and staggers towards the sleek hull.

The hatch of the copter opens. John Smith ducks under the spinning rotors and moves for Lizzy. An imposing figure in his stylish tailored suit and black tactical helmet. She tries to embrace him. John holds her back. He raises his visor and shouts above the noise. "Where is Daniel Morrison?"

"They're all gone." Lizzy babbles in a panic. "I'm

the only one left. I was in the diner when it happened. The whole building shook." Tears streak down her dirty face. "I thought it was an earthquake for sure and I was gonna be buried alive inside there. I can't believe I made it. I'm alive." Eyes as big as saucers as she sobs. "You came for me. You did. You're with the police. Please take me out of here."

John doesn't respond. "Please." She pleads with him. "I'm beggin' you. Help me. Take me to the hospital. In Eagle Pass. You have to get me to Eagle Pass."

John grabs her by the shoulders. "Where is Daniel Morrison?" He shakes her to keep and hold her attention.

"Gone." She swallows and reins in her panic. "Him and that woman. They both left here." She motions to the destruction all around her. "Caused all this. And drove off. Like Bonnie and Clyde. They went and blew up the whole damn place. And poof. On their merry way."

"Which way?" John keeps a hold of her. "Tell me. Which way did they go?"

"Hap. He's…he's dead. Joe Steve. I saw him. He was here, but I can't find him no more." She looks all around and cries. "I watched Hap burn up on the ground, right over there. He stopped screaming, but his body kept burning. Melting. I didn't never see what happened to Lucky. He was driving his semi and I—"

He cuts off her stream of thought with a squeeze and hard shove. John looks over the utter decimation of the station and talks to himself. "He destroys. And runs away. Exactly like this morning. The man sure has one hell of a tell. Doesn't he?" Lizzy shivers in the night, still in shock. Her big eyes never blink and never leave John. He finally turns away and starts back for the helicopter. "He'll be across the border in no time."

"Wait. You can't leave me here. You've gotta take me with you." Lizzy latches onto him. "The hospital. Please. Help me."

"I'll help you." John takes her by the hand and keeps her close. "As soon as you help me. You said, he left here with a woman. What were they driving?" He shakes her to keep her attention. "Tell me. Your Bonnie and Clyde. What did they leave in?"

"I don't know." She cradles against his large chest and shivers. "I can't remember. You. You can do it. Fly me on out of here. Take me away. Please."

John peels her away in disgust and trips her loose legs. She stumbles and lands hard onto the ground with a thud. "Don't leave me here." Lizzy sobs and claws in the dirt. "I didn't do anything wrong." She curls up in a fetal position. "This wasn't my fault. None of it was." She shouts at John. "Help me. Please."

Through the billows of smoke, colorful shadows dance off in the horizon. "Can you see? The lights. In the distance. They're coming." John reaches into his jacket. "You should go." He pulls out a 9mm pistol from a shoulder holster. "Be with your friends." He aims and fires twice into Lizzy.

Surprise edges into her stricken face as she jerks on the ground from the impact of the two shots. The life leaves her wide eyes and bleeds into the ground. "I'm sorry." John turns her over with his boot and fires once more into her chest, to make sure. "But I was never here." John turns his back on her and the burning destruction all around. He walks across sticky asphalt and climbs back into the luxury aircraft. A last look before he secures the hatch closed.

A slow whine from the rotors increases as it lifts off

and climbs high into the sky. The sleek chopper circles the devastation. Through the thick smoke and haze, a rainbow of colorful lights flickers and glows from a fleet of rescue vehicles that head down the roadway and close in on the burning carnage. The helicopter lifts high into the night and moves away from the fires.

****

Down the black and quiet road, a single headlight shines through the dark. The beat-up and bullet-ridden Mercedes keeps a steady pace as it bounces down the rutted causeway. Daniel is at the wheel, Tricia in the passenger seat. Winds blow through the shattered windows. The high-pitched whistle of the winds is the only sound between them.

"Say something." Tricia can't take it anymore. "Say anything." Wind whips through their hair as the tires drone on the endless straightaway.

"Well." Daniel's voice is flat and distant. "I guess I could ask you why. But it would be a waste of time."

Tricia's hands leap up and clench the dash. "Stop the car." Daniel glances over but doesn't slow down. "Pull over." She swallows and grimaces. "I'm gonna be sick."

Daniel takes a second to decide and finally takes his foot off the gas. The vehicle drifts to the side of the asphalt road and comes to a complete stop. The passenger door springs open. Tricia stumbles a few steps and drops to her knees in the cracked dirt. She dry heaves. Spits. Her breathing hitches. She gags and retches as she dry heaves again.

The driver's door opens and closes. "Hey." Scuffed and shredded dress shoes crunch through the gravel, to the edge of the asphalt pavement. "Are you okay?"

"I did…" Tricia pants on the ground, her stomach in

her throat. "I did the right thing. I thought with people around, in public—" She retches again but only coughs and spits up a string of bile. Her dirty sleeve wipes at her pale mouth. "—we'd be fine in a public place. It was the right place to turn ourselves in." She spits in the dirt and pants on her knees.

Daniel leans back against the car. "I'm glad you made that decision for the both of us."

She snaps back at him. "I want to go home." Her sleeve wipes at her mouth again and she rises off the ground. With a bit of a wobble, she manages to stand on shaky legs. "Is that okay with you? Huh?" One foot in front of her; she stumbles away from Daniel.

He keeps watching her. "You feel better now?"

She turns and loses her balance. Daniel reacts to help her. Tricia shoves his hands away. "Get away from me." He lets her go. She stands in the dark and swings a hard fist at him. "What the fuck is wrong with you?" She throws wild punches. "Go on. Scream at me. Shove a gun in my side. But don't stand there with that stupid look on your face and ask me if I feel better." He half-heartedly dodges her blows and doesn't respond to her. Frustrated and exhausted, she stops hitting him and turns away. "For your information. I don't—" She swallows back bile. "—feel better."

Daniel stares off into the darkness down the empty road. "We can't go much farther."

"You can." Tricia stares down the faded yellow line. "Drop me off before the border, and you keep moving."

He picks up a small rock off the tar surface. "Nope." The quartz rolls around in his palm. "No can do." He tosses the rock into the desert dark. "The warning light came on a few miles back. I guess I managed to get gasoline everywhere else except into the fuel tank." He laughs to himself as he opens up the passenger door and reaches inside. "We'll never make it to the border." Daniel closes the passenger door and walks back towards her. "And I'm so tired of running." His shoes click across the asphalt. "I don't remember anything else." He holds out the Mercedes key fob. "You take the car. Head back to what's left of the station. Police will be there by now."

Tricia stares at the key fob. Streaks of mud dried on the silver emblem.

"Go on." Daniel puts it in her hand. "Take it."

She does and holds the black and silver key in the palm of her dirty hand. "You're saying…" He turns away from her; she talks to his back. "You want me to leave you out here?"

"Uh huh. I can't go home." Daniel takes a few steps on the road and talks to the sky. "No matter how much I try to kid myself. That life is over. And I'm really tired of going forward. So, I figure maybe I'll stay around out here." He stares up at the big sky filled with pinpoints of stars. "Give this place a chance. Besides, you can't beat the view."

"You can't be serious." She walks down the road and stands at his side. "You're crazy."

Daniel faces her in the middle of the road. "Figured that out all by yourself, huh?" He turns away from her. "Good for you."

"Hey." She latches onto his arm. "I'm not leaving you again." She doesn't let go. "Both of us. We can go back to what's left of that gas station. There'll be police. Fire. Rescue. For us. And I'll tell them everything. Tell them exactly what happened."

"No." He slides his hand onto hers, caressing her

fingers. And carefully removes her hand from his bicep. "I've been a dead man all day. I should have died in that accident. In fact. I think most of me did." Daniel keeps a hold of her hand. "But I'm down to fumes. And it's over. I really am sorry that I dragged you through all this. But I'm glad you were here." He lets go of her hand. "Now, go away."

Daniel starts to walk away from her and turns on the blacktop. She calls out to him. "What are you doing?" He doesn't respond as he steps off the tar pavement and starts to head into the desert. "Daniel." Her tired voice can't mask her surprise. She shouts after him, "Come back." He doesn't. She chases after him. "You're not running away from me."

A cluster of prickly pear cacti grow wild. Daniel heads through a spread of wild Mexican poppies. He can hear her stumbling after him in the dark. Daniel turns around. She stops.

"Tricia." They stare at each other under the moonlight. "Go back home and have a normal life. A good one. Mine is all finished." He walks away from her.

"Daniel," she calls out to him. "Stop this now. You're scaring me." He keeps moving into the desert until he fades in the shadows of dark night. She shouts out. "I'll go back and get help. You need help. Daniel." There's no response. She waits in the pitch black and decides. A strong stride back through the poppies and onto the asphalt road. Tricia listens in the stillness of the night and cuts off the quiet when she opens the driver's door. She climbs in and starts up the car.

The dashboard lights shine on her pale face. The gas warning light is down to one digital sliver. She hollers out the shattered window. "Daniel?" Nothing. Desert quiet. She shifts into reverse. Tires crack and pop gravel as the car backs up on the road. Tricia steers and hits the gas. The Mercedes heads back down the roadway. One single headlight beam shines through the dense darkness.

Daniel avoids a wall of yucca bushes and clusters of cactus bloom until he stops walking through the desert. He can hear the car's engine recede into the night. A hand moves to his belt. And he brings out the snub-nose revolver. The silver shines in the moonlight. He feels the weight in his hands and clicks open the chamber. His thumb spins the wheel. "Two rounds left." He mumbles to himself. "That's good."

He snaps the chamber closed and starts walking with the revolver down at his side. His voice cracks in the dark. "Just in case I miss the first time."

Chapter Twenty-Seven

A metal roof on the shell of the main building collapses into itself. A shower of burning sparks drift into the starry sky.

An Eagle Pass fire truck is stopped at the edge of the station remnants. Organized chaos all around as sets of canvas hoses are off-loaded and spread out. Busy firemen work the scene. Small groups control pockets of dwindling fire and try to keep the bigger blazes contained.

Parked all along the asphalt roadway, colorful lights flash from four Eagle Pass police sedans and a pair of light fire rescue trucks with markings from nearby Cardona Station.

A loud squawk from the sirens as another ambulance arrives from Maverick County. A police officer flags it to a halt and directs it towards the burnt out Lucky 13 semi-truck.

In the evening sky, the Airbus helicopter hovers high over the destruction. It circles and starts its descent. Wheels touch down on the asphalt roadway, a bit away from the demolished ruins. The side door slides open. Detective Navarro hops out of the bird, glad to have her feet back on firm ground. She hustles under the steady wash from the spinning rotors until she's in the clear. She turns around with a thumbs-up as she shields her face from the cyclone of flying grit and sand.

The SAPD helicopter lifts back off the blacktop and rises up into the sky. Navarro watches the lights on the fuselage twinkle away in the dark.

She heads past the downed truck stop sign and motions to the first police uniform she encounters. "Officer." She pulls out her gold shield and laminated ID. "Detective Roya Navarro. San Antonio police. I need to speak with your ground commander immediately."

"What?" The wide-eyed uniform stares back. "It ain't you?"

She puts her badge away. "Who is the senior officer in charge out here?"

Shouts and alarm from a fire brigade as another roof caves in on a burnt-out adobe building. A shower of fiery sparks flicker and waft into the night sky. He hollers over the ruckus. "Yeah, I'll be happy to tell you when I know something." The skittish uniform officer shakes his head. "I got here minutes ago myself." He leaves Navarro standing alone on the scarred hardpack.

She walks through the hyperactive area and chooses to head on over towards a small group of fireman and paramedics huddled near the largest uncontrolled blaze. "Excuse me." She flashes her gold shield. "I'm looking for whoever is in charge of this operation."

A stern voice in the group speaks up. "Rank and file might be a bit difficult to figure out right now." A man in thick glasses under his fire helmet speaks up. "I'm Lieutenant Steve Freeman. Cardona Station. As you can see, we've got our hands full out here."

She takes in the devastation all around. "I'm with San Antonio PD. I came down here with the Eagle air unit. They're on the way to Maverick County Lake to get a 'copter bucket rigged up and get you all some water.

See if we can help put out these fires for you."

"That's most appreciated." The lieutenant steps away from the huddle. "We'll use whatever help we can get with this mess." He shakes her hand. "You came all the way here from San Antonio? Why? I'd say, we're a bit out of your jurisdiction."

She agrees with him. "I'm on the hunt. You go where it goes. This man I'm after, we're certain he came right through here."

Another structure collapses in a fury of fire. Hoses spray and target the flames that curl and lick into the sky.

"Sorry to say. There's no more here, right here. This place is torched. Hope the owners have plenty of insurance." The fire lieutenant steps away and shouts out. "Josh. Pull your team back. Make a line. I want a defensive line. Come on, let's go. We've gotta contain this angry bitch." He motions to another fireman.

"Lieutenant." Navarro waits to regain his attention. "This person I'm looking for. As far as I know, he may still be out here."

"Well, as of now—" The lieutenant shakes his head. "—bodies are all we've got. It's three and counting. There are no survivors." He looks over various sweaty faces. "Wilcox." And motions over a young paramedic. "Assist the detective here, will ya'?"

"Roger that, L.T." Andrew Wilcox steps over in his white shirt with an emergency medical services patch on his chest. The fire lieutenant falls into a conversation with another fireman as they work out his growing defensive perimeter.

Navarro shakes hands with the fresh-faced paramedic. "What can I do you for, ma'am?"

"I'm looking for someone." She thinks about what

she should say. "Male. Middle-aged. Not a local. Dressed for the city."

"Okay." Andrew follows along. "But I gotta warn you. By the time we arrived on the scene, there wasn't much we could do." He walks away from the firemen cluster. "Come on, I'll show you what we've got."

He guides Navarro across the barren and burnt landscape. They step around flattened metal debris that used to be a row of gas pumps. "These two. I'm sorry to say, it's gonna take forensics out of El Paso to get us a positive I.D." A pair of canvas tarps stand out, staked on the ground. "At best, we're looking at weeks spent combing for matches through available medical and dental records. Both of these bodies were burnt-up bad."

They turn away from the staked tarps and step closer to the warped asphalt roadway. "And this one here." A slick body bag at the edge of the road. "Is a woman. But she didn't die in the fire." He crouches next to the body bag and unzips it. A tuft of blonde hair and a dirty waitress uniform peeks through as its opened. The woman's dead pale face stuck in a rigor of surprise, stares up at the sky. "Multiple gunshots. She bled out on the ground."

"Hey. We've got one," a fireman calls out from a pile of collapsed metal awning debris and destroyed diesel pumps. "He's alive."

Paramedics race over towards a section of collapsed awning. Firemen gather around. "Lift on three. One, two, three." Fire and rescue personnel heave and move a heavy section of metal awning off of Joe Steve.

He's covered in blood and dirt, his ragged cook whites saturated in grime and gas. His right arm was mangled. Seeping cuts and gashes all across his shredded skin and exposed bone. Deep in shock, his wild eyes glassy as they dart around. He tries to sit up and reaches for the sky as paramedics attend to him. One calls out. "Bring the board over here. I want a spinal collar attached. Let's get him on oxygen." An oxygen mask is slipped over Joe Steve's mouth. He tries to claw it off with crooked dirty fingers. The trauma team work to keep his good arm down and they hustle him on the board, over towards the ambulance.

Strobe lights flash as the back of the ambulance is opened and the trauma team work to load him inside. "Stretcher's out. Secure the safety latch." Three paramedics line up on either side of the stretcher. "Let's bring the board on. Okay. I've got the patient. All ready. Roll and slide the board out on the count of three. Here we go. One, two, three." The paramedics transfer Joe Steve securely onto the stretcher. One crouches down to undo the safety latch. The stretcher collapses and the trauma team load it into the back of the ambulance.

"Here." Navarro stops Wilcox before he climbs on board. "Take my card. Call me if he says anything on the way to the hospital."

"Sure." Wilcox looks at the card. "But says anything about what?"

"The man I'm here looking for." Navarro is running out of time. "Daniel Morrison."

"That's who did this, the hit and run guy from the news?" Wilcox cracks a crooked grin. "He's a persistent little fucker, isn't he?" He takes the card and climbs into the rear of the ambulance. "I'll let you know, ma'am." The rear doors close. Red and white lights strobe on and a warbly siren kicks in as the ambulance drives away fast, down the rural roadway.

Navarro walks over towards the cluster of Eagle Pass police sedans. "I need to commandeer a vehicle. And a driver." She shows her shield to a group of uniform officers.

"Gold badge. That's Criminal Investigations, huh. Sweet." A Hispanic woman speaks up. "So where do you want to go?"

"Thank you." She zeroes in on the uniform who asked the question. "It's about twenty miles to the border. Right?"

"Accurately—" The woman shrugs. "—it's more like, seventeen."

"Good." A slight smile breaks through her official police-business facade. "That's where I want to go. Can you help me?"

"Sure. My pleasure." The uniform officer gestures towards the passenger side of a police car. "Corporal Luisa Cruz, at your service."

Navarro introduces herself as they get inside the squad car.

****

The sound of a car engine grows in the still of the desert night. One headlight shines through the dense black. The Mercedes flies down the roadway.

Dashboard lights glow pale green in the cabin. Tricia can't take her eyes off of the low-gas warning light and the single digital sliver left on the gauge. "Come on, baby. We got this." She mumbles to herself. "Get us back there. Come on. You can do it." The single sliver vanishes from the gauge. She grips the steering wheel and keeps her foot on the gas.

The Mercedes starts to sputter on the roadway. A whine as the vehicle sucks up the last drops of available fuel. It hitches and shudders along.

"No, no, no." She keeps her foot to the floor, but the car doesn't respond. The mechanical sounds from under the hood of the German machine sputters and stops as the Mercedes engine cuts off. The car drifts forward on its own momentum.

An array of red lights pop up on the dash. She stomps her foot on the accelerator but gets no response. "No." Tricia slams her fists against the padded steering wheel. "Move, move. Come on you piece of shit. Go."

It doesn't. The Mercedes continues to glide forward. Tires crunch through loose asphalt gravel until the car rolls to a complete stop in the middle of the roadway.

"Don't do this. Not now." Tricia punches the starter button over and over like she's impatiently waiting for an elevator that isn't coming. "Please. Come on. Work for me. Please." The starter motor clicks and whines, but the engine doesn't fire or turn over.

Her balled-up fists pound the dashboard in frustration, until she finally sits still in the eerie evening quiet. The heat and humidity of the night creeps in without the constant blast from the air conditioning. In the quiet, Tricia stares out the windshield at the endless field of stars in the forever sky. Her teeth grit and grind. Her anger levels slowly deplete, until she releases her vise grip on the steering wheel and clicks opens the driver's door.

Tricia slams the driver's door behind her and stands in the center of the road. "Flip a coin. 50/50. One or the other." The faded yellow line seems to extend forever in either direction. "Make up your mind."

She starts to walk, moving away from the dead Mercedes and continuing her journey forward without looking behind her. Insects buzz all around her sweaty forehead. She swats them away but keeps her eyes down on the road and plods forward.

The darkness settles in. An oppressive humidity soaks through her dirty clothes and covers her clammy skin. A light desert breeze is strangled by the damp night air, thick and wet. Her eyes stay glued to the ground as she keeps walking. "Daniel." His name mutters through her chapped lips. "Hold on. I'll get help." She continues to stride forward. Step after step. "Hold on."

She snaps aware in the dark and perks up like a small animal sensing danger nearby. "What is that?" A low rumble grows in the distance. It sounds mechanical. She stumbles forward down the blacktop. A shiver settles at the base of her neck. Her breath caught in her throat.

A glimmer of light on the horizon. It grows into a beam. She can't take her eyes away from the line of light as it expands, brighter and brighter. "Help me." She's not aware of the words leaving her lips as she plods towards the shimmering light. "Here. Please. I'm right here."

The mechanical rumble increases as the light shines even sharper. Headlights appear up ahead. Tricia frantically waves her hands and arms in the air. "Oh, thank God." She jumps up and down in the center of the road. "Over here. Stop, please. Help me." The headlight beam grows even brighter. The mechanical sound increases. It doesn't sound like an automobile. The harsh light shines on Tricia. And it rises into the sky. A wash of dirt and sand blows all around.

Rotors thunder as the mechanical thumping sound of a helicopter roars overhead, barely skimming the asphalt roadway. The harsh spotlight drifts along the desert floor and locks back in on Tricia as she shields herself from cyclone waves generated from the spinning rotors.

The sleek black shark circles her overhead and the engine decreases as it flies and jockeys over the roadway. Tricia stands in shock on the faded yellow line as this giant mechanical insect descends from the starry sky and settles to a stop on the asphalt blacktop.

As the rotors decrease, the main hatch opens. John Smith climbs out of the copter and saunters towards her. He looks like he's on a casual cocktail circuit and not in the middle of a barren roadway in the dark dead of night.

Tricia doesn't blink as this large imposing figure steps up to her and opens the visor on a black helmet. "Car trouble?" She finally stammers out a response. John cuts her off. "I'm guessing you must be Bonnie. But I'm looking for Clyde." John glances around in the dark. "Where is he?"

Chapter Twenty-Eight

A nighttime chill creeps into the evening air as the temperature recedes even further away from the consistent and oppressive heat of the day. The crescent moon shines down on the desert. Shadows fall over cactus clusters and prickly pear bushes.

Daniel slowly and carefully makes his way up a steep embankment. The brittle dried earth cracks, sifts and gives way under his feet as he slips back down a bit. Long fingers clutch and claw at the dried ground until he digs in and gets secure footing. A layer of clammy sweat grows along the back of his neck and drips down his forehead as he pushes forward and continues his way up the side of the slope.

He collapses to the cracked ground and catches his breath. Even in the dim light of the moon, he can make out the rough outline of the endless expanse of desert vista all around him. The croak from his deflated voice breaks through the quiet. "It's gotta be back there."

Daniel peers down the steep hill he climbed and tries to retrace his staggering steps. He searches for the paved rural road but can't spot it in the long shadows of darkness. He collapses down and stays on the dense hardpack. He reaches into his pants pocket and pulls out the snub-nosed wheel gun.

Dirty fingers caress and slide across the slick steel as he feels the weight and studies every inch of the gun in his lap. "What do you think?" His flattened voice is the only sound in the dense dark. "Looks pretty good." He thinks about it as seconds tick away until he finally agrees with himself. "I like it. I mean, look at that view. Even in the dark. What's not to like?"

Nothing answers him. He looks down at the dried earth. "Well, I guess it's as good of a place as any." He digs out a pointy rock that pushes against his thigh and flings it back down the hill. It tumbles away in the dark. "Hey, Jude." His soft and tender voice reaches out to his wife who isn't there. "You always liked it when I called you that. Jude. Except for when we were fighting, I'd call you Judy. You pointed that out to me once." He searches for the memory. "For the life of me, I can't remember when. But I do remember that."

His hand clenches the revolver tight. "I know you can't hear me. But I wanted to say it anyway." Emotions well up as his weary voice cracks and breaks. "I'm sorry. I'm so sorry I put you through all of this. I'm sorry I ran away from our marriage." Tears streak and stream down his grimy face. He stares up at the sliver of moon. "You were right, Jude. I couldn't do it. I couldn't fix us. Only we could fix us. Together."

He picks up the revolver from his lap and squeezes the rubber hand grip. "I wish I would have told you that. You always said we needed to communicate better. You were right. I could'a been honest with you and told you how I really felt."

He cocks the revolver; the chamber advances as the mechanical clicks snap through the dark. "I'm so tired of running. From everything in my life. And I can't go any further." His hand starts to shake as he places the cold steel barrel under his chin and gasps out. "I love you."

He closes his wet eyes tight, his jaw clamped shut. "Good-bye." The word mutters through his chapped lips.

His shaky hands shimmer steady. He holds the silver barrel firm under his chin. He sucks in his last breath and holds it. His finger molds around the cocked trigger. He sits still in the dirt, his body ravaged tight with tension.

A sharp exhale of breath and he flings the gun to the side. It lands on the ground next to a spiny cactus bush.

Daniel weeps, his tired face collapsed in his dirty hands. He blubbers and sobs, sitting alone on the edge of the steep desert slope.

****

Red and blue bubble lights strobe on the Eagle Pass police interceptor as it races down the rural road. It cruises through the night and stays at a consistent speed as crisp headlight beams slice through stagnant dark.

"It's not a bad assignment, you know." Officer Luisa Cruz at the wheel. Her voice fills the cabin. "Working with the Auto Theft and Interdiction unit. For the past three years. Wow. But I mean if they're calling us in. They must be calling in everybody. It's like a... What-d'you call it? All-hands-on-deck. Yeah."

Detective Navarro listens quiet as Luisa drones on. Her tired eyes glued out the windshield as she scans into the desert dark.

"I mean, don't get me wrong. A nice evening out. What's wrong with that? Getting to take a long drive through the countryside. It's a welcome change of pace. At best, my day to day is usually neck-deep with vehicle burglary investigations. Stuck putting the squeeze on crooked car dealerships or underground body shops. Truth is, I've probably combed through every single salvage yard from Fort Bliss to Horizon City. And that goes for junk yards too."

Navarro's wide eyes blink to stay awake. They keep drifting back lidded shut by the endless series of nothing flowing outside the windshield. She reaches for coffee that isn't there and lowers the passenger window a bit to get some fresh air.

"I'm sorry, Detective. Am I talking too much?"

"Oh, no." Navarro shakes her head. "Not at all. I'm,…I can't really…it's hard to explain. Let's say it's been a long day."

"Yeah." Luisa agrees with a smile. "I'll bet."

They drive down the straightaway in silence. Luisa lowers her driver's window down a bit to even out the pressure inside the sedan. The wind whips through the cracks. Hands grip the steering wheel and keep it steady down the straight away. "So." Luisa clears her throat and speaks up. "What exactly are we looking for out here?"

"Well." Navarro sighs and rubs at her temples. "I'll admit, it's starting to feel like a ghost."

"Really? A ghost." A high-pitched whistle of cool night air blows through the cracks in the windows. "Seriously?" Luisa glances over. "I mean. I saw one once, you know. When I was a little girl. I think I was six. I don't know, Maybe seven? Anyway, I do remember this. It was around two in the morning. I got up to pee, and all of a sudden, I see my lovely *abuelita*. She was right there, walking on down the hall. Which wouldn't have surprised me all that much, you know. But she had been dead and buried for more than a month." Her left hand leaves the steering wheel and makes the sign of the cross across her chest. "*Descansa en paz, Abuela*. So. You're telling me. We're out here in the desert dark. Driving around. Looking for a ghost?"

Navarro's about to answer when her eyes widen in surprise. "Watch out."

Rapidly approaching in the headlights, a car sits abandoned in the middle of the road.

On instinct, Navarro reaches and jerks the steering wheel. The police cruiser veers to the right of the rural road and misses the dead car's bumper by inches. A shudder and squeal as it burns and barrels off the asphalt. Tires kick up a funnel of earth as the car skids and planes across the loose ground and tears through pockets of dense brush. The interceptor teeters and barely avoids flipping over as it rocks on sturdy shock absorbers and settles to a halt. Twin headlights shine against a cluster of wild sage and yucca. A shroud of dust dances in the light of the beams.

The passenger car door bounces open. Navarro stumbles from the sedan. She takes a few seconds to get her wits about her. A sharp creak as the driver's door pushes open. Navarro looks around in the dark and calls over her shoulder. "Are you okay?"

In the adrenaline rush, Luisa doesn't answer the question. "What the fuck was that?"

Navarro steps away from the wild sage bushes and heads back onto the road. She closes in on the Mercedes. Even covered in mud and grime, she can make out the purple vanity plate. "Ability."

"Oh. my God in heaven. Was that ever close." Luisa checks over her police cruiser. "We're damn lucky we didn't roll her over." She carefully walks around a thorny cactus briar bush and pulls out loose weeds stuck along the grill and front bumper.

A guttural whine and moan of a distant coyote calls out somewhere in the darkness. Luisa perks up at the sounds of the animal howl. She undoes the safety strap on her holster and holds the butt of her Glock pistol. She decides to catch up with Navarro on the road.

Roya peeks through the blown-out windows and runs a finger across the jagged array of bullet holes all along the side of the car. She opens the driver's door. The cabin is empty. A glance in the back seat to make sure. She leans inside and checks out the interior. An empty Yeti thermos was left in the cup-holder. She touches the car key fob and rubs off some dirt left on the Mercedes logo. She spots and reaches for the small Gucci purse resting on the back floorboards.

"This poor machine's been beat to hell." Luisa walks around the vehicle. "I don't get it. What kinda fool leaves their car in the middle of the road like this?"

Navarro holds out the small designer purse to the officer. "The kind I'm looking for." She walks around to the front of the car.

"Hey, I've got me one of these. Twenty bucks down at the *mercado*." Luisa looks over the purse. "Holy shit. This one isn't from China. It's the real deal." She fiddles with the ornate clasp. "Wow. I've gotta be holding about two, maybe three month's salary right here in my hands."

Navarro touches the hood of the car. "Engine's still warm. They're not far."

"Think they went for an evening stroll out into the desert?" Luisa flips through the purse contents and finds a fancy metal sleeve holding credit and store cards among the cigarettes, random receipts and tissue packets. She pulls out a Texas driver's license. "Is this your ghost? Tricia Kelley, from San Antonio."

"Yep." Navarro nods back. "She's one of 'em."

"Vanished without a trace." Luisa looks up and

down the empty road. "So, the blonde *fresa* leaves her car. Keys. Hell, even her gosh-dang, cash-dripping bag from the house of Gucci. Could be, she was abducted?" Lusia closes the purse. "I mean, you're out here busting ghosts. Maybe you should be searching for aliens? And I'm not talking about the illegal kind."

The Mercedes engine cranks over but doesn't catch. One headlight flutters and flickers to life. It shines on the worn asphalt. She holds the key fob and hits the starter button again. A whine from the engine but the car doesn't turn over. Navarro sits in the driver's seat and peers out through the blown-out window. "Out of gas?"

"Uh huh. Battery's good. The engine's trying, but there's no fuel for the fire." Lucia drapes the Gucci purse over her shoulder. "And we didn't pass anybody walking on by with a gas can. So, using my police deduction skills. I guess our ghost alien headed that way."

"Give me a hand over here, will you." Navarro shifts the car into Neutral and gets out. "Help me push this thing off the road."

Lucia puts her back into it. The dead car starts to drift forward a bit as it inches off the pavement. Navarro pushes from the driver's side and steers it to the side. Tires crackle through the loose gravel right at the edge of the asphalt. Navarro sits back inside the car and applies the brake. Rear red lights flash in the night. She locks the parking brake.

"Good to go. Mystery solved." Luisa wipes her hands on her uniform. "You want me to radio this in, Detective?"

"Not quite yet." Navarro stays in the driver's seat and drums her fingers on the steering wheel. "Let's see what we find out there on the road, before we call in the calvary." She gets out of the Mercedes and closes the door behind her.

Chapter Twenty-Nine

The darkness is dense and thick under an endless field of pinprick stars. They glitter and twinkle high in the night sky.

Daniel stays seated in a fetal position on the desert hardpack, overlooking the steep drop and the barren landscape. A cloud of angry mosquitos buzz around his matted hair. He ignores the persistent pests and keeps his head buried in his arms with his knees pulled up to his chin. A constant whine from the needy bugs as they search for exposed skin and fresh blood. He doesn't have the energy or desire to swat them away. He remains in his deep funk as the shroud of insects constantly hover and drone.

A faint noise flutters in the distance. It grows louder than the loopy high-pitched insect whine. Enough for him to peek his head up. Hungry mosquitos take advantage of the moment and land all along sweaty skin. Daniel swats and kills bugs as he springs up to his feet. Streaks of dead mosquitos and wet blood smear along his neck and into the rough stubble on his cheeks.

The foliage starts to shiver. High wind gusts pick up along the embankment. A cluster of cactus bushes pendulum in the intense breeze. Pockets of sage brush sway as a wall of grit blows all around. A mechanical sound sweeps in and overpowers.

Daniel shields his eyes and peeks up into the night

sky. Red and green lights flicker among the field of stars. As if from the heavens, a bright spotlight pops on and starts to sweep across the desert floor. Cyclones of sand flies all around. Daniel keeps his tattered shirt sleeve stuck over his bloodshot sunken eyes as the spotlight dances in the dark. It climbs the embankment and passes over him. The light rotates back and settles on Daniel. The pool of light widens.

Twin rotors thunder as the Bell helicopter coasts and glides overhead. It circles the embankment like a sleek predator stalking its prey. The spotlight leaves Daniel and drifts across the wild growth and hard ground. It stops on a nearby clearing.

Daniel glances at the discarded pistol, hidden in the shadows of cactus bushes. He starts for it but stops as the fierce gusts pick up and blow even harder. Dust devils swirl all across the desert floor as the black bird descends from the dark sky and hovers off the deck. Daniel squints his eyes and shields his face from the swirling windstorm. Rotors thunder as the Bell helicopter drifts overhead. Daniel still stays at the edge of the embankment as the mechanical beast drops and bounces on its skids. It settles down secure onto the ground. The engine dies down. Daniel stares into the reflective hull as the rotors slowly spin and rotate to a stop.

Night turns into day as the bright spotlight kicks back on. Under the intense glare, Daniel shields his gaze. He can't see anything but a field of spots. He perks up to the sounds of mechanical clicks. Clasps release, and a hatch on the copter opens. "Mr. Morrison," a stern voice calls out. "Daniel Morrison."

"Yes." Daniel still tries to adjust to the harsh light." That's me."

"And I am brought triumphant through the air." The voice responds. "The judge of both the quick and the dead." Daniel can hear boots crunch into dirt. "Moroni. Chapter 10. Verse 34."

He can make out the fuzzy outline of a man walking towards him. Daniel's voice is hoarse and worn. "Are you the police?"

"Ha." The firm voice replies with a chuckle. "Hardly."

Daniel blindly blinks at the hazy figure. He can make out the shoulders and stocky frame of a large man in a dark suit. "Who are you?" Daniel cowers.

Thick calloused hands dart forward, snatch him close and hold him tight. "John. My name is John Smith. And I am here to take what is left of your life." Daniel doesn't get out a word as John grabs him by the windpipe and manhandles him. "It's true. That's why I'm here." His free hand frisks him for any weapons. Daniel tries to speak and struggle but John's grip is strong. He stops choking him and jerks him close. "We haven't formally met. But your reputation precedes you. Oh, yes."

One last sweep and check between Daniel's legs. Satisfied, John shoves him to the ground. His tone is nonchalant. "I must say. It's nice to finally put a face with the name."

"Go on then." Daniel stays down. "Kill me." Drained and defeated, he speaks to the sod. "Get it over with. I can't do it myself. I tried. But I can't."

"I'll admit—" John walks around and smiles down at the pathetic figure groveling on the ground. "—we had a devil of a time tracking you down."

Daniel turns his face up to the stalking man. "Kill me," he shouts out, his raspy voice echoes in the dark.

"What are you waiting for? Do it."

John shakes his head. "I wanted you to see me." He circles around the man in the dirt. "And suffer. As I have." John stops and backs up a few steps. "I want you to feel every sordid little bit of my sorrow and pain." He bellows triumphantly as he delivers a swift hard kick into Daniel's rib cage. Daniel coughs out blood as bones break. He crawls on the ground with frantic gasps and wheezes from the strong blow.

John savors the moment and continues pacing around him. He finally crouches down with a growing crescent grin. "And once I have gotten my fill of your pitiful anguish and pain. Why then. Yes. I can kill you." He grabs Daniel's tattered shirt and pulls him close.

In a spasm, Daniel coughs and sputters out a wheezy laugh. "Blood money. What a joke." John doesn't wince from the crimson spray of warm spittle on his face. "My entire life," Daniel mutters through the copper taste in his mouth. "turned to shit. For nothing more than a payday."

John wraps a hand through his limp and greasy hair. "Oh, please." He lifts a wheezing Daniel off the ground. "Don't be so melodramatic." He tosses him back onto the hard surface and walks towards the sleek fuselage. He speaks over his shoulder. "I have a present for you."

Daniel blinks in the bright spotlight and tries to focus as he watches the menacing figure stalk back to the helicopter and slide open a side door. He reaches inside and pulls out a long bundle. It lands to the ground with a thud. John drags the bundle over towards Daniel. He can't make it out at first. His puzzled and pained expression turns to shock. It's Tricia, her arms and legs bound tight. Coarse rope crisscrossed across her torso and legs. An oily red bandana used to gag her mouth. She's tugged and dragged over until her ghostly pale face is glaring at Daniel on the cold ground. Her wild and wide eyes are full of terror. The putrid stench of fear wafts off of her. She burns at Daniel and never blinks.

"'Just as another person has received injury from him—' " John wipes his hands on his flight jacket. "—so, it will be given to him.' Do you know that one?" He prods Daniel with his steel-toed boot. "You might have heard it as an eye for an eye. And the way I see it. You took my person from me. Now, I'll do the same to you."

"I didn't take anything from you." Daniel turns his panicked face up to John and speaks over the intense pain. "Please. Listen to me. I didn't do anything wrong."

Tricia whimpers through her bonds, the bandana stretched across her mouth soaked with saliva. Clammy sweat runs off her in a river. An audible muffled gasp as John crouches down next to Tricia's prone body and grabs her by the bicep.

"You didn't do anything? That's your pathetic excuse? For murdering my love. Okay. Well, I am about to do something. And I want you to watch every second of it. Personally, I wish this was your wife. But take comfort in the knowledge that I will visit with her soon enough." John grabs Tricia by the hair and lifts up her head. "I don't know if you really care for this woman. But your hostage is the best I could do on short notice." John pulls a large hunting knife from its sheath. He brings the shiny silver blade up to Daniel's face. "My girl is gone. For good. And you took her away from me." The sharp blade sways and dances in his eyes. "Yes, you did that." The blade inches closer to Daniel's left eye. "Tell me. About this morning. Did you witness the light of her life snuff out like a candle? Her mangled body, discarded like trash on the street after you plowed into her?"

"No." Realization hits Daniel like a splash of ice water. "I didn't kill her." He tries to move but his broken ribs splinter through him with sharp pain. "The car wreck. It was an accident."

"An accident?" John uses the blade to wave the words away. "Who hit who is trivial. What matters is. She's gone." He snatches Tricia tight and brings the blade up to her throat. "Okay. Time for the wet work. Careful, now." Tricia's scared shrieks and tearful moans resound as the cold steel blade pushes and snugs against her slick and sweaty skin. "You're in the splash zone." John grins as he keeps Tricia in a tight grip, ready to cut her throat from ear to ear. "An eye for an eye. Now you watch. Watch her life force drain away."

He glances up at Daniel, but he isn't paying any attention. John's Cheshire grin melts away as he sees Daniel crawl slowly in the dirt. "Where are you going?" He chuckles. "I heard them break myself. At least, two. Maybe three ribs." John removes the blade from her neck and releases Tricia. She drops back to the ground with a drawn out and muffled sob.

He gets up and holds the large knife down to his side. "You're going to burn out, exerting energy like that. Huh." He paces Daniel's slow pace and speaks with a smile. "Look at you go. Oh, that's gotta hurt. I bet it feels like dragging yourself across broken glass. Am I right?"

Daniel doesn't stop crawling. John snickers with surprise. "Mr. Morrison. If you don't mind me saying. You're being quite rude. It's never polite to turn your back on company."

Dirty fingers continue to clutch and claw at the hard

earth. Daniel sobs and strains under the pain but keeps inching forward.

"Here I am, being courteous. I even warned you about the bloodletting. Hello? You really should focus on what's at hand." He keeps up with Daniel's tortoise speed. John toys and twirls the large knife with a smirk on his face. Daniel doesn't stop. John shakes his head and asks, puzzled. "What are you doing?" Daniel doesn't answer. His sticky sweat covered face contorts through waves of intense pain as he pulls himself along.

"That's enough." John shoves his boot into the center of Daniel's back, pinning him to the hardpack. "Where are your manners? How about showing me some. Here I am, about to slit this woman's throat and you're…" John fades off as he spots what Daniel was crawling for. The silver wheel gun shaded under a cactus blossom. "Sorry. Excuse me." Daniel wheezes as John puts all his weight on his boot and steps on his back. "Only for a minute." John walks over and crouches down. "Well, well, well." He picks up the snub-nosed pistol and looks it over. "What have we here?" Daniel pants in the dirt and watches with desperation as John clicks opens the chamber and spins the wheel. "Hmmm. How very appropriate. Two shots left."

Daniel rapidly stammers a response as John strides over and drags him back across the gritty ground. He tugs him along and brings him right back where he was, facing Tricia's frightened face on the hard silt.

"Please, listen." Daniel babbles in a panic. "It was an accident. I didn't mean to hurt anybody. Please, you have to listen to me. You have no right—"

"Rights? Because of your idiocy, crawling along through sheer stupidity, I've got your gun." John closes the chamber with a snap. "And that's all the right I need." He stands over the two bodies and aims the gun between them. "One bullet each. And if you're still kicking, well, we can leave what's left of your lives for the wild bobcats and hungry coyotes. So. Who wants to go first? Speak up. Any volunteers?"

"Don't." Daniel begs and pleads. "No. Don't do this. Please."

John scowls down at him. "Stop crying, you pussy." He turns to Tricia. "How about we go, ladies first. What do you say?" John cocks the pistol. "Works for me." He settles the barrel on Tricia's back.

"Stop." A loud voice echoes from the dark.

"Put the gun down." John turns towards the sound.

The voice calls out. "San Antonio police. Drop your gun. Right now."

John stays put, standing over both bodies, the wheel gun still aimed at Tricia.

Officer Lucia Cruz steps from the shadows around the helicopter and into the glow of the spotlight. "Don't do it, Fella." She has her weapon trained on John. "Stand down." John doesn't react or show any emotion. He keeps his raging eyes locked on Tricia and Daniel.

"I won't say it again." Detective Roya Navarro steps into the light, with her revolver squarely aimed. "Last chance." She takes a few tentative steps closer. "Do you really want to force us to shoot you?"

"Ha. You can't stop me." John stands over the two shaking bodies and shouts. "I'm a resurrected being." He keeps the pistol firmly gripped in his hand. "And I'll live forever." He rages at the two officers with unblinking eyes. "I'm ready to die." His voice decisive in the face of their aimed weapons. "Into the pits of fiery hell below.

We are all gonna go."

Daniel seizes the moment. He fights through the pain and reaches up for John's flight suit. He grabs and tugs him back.

John pulls the trigger. The gunshot shatters the desert quiet, and he fires blindly into the earth. He staggers and trips over Tricia. He teeters with a yelp and tumbles all the way down the steep embankment.

Daniel collapses back onto solid ground with a wet grunt. Tricia shouts out in a muffled panic through her saliva-soaked gag.

"Eyes. Eyes." Navarro hollers out. "I want eyes on him."

Lucia grips her pistol tight. "On it." She clicks on a flashlight and cautiously approaches the edge of the steep drop.

Navarro keeps her revolver ready and wits about her. "You got him?" The anxiety in her voice on a razor's edge. "Talk to me."

Lucia aims the flashlight beam down the slope. "I got him."

Navarro joins her at the lip of the drop.

The flashlight picks up John at the bottom of the ravine. His neck bent and twisted around at a sharp angle. He doesn't move.

They continue to shine the beam of light onto his contorted body. Both officers hold their aim steady as they catch their breaths and reign in their tensions.

Chapter Thirty

He couldn't make out the song on the radio. It was slow and soothing. Easy listening with a repetitive beat. The voice of the singer was moody quiet and seductively steady. Something about a blue Spanish sky. As the horn section kicked in, his mind drifted along in comfort wrapped in the warm blanket of sound. Until his thoughts rapidly raced to the surface.

Daniel's eyes spring open. He blinks and focuses on the bright lights shining down as he glances around.

A tight space of compartments and cubbies from floor to ceiling. Small monitors pulsate as they respond to sensors stuck all along his body. He follows an IV drip. The thin tube runs from the plastic bag and back to his bandaged arm, the exposed skin covered in scratches and welts. He looks down at his battered body stretched out on a gurney. Fresh bandages wrapped around his bare chest. "Where am I?" Daniel speaks to no one, his voice cracked and groggy. "Hello. Is anybody there?" He starts to sit up, until the handcuff chain pulls tight against the metal handgrip on the gurney. Bleary eyes focus as he follows the chain to the other cuff, wrapped around his grimy wrist. He lifts his arm up as the chain clanks and clatters against the metal.

His energy sapped by fatigue and painkillers; he falls back onto the gurney. The steady beep from the heart monitor fills the tight space.

The rear double-doors of the ambulance open wide. The morning sunrise crests over the desert hills. In the horizon, a kaleidoscope of red and yellow bleeds into the big Texas sky. A colorful spread of wildflowers and cactus stand out from the brush and scrub. A phalanx of police officers and paramedics dot the road. Eagle Pass police cars parked all along the asphalt sides. The whoop of a siren whine emanates from another ambulance as it pulls out and heads down the flat straightway.

Roya Navarro climbs into the back of the ambulance and closes the doors behind her. The steady commotion from outside sealed off as the soothing sounds from the radio fill the rear cabin. She opens a jump-seat and sits next to the gurney. She waits until she's settled before saying anything. "How are you feeling?"

Daniel doesn't reply at first. He takes a deep breath, and hoarse words finally croak from his dry throat. "I've been better."

"Yeah, I can imagine so." Navarro looks all around the cramped space. "You know, I'm on zero sleep, thanks to you. Without a coffee IV, I'd be in one of these busses myself."

"Can you tell me. Is she okay?" Daniel's eyes well up with emotion. "Where's Tricia?"

"She's at Fort Duncan Medical over in Eagle Pass." Before he can ask, Navarro tells him. "She's safe. Looking at a few nasty scrapes and bruises but she'll pull through. You seemed to have gotten the brunt of it."

Daniel doesn't say anything but is relieved to hear the news.

"She's talking. Freely." Navarro continues to watch him. "I've gotten one update on her witness statement." Roya adjusts on the uncomfortable seat. "And I must say.

she's telling us quite the story."

Daniel doesn't look over at the detective. He talks to the ceiling. "I'm glad to hear she's okay." He starts to move on the gurney and winces from the pain.

"Stay put." Navarro starts to get up. "I'll get you a paramedic."

"No, I'm good." Daniel shakes her off. "I've got too many drugs in me already." He settles back down. "I'm fine. Really."

Navarro stays in the jump seat. Daniel turns to look at her. "That crazy man. He dropped out of the sky. I never saw him before. Said his name was John. He was gonna kill us, and—"

"He's dead." Navarro thinks for a second and decides to tell him a bit more. "Enroute to the Fort Duncan morgue. EMT's called it a Hangman's Fracture. Broken neck."

Daniel settles back on the gurney. Navarro watches his every move.

The easy listening song on the radio fades out. A morning DJ's soothing voice fills the cabin. "92.7, KINL. It's the top of the hour here on the morning scramble. And here are your current headlines. Breaking news on out of central Texas. House District 21, congressional candidate Hayden Grant passed away last night, of natural causes. For more information, we go to KTXU - San Antonio for an update."

An excited and breathless voice fills the cramped cabin. "This is Gary Grey, KTXU. Reporting live from Cordillera Ranch. All of us, gathered here, anxiously awaiting further details on the political shockwave that has occurred here this morning with the death of Hayden Grant. Public officials are being rather tight-lipped until their official news conference gets under way in less than an hour."

Navarro gets up from her jump seat and moves towards the front of the ambulance.

Gary Grey's voice continues to spit rapid-fire. "From his humble beginnings in Texarkana, to a smooth road paved all the way to Austin. Hayden Grant was a political power player who was certain to clench victory this November and take his seat in the D.C. Capitol. What his passing does to the political horse race here is anybody's guess. This House seat has been locked in Republican hands since—"

Navarro clicks off the radio dial. She takes a deep breath and soaks in the quiet. She starts back for the gurney. Steady pings from the heart monitor fill the tight cabin. "It's a brand-new day." Roya stands over Daniel and looks down at him. "And I guess that makes you yesterday's news."

"Just like that." Daniel looks down at the handcuff. "It sure doesn't feel over." He rattles the cuff against the metal gurney. His arm goes slack. "So, what happens to me now?"

"If you want my medical diagnosis." Navarro takes a seat next to him. "You seem stable enough to travel. Once the medical tech signs off on you. We'll transport you to a hospital bed in Eagle Pass. I've asked SAPD to bring your wife there as well. She's anxious to see you." She takes a set of keys from her jacket pocket and grabs his arm. "And then we'll get you both back home to San Antonio." Navarro unlocks the cuff from around his wrist. Daniel stares up at her. She glances at him. "It probably doesn't need to be said, but I'm gonna say it out loud anyway." She undoes the other cuff from the gurney and slips them back into her pocket. "You better not run on me."

"I'm not going anywhere." Daniel flexes his raw wrist.

"Good." Navarro gets up and opens the rear doors of the ambulance. "Then I'll let them know we're ready to go." Before she climbs out, she turns back to him. "Hey. Do you mind if I ride back here with you?"

"No." Daniel shakes his head. "Not at all."

"Appreciate it." She jumps down onto the asphalt. "I've still got some questions for you."

He tries to smile back. "I'll tell you everything you want to know."

Navarro closes the double doors behind her. Daniel falls back on the gurney and stares up at the lights in the ceiling. He closes his eyes and soaks in the quiet and comfort.

A word about the author...

Sean Bridges was born in Wiesbaden, Germany. He's an A.M.P.A.S. Nicholl award-winning screenwriter and author. He's a Stephen King Dollar Baby with his festival winning audio production of *One for the Road*.

His Audible Parade Productions created a serial audio thriller, *Triple Six* and a horror/suspense audio series, *Parasite Zero*. He lives in the Texas Hill Country.

Thank you for purchasing
this publication of The Wild Rose Press, Inc.

For questions or more information
contact us at
info@thewildrosepress.com.

The Wild Rose Press, Inc.
www.thewildrosepress.com